Another half an hour went by, and Alonzo was just beginning to relax again when an acrid scent tingled his nose. *Smoke*. His first thought was that it must be Indians, but no, they wouldn't give themselves away like that. It must be whites, then. Eager for the cover, since it might discourage his stalker if the killer was still back there, he brought his horse and the pack animal to a trot.

Pounding around yet another turn in the river, Alonzo abruptly had to draw rein.

Before him spread a wide clearing. In the middle a campfire burned, and beside it lay a man on his back, resting.

Alonzo thought that was strange. The man had to have heard him. Why hadn't he sat up? Then he saw that the man's shoulder was bandaged, and handcuffs were clamped to his wrists.

Before the significance could sink in, another man stepped out of the trees, holding a leveled Winchester. . . .

Also by David Robbins

Thunder Valley
Blood Feud
Ride to Valor
Town Tamers
Badlanders

GUNS ON THE PRAIRIE

DAVID ROBBINS

A SIGNET BOOK

SIGNET
Published by New American Library,
an imprint of Penguin Random House LLC
375 Hudson Street, New York, New York 10014

This book is an original publication of New American Library.

First Printing, September 2015

For more information about Penguin Random House, visit penguinrandomhouse
.com.

ISBN 978-0-451-47290-8

Printed in the United States of America
10 9 8 7 6 5 4 3 2 1

Penguin
Random
House

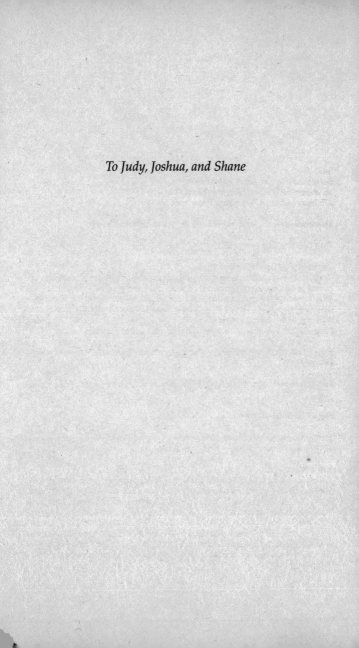

To Judy, Joshua, and Shane

1

———◆———

The one-armed rider came out of the woods and drew rein on the crest of a hill overlooking a small farm. Placing his right hand on his saddle horn, he grinned. "It looks plumb ripe for pickin', doesn't it, Archibald?"

His horse, a bay, pricked its ears at the mention of its name.

"Let's get to it, shall we?" the rider said eagerly. "I'm hungry enough to eat one of those cows."

The rider wore a loose-fitting blue uniform. Patched at the elbows, and with a tear in the left pants leg, it gave the impression he'd worn the uniform a good many years. So did the gray in his hair and mustache. His sparkling blue eyes and complexion, though, hinted at youthful vigor and vim. The effect made it hard to guess his age. He could be anywhere from twenty to fifty.

Halfway down the hill the rider again drew rein. "I'm gettin' careless. I forgot I washed up in that creek this mornin'." Dismounting, he searched about for a patch of bare earth. Finding one, he scooped at the dirt with his fingernails, then rubbed a little on his cheeks, forehead, and neck to further disguise how young he truly was. "Don't want to overdo it," he said to the bay.

Climbing back on, the rider stared at his empty left sleeve. "It's a darned nuisance but it never fails to work."

He clucked to his mount and presently they reached a fenced pasture where half a dozen cows grazed or lay watching him with idle interest.

The farm wasn't much, a house and a barn and a chicken coop, but the buildings were well tended, and that gave the rider hope. "They keep the place up," he said. "That usually means hard workers, and hard workers usually have more than layabouts, don't they?"

The sun had barely cleared the eastern horizon, and the farm was stirring to life. Clucks came from the chicken coop. Smoke curled from the chimney atop the house. A large wagon filled with manure, the team already hitched, stood between the barn and the coop.

The barn door was open, and as the rider approached, out of the barn strode a big-boned middle-aged man wearing bib overalls and a straw hat and carrying a pail. He drew up short, his eyes narrowing, his other hand curling into a fist.

"What do we have here?"

The rider smiled his friendliest smile and brought the bay to a stop. "How do, mister? I hope you don't mind my bein' on your property. I'm just passin' through and was wonderin' if I could maybe buy me a meal."

The farmer studied him and the bay. "You've come a far piece."

"Yes, sir," the rider said politely. "All the way from Kansas City, in fact. I'm headin' west to the mountains."

"You're off the beaten trail by a long shot."

"I reckon I am, at that," the rider admitted, and chuckled. "I figure I'll find Denver eventually. Folks say it's right big."

"Denver, you say?"

"Yes, sir. I hear it's boomin', and I figure there'll be work to be had, even for someone like me."

The farmer glanced at the rider's empty left sleeve, hanging limp at his side. "Lost that in the war, did you?"

"Yes, sir. And you'd be surprised at how many folks won't hire a cripple."

"That's not very Christian."

"No, sir, it's not," the rider said sadly.

"We don't see many in uniform these days," the farmer mentioned. "It's been, what, a dozen years, or thereabouts."

The rider touched his dusty shirt. "These are the only clothes I have."

The farmer came closer. He looked at the rider's waist and then at the saddle where a scabbard would be. "Why, you're not armed."

"No, sir," the rider said. "I gave up guns when I mustered out. I had enough of them in the war."

A hint of friendliness came into the farmer's face, and he unclenched his fist. "That's admirable. But it might not be wise. You're headed into dangerous country. West of here there are hostiles. To say nothing of all the outlaws and hard cases."

The rider shrugged. "I've put my life in the hands of the Almighty. What will be, will be."

"What's your name, anyhow?"

The rider happened to notice a pump over by the farmhouse. "Waterton," he said. "Jules Waterton."

"Well, Mr. Waterton—"

"Corporal Waterton, if you don't mind," the rider

said. "I'm not in the army anymore, but I still like to be called that."

"Corporal Waterton," the farmer amended, and hefted the pail. "I just got done milkin', and the missus and me are about to sit down to breakfast. How would you like to join us? I'm sure Martha won't mind."

"I don't want to be any bother," the rider said. "And I can pay."

"The meal is free," the farmer said. "It's the least we can do, given what you lost in the war."

"I never ask to be treated special," the rider said. "I can make my own way."

The farmer smiled. "I'm sure you can, Corporal. I admire that. But let us treat you anyhow. I'm Sam, by the way. Sam Carson."

"Pleased to meet you."

Carson conducted the rider to the pump and told him to help himself while he went in to break the news to his wife.

"I'm very grateful, sir." The rider dismounted, putting on a show of moving stiffly to add to the illusion that he was old. The moment the front door closed on the farmer, the rider chuckled. "This uniform does the trick every time, Archibald." He worked the pump handle until water spurted, then cupped his right hand and raised it to his lips.

It wasn't two minutes that the door opened and out came Sam and Martha Carson. She was what some would call pleasingly plump, with a face that made the rider think of the cows in the pasture. Her dress was homespun, and she wore a white apron.

The rider doffed his hat and gave a little bow.

"How do you do, ma'am?"

"Corporal Waterton, is it?" the woman said.

The rider nodded. "I'm awful sorry to bother you. I

told Sam, there, that I'm willin' to pay for breakfast but he wouldn't hear of it."

"Neither will I," Martha said. "Come on in and I'll set another place. We don't often get visitors."

"We're a bit far out," Sam said.

"You have a nice farm," the rider said. "It shows a lot of hard work went into it. My pa used to say that hard work is good for the soul."

"Your pa sounds like he knew what he was about," Martha said.

"He did," the rider said, and grew sorrowful. "He died while I was off fightin' to free the slaves. I never got to attend his funeral."

"I'm sorry to hear that," Martha commiserated, and beckoned. "Come. Join us. I have bacon on the stove and don't want to burn it."

"Whatever you say, ma'am."

A long parlor brought them to an immaculate kitchen. The floor was clean enough to eat off of, gleaming utensils hung on the walls, and in a frying pan, long strips of bacon sizzled.

The rider inhaled and happily grinned. "Smells just like home when I was a boy."

"We always wanted children," Martha said. Taking a fork, she speared a bacon strip and turned the strip over. "But it wasn't meant to be."

"I would have liked a son," Sam said. He indicated a chair. "Have a seat. Make yourself comfortable."

The rider eagerly complied. Two plates and silverware had already been set out, and shortly Martha brought over a plate for him.

"Here you go. It's about ready."

"My belly is rumblin' like a starved bear's," the rider said.

Sam sat the head of the table and made a tepee of his

hands. "It's none of my business, but what do you plan to do with your life? Ten to twelve years is a long time to wander where the wind takes you, and I have the notion that's exactly what you've been doing."

"You have me pegged," the rider said, and chuckled. "I've been livin' hand to mouth for so long, I don't know any other way."

Martha took cups and saucers from a cupboard, placed them in front of her husband and their guest, and went to the stove for the coffeepot. "Tell me a little about your travels, if you don't mind. I haven't done much traveling, and I do so love to hear about other places."

"Martha, don't bother the man," Sam said.

"That's all right," the rider said. "It'll be my way of thankin' your missus for her generosity." So saying, he launched into an account of how, after he was discharged, he drifted through a number of Eastern and Southern states, taking jobs where he could get them, and finally decided to try his luck west of the Mississippi River. "It's all folks talk about. 'Go West, young man,' that newspaper fella said. Well, I'm not so young anymore, but I reckoned it was high time I took his advice."

"You certainly look younger than your years," Martha said.

"Even with the gray in my hair?"

Martha nodded. "It's your face. As smooth as a baby's bottom, my mother would say. It doesn't go with that hair."

"I'll have to remember that," the rider said with an odd grin.

Sam Carson coughed. "Enough of that. Is the food ready, or what?"

"Oh." Martha got up and hustled about, and soon a

heaping bowl of scrambled eggs and a long plate of bacon, and a stack of toast joined the butter dish and the sugar bowl in the center of the table. "Dig in," she encouraged them.

The rider took her urging to heart. He filled his plate to overflowing and ate as if ravenous. The farmer and his wife looked on and shared smiles.

Only when he'd wiped the last bits of egg from his plate with the last bit of crust in his hand did the rider sit back, pat his stomach, and say, "That was right fine, ma'am. Sam is right lucky to have such a good cook for his helpmate."

"Oh, pshaw," Martha said, and blushed.

"I have to be careful," Sam said, and patted his own belly, "or I'll end up like our sow out in the barn."

"Speakin' of which," the rider said. "I don't suppose I could rest in there a while? Out of the sun? I could use a nap after a fine feed like this, and my horse is a bit tuckered." He quickly added, "It wouldn't be for more than an hour or two, and then I'll be on my way."

"Nap as long as you like," Martha said.

Sam pushed his chair back. "I have manure to spread and a shutter to fix, so I'll be busy. You rest up and head out when you please."

The rider gave them a kindly look. "You're the salt of the earth, the both of you. I wish you all the best, your whole lives long."

"Why, aren't you a dear?" Martha said.

Stretching, the rider smothered a yawn, and stood. "See how tired I am? A pile of straw would be like a featherbed right about now." He thanked them, shook Sam's hand, and made his way out the front. Taking hold of the bay's reins, he led his animal into the barn. No sooner were they out of sight than he stepped to his saddlebags. Taking out a coiled gun belt with a Colt in the holster, he palmed the six-shooter, replaced the belt in his saddlebag, and tucked the Colt under his belt. Pulling his shirt out to hide the revolver, he said to Archibald, "Just in case."

The ladder to the hayloft posed no great difficulty. He lay on his back and rubbed his left shoulder. It wasn't long before he heard heavy footsteps.

"Jules? Are you in here?"

"Up in the loft," the rider replied in a sleepy voice. "If that's all right."

"You sleep away," Sam Carson said. "Sorry I disturbed you."

When the farmer's footfalls faded, the rider descended. Peeking out, he saw Carson about to climb on the manure spreader. A flick of the reins, and the farmer headed for his fields.

"Couldn't ask for better," the rider happily declared. Turning, he ran the length of the middle aisle to the rear door. The latch rasped when he pressed it. Squinting in the bright sunlight, he sidled to the corner. Forty feet of open space separated the barn from the house. "Can't be helped," he said, and took off like a shot, racing to the back of the house. Ducking under the kitchen window, he removed his hat and peered in.

Humming as she worked, Martha Carson was busy washing and drying the dishes.

Quickly, the rider sprinted to the front. He'd paid particular attention and knew that the front door wouldn't squeak when it was opened. And he wasn't wearing spurs, so his bounds to the stairs were as silent as an Apache's. Swiftly climbing, he glided to the bedroom. The bed was made up, the flowered quilt smooth as glass. A chest of drawers gleamed with polish. He tried the drawers first. There were the usual clothes, undergarments and socks, shirts and blouses. In the top left were a folding knife, a tobacco pouch and pipe, and other manly things. In the top right there were a necklace and several rings. He was tempted but left them be.

Rubbing his chin, he turned to the bed. "It's nearly always the bed," he whispered to himself, and hunkering, he shoved his hand under the mattress and groped about, moving from top to bottom. Nothing. Hurrying around to the other side, he repeated his groping. Suddenly he froze, and smiled.

Some people kept their money in pokes, some in tin boxes, a few in jars. This time it was a leather pouch. He flipped it open, saw mostly coins, double-eagles and the like, and a few bills.

Clutching the pouch to his chest so it wouldn't jingle and give him away, he hurried to the stairs and was about to go down when he realized the humming had grown louder.

Martha was coming down the hall.

Backpedaling, the rider retreated into the shadows. He could see the top of her head, and hoped she would go on by.

Instead, she started up the stairs.

2

When Federal Deputy Marshal Jacob Stone rode into Hebron, Nebraska, he wasn't expecting trouble. Hebron was a small farming community, its residents as peaceful and law-abiding as Quakers. Hebron didn't even have a saloon. So when he wearily drew rein at the hitch rail in front of the general store, the last thing he expected was for the owner to come hurrying out with half his face swollen and black-and-blue.

It startled him, and it shouldn't have. Stone had worn tin for a good many years. More than any other Federal lawman on the frontier. By all rights he should have handed in his badge and taken to a-rocking by now. In fact, his superiors had been putting pressure on him to either do just that or agree to a desk job.

Stone would rather be shot. He couldn't think of anything worse than sitting behind a desk all day, pushing papers. It would be a death in itself.

For almost forty years now, in several jurisdictions, he had dutifully done his job to the best of his ability.

He liked always being on the go, never staying in one place too long. Liked the sky over his head for a ceiling and the ground under his feet for a floor. He could no more sit at a desk all day than he could give up his pipe. It was his one vice, and the reason he'd stopped at the store—to buy tobacco.

The owner came to the hitch rail and pointed at the ruin of his face. "Do you see, Marshal?" he practically wailed. "Do you see what they did to me?"

Stone had to think to recollect the man's name. "Mr. Applebaum, isn't it? Looks like you stuck your face in front of somebody's fist."

Applebaum was portly and balding. He had thick lips, which quivered when he was mad, and he was furious. Gripping the rail, he stabbed a thick finger at Stone. "Was that supposed to be funny? Why are you just sitting there? Didn't you hear me? Go after them. They might still be out there."

"Simmer down, Mr. Applebaum."

"I'll do no such thing. They deserve to be shot, those animals. Riding in here and doing the terrible things they did."

Stone was aware of others coming from all directions. The sleepy little hamlet was coming alive. "You need to stay calm," he said politely. He was always polite, always courteous. Back in his day, that was how folks did. There was none of the sass and rudeness so common these days.

"Calm, my ass," Applebaum said.

Stone bent forward, his gray eyes flinty. "And watch your language. There are ladies comin'."

"What?" Applebaum said. "Who cares about that? Look at my *face!*"

Before Stone could reply, a heavyset woman who waddled when she walked came up and placed a pudgy hand on his leg.

"Have you heard about them, Marshal? Have you heard what they did?"

Half a dozen people ringed Stone's roan, all of them talking at once. They stopped when he held up a hand and barked, "Enough! I'll take you one at a time. After I climb down."

The woman waddled back, saying, "Well, I never."

Stiffly dismounting, Stone put a hand to the small of his back. Long hours in the saddle tended to bother him some. In his younger days, he could ride forever and not feel a thing.

Stepping onto the boardwalk, Stone caught sight of his reflection in the store window. At five feet, ten inches, and spindly of frame, he was hardly imposing. His gray hair, and the gray on his chin when he didn't shave, lent him a grandfatherly look. His hat, his clothes, were plain, his boots ordinary. Even the Colt on his hip was an over-the-counter model. There was nothing flashy about him at all, nothing to draw the eye except the badge on his shirt.

The townspeople were looking at one another and some of them fidgeting as if they couldn't wait to say what they had to. Up and down the street, more people were coming.

"Suppose you give me the facts, Mr. Applebaum, and then I'll point at each of you and you can each have your say."

Applebaum pointed at his face again. "You see this? The two of them did this. Beat me with their pistols. They must have struck me ten or eleven times."

Stone doubted it. Anyone hit that many times, their face would be pulped. "Two who, Mr. Applebaum? How about you back up and start at the beginnin'."

With an effort, the store owner composed himself,

and coughed. "Very well. I apologize for yelling at you. But I'm terribly upset."

"We all are," the heavyset woman said. "They took our town over and terrorized us."

"You'll get your turn, ma'am," Stone said. "Go on, Mr. Applebaum."

"It was yesterday, toward sunset, that they rode in. Two of them. Scruffy sorts. They hadn't bathed in ages, and they were wearing guns. You know the kind."

Stone refrained from pointing out that on the frontier, guns were as common as teeth. "Can you describe them better? Did you hear their names?"

"Franks and Loudon, I heard them say," Applebaum said. "Franks is tall and has a scar. He did most of the talking. Loudon didn't say much but he's the mean one. The one who struck me when I didn't move fast enough to suit him. Then Franks hit me, too." He closed his eyes and shuddered.

"Go on," Stone encouraged him.

"Well, they came into my store and looked around as if they were going to shop, but then they came to the counter and the one called Franks asked me if I had any liquor. I told him we don't have a saloon, and he said that wasn't what he asked. He looked at me and sort of bared his teeth and asked if *I* had any liquor. I told him I had a bottle of whiskey that I hardly ever touch, and he told me to fetch it. When I said it wasn't for sale, that's when he hauled me over the counter and Loudon hit me. Franks stood over me and asked where the bottle was, but I was so shocked, I couldn't answer. So he hit me, too."

Stone frowned. He knew where this was going. He'd seen it before, more times than he could count. "They forced you to tell them and treated themselves."

"If by 'treat' you mean they drank the bottle dry, and it

was nearly full, then yes," Applebaum said. "They left me on the floor, and went around smashing things and turning my shelves over. You should see it in there. My store is a mess. They must have done hundreds in damage."

Stone turned and looked through the window. The place was indeed a shambles.

"The more they drank, the more they carried on," Applebaum was saying. "I don't know why they picked on me. I hadn't done anything."

"Men like that don't need an excuse," Stone said.

The heavyset woman couldn't curb her impatience any longer. "That's not all they did. They came out into the street and began shooting at people, and laughing all the while."

"Did they hit anyone?"

"No, but what does that matter? They were shooting at us. That was enough." She pointed up the street. "They shot out the window to the feed and grain, too."

Stone hadn't noticed the shattered glass when he rode in. But then, he was bone tired.

"They demanded more whiskey, Marshal," another man said. "Warned that they'd hurrah the town if we didn't give it to them."

"And did you?"

Yet another townsman spoke up. "I had a bottle I kept for special occasions. I gave it to them and pleaded for them to go and leave us be."

"And did they?"

Applebaum answered. "They rode out to the wash north of town and made camp. Built a fire and sat there drinking, as brazen as anything. We know because Levi's oldest boy snuck out and took a look."

"They might still be there," the heavyset woman said. "You can catch them if you hurry."

Stone glanced skyward. The sun was only a few hours high. The pair might still be there, at that. Stepping to the roan, he swung back up.

"Be careful, Marshal," Applebaum said. "They're dangerous."

Stone would have been inclined to think the pair had just gotten carried away, except that they'd beaten the store owner *before* they got their hands on his liquor. "I'll have a talk with them."

"Talk?" the woman snorted. "You should arrest them. It's indecent, what they did. Scaring people like that."

"Don't forget my face," Applebaum said.

Some of the others started talking all at once.

Stone reined around.

"The wash isn't far, Marshal," a man called out. "You can't miss it."

Hebron fell behind him. He hadn't gone a quarter of a mile when tendrils of smoke drew him to the east. He left the road, holding the roan to a slow walk. The smoke made it easy. When he was fifty yards out, he drew rein and advanced on foot, his hand on his Colt.

The pair were bundled in their blankets, asleep. An empty bottle lay in the dirt between them. They'd had the sense to use picket pins for their horses but hadn't stripped their saddles. The fire had burned low but hadn't gone entirely out, which explained the smoke.

Stone squatted on the rim, rested his arms across his knees, and studied the troublemakers. He had a long memory when it came to faces, particularly those who were wanted, and neither jogged his recollection. That was good. Hardened outlaws were more apt to resist, and he could do without the aggravation. Clearing his throat, he hollered down, "Mornin', gents."

Neither so much as stirred.

"Mornin', gents," Stone yelled a little louder. "Rise and shine. You've got some explainin' to do."

One of them rose onto his elbows and sleepily looked around. "What?" he said thickly. "What was that?"

"I said mornin'," Stone said.

Blinking against the glare, the man squinted up at him. "What was that? Who the hell are you?" He had straw-colored hair and was missing part of his left ear.

Standing, Stone tapped his badge.

The man sat bolt upright. "A lawdog!" he exclaimed, and glanced at his companion. "Loudon! Loudon! Wake up."

"You must be Mr. Franks," Stone said. He stayed on the rim, his hand still on his Colt.

Franks was struggling to collect his wits. He vigorously shook his head, and winced.

"I hear you boys drank a lot last night," Stone said. "Your noggin must be hammerin' right about now."

"Well, hell," Franks said. Jamming his hat on, he threw his blanket off. He'd fallen asleep fully clothed, with his gun belt on. Either his six-shooter, a Remington, had fallen out, or he'd set it beside him. He went to reach for it.

"Don't," Stone said.

Franks froze. "What is this?" he demanded.

"I hear you pistol-whipped a man," Stone said. "You and your pard."

Loudon picked that moment to roll over. He had black hair and close-set dark eyes, and was scowling. Smacking his lips, he gazed confusedly about. "What's all the racket? What's goin' on?"

"We have company," Franks said. "A tin star."

That woke Loudon right quick. He, too, sat up, his blanket sliding around his waist. "Him?" he said, spotting Stone.

"You see anyone else?" Franks said.

"What is this?" Loudon said. "We didn't do anything."

"The storekeeper's face says different," Stone replied. "So does his store. And there's the matter of the feed and grain window, and shootin' the town up."

"Well, hell," Franks said. "We were just havin' fun."

"That's right," Loudon said. "Sowin' some oats is all we done."

"You sowed a little hard," Stone said. "I'm afraid I'll have to ask you to collect your things and come with me."

"Well, hell," Franks said. It seemed to be his favorite expression. "Can't we just agree to pay for the damages?"

"We don't know what they are yet," Stone said, "and that's not up to me, anyhow. It will be for the judge to decide."

"Are you arrestin' us?"

"Afraid so," Stone said. He was watching Loudon, who had placed his hands flat on the ground close to his blanket and his hips.

"Well, hell," Franks said.

"If it was only drunk and disorderly, I might be willin' to let you go if you could pay the damages," Stone elaborated. "But you had to go and beat Mr. Applebaum."

"We only hit him once," Franks said.

"Each," Stone amended. "With your six-guns."

"All we wanted was a bottle," Franks said. "All he had to do was give us one without any fuss. But he went and lectured us on the evils of drink."

"So you hit him."

"I wasn't in no mood for no lecture," Franks said. "I told him to shut up and he wouldn't."

"That's a poor excuse," Stone said. "Now how about the two of you put yourselves together so I can take you back into town?"

"Maybe we don't want to go," Loudon said.

"I'm the law," Stone said.

"That don't make you God Almighty, you old geezer."

Franks glanced at his partner. "Loudon, don't."

"I hate high and mighty," Loudon said. "I hate it more than anything." He gave his head a vigorous toss, as if to fully wake up.

"No, I say," Franks said.

"Do you *want* to go to jail? I sure as hell don't. And I sure as hell won't." With that, Loudon jerked his hand out from under the blanket and pointed a revolver.

3

―――――

The rider reached the bedroom in several long bounds. Darting around the bed, he yanked the closet door open, crouched, and slipped inside. Long dresses filled half of it, and he slid behind them, leaving a gap so he could see out. He left the door open a couple of inches, enough that he could see the doorway and part of the bed.

None too soon.

Martha appeared. She was humming to herself. She crossed out of his line of vision, toward the chest of drawers. He heard a drawer scrape open. Whatever she was after didn't take long to find. The drawer scraped again and she reappeared, about to depart. Unexpectedly, she glanced at the closet.

The rider held his breath. She might remember that the door had been closed and wonder why it was open. But no, after a few moments she walked out, humming softly as before.

The rider quietly let out his breath. The last thing he

needed was to be caught. He prided himself on always getting away clean. Not that there hadn't been a few times when he'd been lucky to make it out alive.

He stayed put several minutes, just to be safe. Finally easing out, he crept to the door. From downstairs came the clatter of pots.

On cat's feet he descended and was out the front with Martha none the wiser. There was no sign of Sam. Hastening to the barn, he shoved the pouch into his saddlebags, brought Archibald out, and rode at a walk until he was sure he was out of earshot. Then he gigged Archibald to a trot, back to the hill and up it into the woods.

His packhorse was right where he'd left it, dozing. Climbing down, he unbuttoned the uniform shirt and eased his left arm from behind his back. The arm was a little stiff from being bent behind him for so long, and he flexed it and moved it up and down. Satisfied, he shoved it into the sleeve, untied the lead rope, and got out of there.

He had no doubt that if Sam Carson and his wife discovered the theft, Sam would be after him with a shotgun.

"Let him," the rider said to Archibald, and grinned. "That was pretty slick, huh?"

The rider used his heels and held to a trot for about half a mile. That should be enough, he reckoned, that he could relax some, and he slowed.

The day was sunny and bright. Butterflies fluttered about a patch of wildflowers, and songbirds warbled.

"Yes, sir," the rider happily declared. "Life is lookin' good."

It hadn't always. In his mind's eye he flashed back to when he was ten, to that horrible day when his ma died of the consumption that had slowly been killing her for years. His pa went to pieces and took to the bottle, sucking the bug juice down as if there would be no tomorrow. Which, in his pa's case, turned out to be the truth. In less than a year his pa was dead, too.

The worst day of all was the day of his pa's funeral. His aunts and uncles brought him home and sat in the parlor discussing what was to be done with him. They didn't know he was eavesdropping, didn't know how it crushed him to hear them say that none of them wanted to take him in. One uncle flat-out said he wasn't their responsibility. An aunt said that she already had four kids and couldn't afford to raise another. Another aunt, a spinster, said that she'd never wanted children, and wasn't about to change her ways because "the black sheep of the family,"' as she called his pa, had drunk himself to death.

The upshot was that they decided to put him in an orphanage.

Four years. That was how long he was stuck there. Four years of pure hell. Four years of being switched for the slightest infraction. Four years of barely enough to eat, of threadbare blankets in the cold of winter, of hand-me-down clothes that never fit, of shoes that were either too tight or too loose, of lights out at eight and always up at five, of scrubbing and sweeping and not being allowed to visit the outhouse without permission.

Was it any wonder he'd hated it? Was it any wonder that one day he decided enough was enough, and snuck out in the middle of the night? He hiked over ten miles to the city.

Chicago. He hadn't known much about it at the time, except that there were an awful lot of people and it would be easy to lose himself amid the teeming throngs. Nearly three hundred thousand, he would learn, and growing by leaps and bounds.

It was a whole new world. A scary world. At first he scrounged in the trash and refuse bins in alleys for food. He slept in discarded crates, in empty houses, anywhere dry and somewhat safe.

In time he graduated from refuse to thievery. He'd swipe fruit from stalls, snatch clothes from street vendors. He learned that other urchins were adept at picking pockets, so he became adept at it, too. His early attempts were clumsy, and only his fleetness of foot spared him from winding up behind bars. He might not have improved much if he hadn't made the acquaintance of Old Tom, who was a master at relieving others of their valuables. Old Tom taught him the most valuable trick of all. Being quick was fine, and having a light touch was dandy, but the true secret to being a successful pickpocket was what Old Tom called "the art of distraction." Which was a highfalutin way of saying you bamboozled your victim.

A common method was to bump into someone, hard, and then, while saying how sorry you were, you patted and smoothed their clothes while relieving them of their purse.

His own favorite was to carry a jug of water around, and when he spotted a well-dressed mark, he'd intentionally walk into them just as he started to take a drink from the jug, spilling water all over.

Old Tom and some others were friendly enough, but the streets were a dangerous place. He wasn't the only one scrabbling to stay alive. The city was packed with immigrants, many of them barely getting by. And then there were those without anywhere else to live, and no family, besides. Street urchins, they were called. Like wolves, many roamed in packs, and like wolves, they were fiercely protective of the streets they roamed.

Twice a pack had caught him unawares.

The first time, it was late at night, and he was in a part of the city he'd never explored before. He was searching for a place to sleep when, without warning, he was jumped. Over a dozen sprang out of the darkness, but only a few of the older ones came at him with clubs. That was what saved him. If all of them had attacked at once, he'd have been overwhelmed. As it was, he'd barely escaped. Twisting and dodging, he'd taken blows to the shoulder, chest and arms, and then he was through them and ran with all the speed he could muster. Howling and yelling, the pack gave chase, but in the dark he was able to slip away.

The next time was more serious.

He'd been in the city a couple of years. He knew it like the back of his hand, and grew overconfident. He'd decided to spend the night in a seldom-used shed at the stockyards. He had slept there before, and wasn't expecting trouble.

Little did he know that a new gang had claimed the stockyards as their territory, and as he stepped up to the shack, he was suddenly ringed by boys bristling with knives and clubs.

Their leader waved a knife and demanded money, "or else."

Every cent he had at the time, he'd come by the hard way. He decided he would be damned if he'd hand it over. He'd pretended to give in, nodding and saying, "Sure. Whatever you want." He'd made as if to reach for his poke—and kicked the leader where it would hurt the most. Unfortunately, the leader had oysters made of lead and came at him in earnest, intent on relieving him of his life.

He'd tried to flee and been shoved back by some of those who ringed him. He would have died, then and there, but the leader toyed with him like a cat with a mouse. As it was, he was cut four times. Not deeply, not to where the cuts were life-threatening, but they hurt and they bled, and he was sure he was a goner.

In desperation he'd leaped at the older boy and gouged a fingernail into the boy's eye. The gang leader shrieked and clutched at his face.

The next was hazy. Somehow, he wrenched on the leader's arm and got hold of the bloody blade. He attacked the circle, swinging wildly, voicing savage cries. To his amazement, they gave way, and he'd fled into the night.

That was it for Chicago. He'd laid up for a week. By then he was healed enough to jump on a freight train headed west. He didn't care where he ended up. One city was much like any other, or so he'd reckoned.

Kansas City proved him wrong. Compared to the hustle and bustle of Chicago, it was downright lackadaisical. The pace of life was a lot slower, the people a lot friendlier. That the population wasn't much over thirty thousand might have had something to do with it.

He continued to ply his pickpocketing craft and took up gambling, in a small way. He made enough that instead of living on the street, he rented a room at a boardinghouse. He dressed better, and ate better, and might have stayed there forever if it hadn't been for the Finch episode.

Oliver Wendall Finch was a leading citizen. A banker, he had made his first million by the time he was forty, or so the story went. Now past sixty, he indulged his one vice—bucking the tiger—every chance he could. Finch happened to frequent the same saloon—the Frontier House—that the rider did. Why, he never could figure out. With all the money Finch had, it made more sense for him to spend his time at one of the luxurious gambling palaces.

As curious as everyone else, he'd joined the onlookers watching Finch play one night, and noticed that Finch was a heavy cigar smoker. A lot of men were. There was nothing unusual in that. But it gave him an idea.

At any hour of the day or night, a person could find a hawker selling virtually anything under the sun. Cigars included. Hastening out, he'd scoured nearby streets, and as fate would have it, found an elderly man selling cigars. He offered to buy every one, plus the tray the old man carried them in. The old man was reluctant. He had to offer twice what the cigars would have fetched—on average, two for fifteen cents—and throw in another couple of dollars for the tray.

Then he posted himself outside the Frontier House, and waited. The moment Oliver Wendall Finch came through the batwings, he began bawling, "Cigars for sale! Get your cigars here! Finest quality!"

The truth was, he couldn't tell a good cigar from a bad one if his life had depended on it. He was taking a gamble.

Finch stepped to a carriage and was about to climb on when he heard the cry and glanced over.

Hoping against hope, he hollered, "Cigars! Cigars! From five cents to twenty-five!"

Finch came over. "Twenty-five?" he said. "Let me see your selection, young man. What brands do you carry?"

He hadn't bothered to find out. The important thing was to lure Finch close. And now, as Finch reached toward the tray, he pretended to stumble and upended it onto Finch's legs and shoes.

"My word!" the great man had exclaimed. "Let me help you."

Together, they bent and collected cigars. They were so close that Finch didn't think anything of it when they bumped shoulders. So close, that his hand darted in and under Finch's coat and out again without Finch being the wiser. They finished picking the cigars up. Finch examined a few, produced a coin from a pants pocket, and bought a couple.

He would never forget the feeling he had, watching the great man clatter off in the carriage, the great man's wallet in his own jacket. The snatch had been flawless. Quickly setting the tray down, he hurried to his room at the boardinghouse to collect his belongings.

He didn't look in the wallet until he was ready to leave. Seated on the bed, every nerve tingling, he opened it and counted the thick sheaf of bills. Six hundred and forty-three dollars. For him, a fortune.

Giddy with delight, rolling back and forth, he'd laughed until tears trickled from his eyes.

A knock on his door brought his glee to an end. His landlady said that a constable was there to see him.

He went out the window. His room was on the second floor. He dropped his bag, hung from the sill, and dropped. Fear lent wings to his feet, and the next morning, he bought a horse and took the road to Atchison, Kansas. He had a hankering to see Denver, but to get there he'd have to cross nearly six hundred miles of hostile-infested countryside. By his lonesome, he invited an early grave. So he sold the horse and bought a ticket on the Butterfield Overland Despatch. The man who sold him his ticket told him that the stage line might be shutting down soon because it couldn't compete with the railroad.

That was a shame, because he enjoyed the trip. Relay stations at regular intervals were welcome breaks. The food was tolerable, and he got to see a lot of prairie country.

The other passengers talked a lot about Indians, but they didn't see a single hostile the whole way.

Denver suited him down to his marrow. It used to be known as Denver City until it was picked as the new territorial capital. Thanks in large part to the Pikes Peak gold rush and a silver boom in the high country, Denver became a hub of commerce and travel. It also, he soon discovered, was a hub of corruption.

Saloons and sporting houses outnumbered churches twenty to one. Card sharps, confidence men, and ladies of ill repute thrived.

For a pickpocket, Denver was a feast of opportunity. But it wasn't enough. He yearned for something more. Something that would reap the kind of money he'd gotten from Oliver Wendall Finch. He'd picked Finch's pocket, sure, but he'd done it while impersonating a cigar hawker.

Impersonation. That was where the big money lay. To that end, he came up with a scheme to fleece several of Denver's elite out of a lot of cash. He thought his brainstorm was brilliant.

He never expected to be lynched.

4

———◆———

Federal Deputy Marshal Jacob Stone never knew it to fail. Liquor and stupid went hand in hand. He couldn't count the number of drunks he'd had to confront in his long career. And a lot of them ended as this one was about to end: badly.

Stone knew that Loudon was going to draw before Loudon did. He could tell by Loudon's attitude, his tone. Men like Loudon did what little thinking they did with their six-shooters.

Stone, on the other hand, prided himself on being a thinker. He'd often said that any man who toted tin should use his brain more than his six-gun. Unfortunately, in this instance, he was forced to use both. He drew his Colt even as Loudon raised that revolver from under the blanket, and shot him in the shoulder. At the blast, Loudon was knocked onto his back and his six-gun fell from fingers gone limp.

Franks sat there in shock.

"You shouldn't ought to have tried that," Stone said.

Scarlet was spreading down Loudon's shirt. He stared at the wound as if he couldn't believe his eyes. "You shot me," he bleated.

"You point a gun at a deputy marshal, what do you expect?" Stone descended into the wash, keeping them covered.

Franks found his voice. "You damned jackass," he said to his pard. "You're no gun hand."

Seemingly fascinated by his own blood, Loudon replied, "I don't want to go to prison over raisin' a little hell."

"You won't," Stone said. "You'll go to prison for tryin' to kill me." He kicked the revolver out of reach, tossed Franks's revolver to one side, and stepped back. "See to your friend."

"I'm no doc," Franks said. But he knelt next to Loudon and gingerly probed the hole in Loudon's shirt. "He's bleedin' bad."

Stone could see that himself. He could have saved himself some trouble and shot Loudon dead, but that was another thing about him. He never killed unless absolutely necessary. He'd much rather take them in alive. Even if it sometimes meant putting his own life in peril. "See if the slug went clean through."

"How do I do that?"

Stone began to wonder if the pair had a brain between them. "Lift him up and look at his back."

"Oh." Franks slid his hands under Loudon, partly raised his shoulder, and peered under. "Yep. There's a hole on this side, too."

"Good," Stone said. "Now untie one of the horses and pull out the picket pin you used."

"What do you want with a picket pin?" Franks asked in surprise.

"To clean between my teeth."

Franks didn't hide his confusion. "What are you talkin' about? Picket pins are too big to use as toothpicks. How can . . ." He stopped. "Oh, you're pokin' fun."

"Pull out a pin."

Clearly puzzled, Franks did as he was told. He had to work at it. The pin was in deep. Finally he held it up. "There. You want me to climb on and ride for help?"

"Sure," Stone said. "I'm as dumb as you." He pointed at their smoldering campfire. "Get that burning again, then stick it in there until it's red-hot."

"The pin?"

"No. Your head."

Muttering, Franks gathered some brush and added it to the tiny flames. Soon a fair fire crackled, but it wouldn't last long.

"Get to stickin'," Stone said.

Franks thrust the end of the picket pin in the flames. "You like makin' fun of folks, don't you?"

"It keeps me entertained."

Loudon had clutched his shoulder and was gritting his teeth. He let out a groan, then said, "It hurts somethin' awful."

"Bein' shot will do that," Stone said.

"You're a hard man, Deputy," Loudon said.

Stone felt no pity. The man had brought it on himself, and was too dumb to appreciate the favor he'd done him. "If I was, you'd be dead."

Franks had a bigger concern. "What happens once we stop the bleedin'? What do you aim to do with us?"

"Take you to Ogallala and lodge you in their jail," Stone replied. "After that, it's out of my hands."

"I have pretty near fifty dollars in my saddlebags," Franks said. "I don't suppose you'd take it and let us go?"

Stone stared.

"What?" Franks said.

"You expect me to take a bribe?"

"Why not? I hear tell the law does it all the time."

"Not this law," Stone informed him. For forty years, he'd enforced it the best he knew how. Never once had he stepped outside it himself. Yes, he knew of deputies who had, but they were few, and the bad apples were always weeded out. He'd done some of the weeding himself.

"My pard is right," Franks said. "You are high and mighty."

"Some gents," Stone said, "shouldn't be let loose without a keeper." He motioned. "How hot is that pin?"

Franks bent down. "It's not red yet."

"I feel dizzy," Loudon said, his Adam's apple bobbing. He lay flat and forlornly gazed skyward. "I ain't ever been shot before. It's not like I thought it would be. It don't hurt much. And the smell of my blood is makin' me queasy."

"You're still breathin'," Stone pointed out.

"Barely," Loudon said, and mewed like a kitten. "I've never had a day start worse than this one."

"Pitiful," Stone said.

"Why are you pickin' on me? Ain't it enough that you shot me?" Loudon let out a gasp. "Lordy, I feel weak. I might pass out."

"Good," Stone said.

"That's harsh," Franks said.

"He'd do us a favor if he did," Stone said. "We don't want him thrashin' around when you stick that pin in him."

"When he does what?" Loudon said.

"We have to stop the bleedin', and Hebron doesn't have a sawbones," Stone enlightened him. "Usin' a picket pin is a trick I learned in Texas in my younger days."

"You're a Texan?" Franks said.

"Born and bred. I never intended to end up in Nebraska, but here I am."

"A Texican. It figures."

"How so?" Stone said.

"Everybody knows Texans are mean as hell."

"It's not that so much," Stone said, "as we don't abide dumb."

"There you go again."

Stone sighed. They didn't breed badmen like they used to. In the old days, hard cases were really hard. This pair were muffins compared to some of the outlaws he'd tangled with.

Franks bent forward again and nearly put his forehead in the fire. Snapping back, he said, "That was close."

"Lord help me," Stone said.

"What are you on about now?"

"I can't wait to reach North Platte." Stone was eager to be shed of these simpletons.

Franks took the picket pin from the fire and held it up. "Is this hot enough, the tip a little red?"

"It will do," Stone said. "Unbutton your pard's shirt, and get to it."

Franks looked uncertainly at Loudon. "Get to what exactly?"

"Where are you from?" Stone asked.

"Why do you want to know?"

"Where?"

Franks frowned. "I was born in Ohio, but I don't see what that has to do with anything. I haven't been back in pretty near fifteen years."

"I know a gent from Ohio," Stone said. "He can actually think. So it must be you and not the state."

"You are damned hilarious."

"Open the shirt and stick the pin in the hole. And be quick about it before your friend bleeds to death."

Franks blinked and blanched. "Stick it in the hole?"

"How did you two tree that town? Kittens are more fierce," Stone said in mild exasperation. "Yes, you stick it in the hole to stop the bleedin' and cauterize the wound so it won't become infected. In case you haven't heard, more people die of wounds than they do from bein' shot."

"I know that," Franks said. "But still."

Stone shrugged. "It's up to you. He's your pard. Do you want him to live or not?"

"I think I hate you," Franks said.

"I'll try not to let that hurt my feelin's," Stone said. "Now get to pokin' or you'll have to stick the pin in the fire again."

"Oh, Lordy," Franks declared. "What a day."

He fumbled at the buttons and carefully peeled the blood-wet shirt back to expose the wound. It was still bleeding but not as profusely. When he picked up the picket pin, Stone stopped him.

"Stick it in the fire again."

"Do I have to?"

"No. You can stick it in him cold. It won't seal the wound and won't stop the bleedin'. But it should help any infection get worse, and with a little luck, you can bury him in a week or so."

"You're the most peculiar lawdog I ever met." Franks held the pin in the fire again. "Mind if I ask you a question while we wait for this to heat up?"

Stone had noticed a boulder that suited him as a

seat, and he roosted before responding, "So long as it's not personal."

"Why do you keep doin' what you do?"

"I told you," Stone said. "Not personal."

"What's personal about that?" Franks rejoined. "I only ask because you look to be as old as Methuselah. Most would have quit before they got so many wrinkles. How come you stick with it?"

"I like to travel and meet jackasses."

"I mean it. I'm really curious."

Stone suspected Franks was stalling in hope of turning the tables, but he answered honestly. "I had a friend once. My best friend in all the world. He was a lawman, like me. One day, oh, about ten years ago, he decided he'd worn a badge long enough, and it was time for him to buy a small house with a porch so he could while away the rest of his days in a rockin' chair."

"Nothin' strange about that," Franks said. "Folks like to rock when they're old. My grandma used to say it reminds them of when they were infants and were bein' rocked by their mas."

Stone had never thought of that. It struck him as half-brilliant.

"'Course, she was addlepated," Franks went on. "How can anyone recollect bein' rocked by their mothers when they weren't even old enough to tell their fingers from their toes?"

"There's hope for you yet," Stone said.

"So your friend had his rockin' chair?" Franks prompted. "How does that account for you not havin' one of your own?"

"About a year after he retired, his grandson went over one mornin' and found him in that rocker, dead as a doornail, and stiff, to boot. The doc said his heart gave out, but I knew better."

"What did he die of, then?"

"Uselessness," Stone said, scowling at the memories being stirred. "We had a talk, him and me, not long before he passed away, and he mentioned how useless he felt. He didn't have anything to do anymore besides go fishin' now and then and sit in that rocker and rock."

"So you won't quit because you're afraid the same might happen to you?" Franks scratched the stubble on his chin, and nodded. "I reckon that makes sense. Everybody should feel like they're of some use. I did, back in my cowboyin' days. Then I got too big for my britches and took up with Loudon, and I've been pretty much useless ever since."

"I'm surprised you'd admit it."

"We are what we are," Franks said. "No use tryin' to hide it."

"Some of your grandma must have rubbed off on you."

"Beg pardon?"

Stone had come to a decision. He'd long since learned to weed out the truly evil from the so-so. "When you're done stickin' him with that picket pin, you can go."

"Go where?"

"Anywhere you want."

Franks's jaw dropped. "Am I hearin' right? You're lettin' me go?"

"Provided you leave your pistol and your rifle and pay for the damages you and him caused."

Franks beamed, then scowled. "We don't have much money. Not enough to pay for all that."

"You can work it out with Applebaum and the owner of the feed and grain," Stone said, and wagged his Colt at him. "Mark my words, though. I'll keep in touch with them—and if you go back on your word, I'll hunt you down."

"I believe you." Franks jabbed a thumb at Loudon. "What about my pard?"

"He pistol-whipped Mr. Applebaum and tried to shoot me. He doesn't deserve a second chance."

"Thank God I do!" Franks exclaimed.

"Thank somebody," Stone said.

5

BACK THEN

The City of Sin. The Mile High Bordello. Queen City of the Plains. Those were a few of the nicknames Denver had earned in its short existence.

He took the name Robert Grant. It had a nice sound to it, an honest sound. And easy to remember. "Robert" came from the first name of the most famous Southern general during the Civil War. "Grant" was the name of the most famous Union general, and later President. He also took a room at the Carlton. It wasn't the most prestigious, but it had a reputation for quality and he wanted to give the impression he was a man of quality.

The key to impersonations, he'd decided, was to make them as real as possible. No detail was too small to prevent people from suspecting he was a fake.

The idea for his scheme came to him by chance. In order to better acquaint himself with the city, he bought a copy of the *Denver Weekly Times*. The main page had a story about how Colorado was expected to be admitted to the Union in the next year or so, and how there was talk of Denver becoming the state capital.

An article on the last page interested him more. It was headlined "Where Is the Charity?" According to the journalist who wrote it, Denver was a city of two classes, the rich and the poor. Mansions were springing up right and left, thanks to strikes in the gold fields and the silver lodes. Savvy businessmen who catered to the needs of the hordes of the money-hungry were making their own money hand over fist. But a lot of people, the majority, barely got by. They lived hand to mouth. Hundreds could barely afford their next meal, let alone a roof over their heads.

"Where is our sense of Christian charity?" the journalist asked. "Why do we let women and children go homeless? Why must a mother with a newborn plead for the money for milk on a street corner? Why must a miner who lost his legs in a mine collapse beg for the sustenance the rest of us take for granted?"

The journalist went on to appeal to Denver's well-to-do to open their pocketbooks and purses to those in desperate plight. What was needed, he wrote, were new charities that would work to feed and clothe those who, through no fault of their own, were in great need.

Reading the account, he had his brainstorm. It was as if a keg of black powder went off in his head. Over the next several days, it was all he thought about.

The impersonation he had in mind would be easy to carry off. And it wouldn't cost much to get started.

The next day he visited a printer. He had cards made up. THE DENVER BENEVOLENT ASSOCIATION, they read, along with his name and his address at the Carlton, in case anyone checked up on him. He liked that word, "benevolent." He remembered it from the Sisters of Benevolent Mercy in Kansas City, nuns who served meals to those down on their luck.

Wearing his suit and looking his very best, he started at one end of Larimer Square and went from business to business, introducing himself and asking if they would like to contribute to the poor and needy of their fair city. The money, he assured them, would go to feed and clothe those in desperate need.

At the very first business he visited, a place that sold tools and the like, the owner offered to give him fifty dollars but said that he'd need a receipt for accounting purposes.

Smothering his panic at his blunder, he patted his pockets and laughed and said, "Wouldn't you know it? I left them in my room. There are days when I wonder if my head is attached."

"That's no problem, Mr. Grant," the owner said. "I always have extras. I buy receipt books by the dozen. Cheaper that way."

He'd never known there was such a thing. It was a godsend. Nearly everywhere he went, they wanted a receipt, too.

By the end of the day, to his considerable astonishment, he'd collected close to five hundred dollars. That night, he spread the money out on his bed and threw a few bills into the air and silently laughed at how easy it had been.

He didn't overdo it. He went out once a week, always to a part of the city he hadn't been to before.

For several months all went fine. He lived well, ate well. He gambled now and then, but judiciously.

Then one day he was strolling along Broadway and saw a bronzed plaque on a brick building. The Denver Businessman's Club, it announced. He figured it was worth a try. Going in, he introduced himself and gave

a card to the receptionist. Presently she escorted him
down a long hall to the manager's office. A short, heavyset man named Owlsley pumped his hand and bid him
take a seat, then went around a large mahogany desk.
Owlsley was holding the card.

"The Denver Benevolent Association? I don't believe
I've ever heard of your organization before, Mr. Grant."

"We've been around a while now," he said glibly. "Our
work with the poor is well known." He mentioned several businesses that had contributed, adding, "The poor
are in need of so much. Maybe your club would consider helping out?"

"It's not *my* club," Owlsley said. "I merely run it for
some of the wealthiest men in the city. The membership
is restricted, you see."

"The Association would be grateful for anything they
can give." He patted his pocket. "I'll provide a receipt, of
course."

Owlsley sat back and tapped the card against his
double chin. "If you don't mind my saying, you seem
a trifle young for your line of work."

"How old do you have to be to want to help people?"

"It's just that most your age seldom take much interest in the welfare of others. They are too involved in
their own lives."

"I lived on the street once," he said. "It taught me a
few things."

"Indeed it would," Owlsley said. He looked at the
card and set it on his desk. "Tell you what. I'll broach
the subject of a donation with the members, and if they're
willing, make a generous donation. Come back in a few
days and I should have your answer."

It sounded reasonable. He thanked Owlsley, shook
his hand, and went out with visions of the largest do-

nation yet swimming in his head. That night he visited his favorite saloon. He drank a little, gambled a little, and was on his way back to the Carlton by eleven.

Halfway there, a feeling came over him. A strange feeling that he was being watched. He stopped and looked around, but the few people he saw weren't paying any attention to him.

He didn't want to give the impression he was over-eager, so he let four days go by before he paid another visit to the Businessman's Club. The receptionist was gone a while. When she returned, she apologized. Mr. Owlsley was tied up in a meeting. Would he be willing to come back that evening, say, about nine o'clock?

He thought that was a little late, but he agreed. He idled the rest of the day away, and at a quarter to nine, rapped the knocker on the club's door. To his mild surprise, Owlsley, himself, opened it.

"Mr. Grant! How nice to see you again. Come in. Come in. I have good news for you. Let's go up to my office, shall we?"

Only a single lamp was lit. The hall was plunged in shadow. Owlsley held the office door for him, and he went in and drew up short.

Another man was behind the desk. A spindly man in expensive clothes, his hands resting on the ivory handle to a polished cane. He had graying hair and muttonchops, and a nose hooked like a hawk's beak.

On either side of him stood a pair of big men with broad shoulders, virtual living statues.

"What's this?" he blurted as Owlsley closed the door behind them and stayed where he was, effectively blocking the only way out.

The older man reached to the desk and held up the card. "Robert Grant, is it?" His voice was an ominous growl.

"That's right," he answered, smiling. "And who might you be?"

"Have a seat, Mr. Grant."

He went on smiling as he sank into a chair, but the hairs at the nape of his neck prickled.

"You've stepped in it, Mr. Grant," the man said.

Shamming innocence, he twisted to look at Owlsley. "What is this, Mr. Owlsley? Who is this man, and why is he treating me this way?"

"Tell him, Owlsley," the man said.

The manager had broken out in a sweat. "You're addressing Mr. Ebidiah Worthingon. His name might be familiar. He is the founder of the Lucretia Mine and Silver Company, perhaps the most famous in the territory."

"Perhaps?" Ebidiah Worthington said in that growl of his.

Owlsley coughed. "Mr. Worthington is one of the wealthiest men in Colorado, if not the country. He, in fact, also founded this club, which I manage for him."

"Get to the point," Worthington said.

"Yes, sir." Owlsley paused. "As a matter of course, I report all matters of consequence to Mr. Worthington. I mentioned to him that you had stopped by and asked how much the club was willing to donate to your cause."

"And as a matter of course," Worthington mimicked Owlsley, "I had you investigated."

"What?"

"You heard me, boy," Worthington said. "I didn't get where I am by letting others take advantage of me."

"I don't believe this."

"Start believing it, boy," Worthington said. "You're in very deep trouble. You and your confidence scheme."

"I represent the Denver Benevolent Association—" he began.

Worthington held up a hand. "Stop. Don't insult me. You see, initially I planned to donate a thousand dollars. But I thought I should check on the uses to which the money would be put. Some charities raise a lot of money for worthy causes but very little of what they raise goes to the cause. Imagine my surprise when I learned that you, in fact, have no cause. All the money you collect goes to yourself." His thin lips curled in a sneer. "As best I can determine, you simply had cards printed and set yourself up as your own charity. Your gall astounds me. Your greed appalls me."

"Greed?"

"What else would you call it, Mr. Grant? If that's even your real name, which I very much doubt."

"I just wanted money to live on. I didn't take a lot from anyone."

"You took enough, you despicable cad," Worthington said. He tapped his fingers on his cane. "What's your real name, by the way?"

He went to reply.

"Bear in mind," Worthington broke him off, "that if I sense you're lying, these men next to me will break your arms and your legs and whatever else I want broken."

He barely hesitated. "Alonzo," he said. "Alonzo Pratt. My folks died when I was young and I was raised in an orphanage until I escaped and made my own way in the world."

Worthington stared intently at him, as if trying to peer into his very soul. "I believe you."

"Thank you."

"But if you think your little tale of woe will sway me, you have another think coming," Worthington said. "What you have done is despicable."

"Killers and robbers do worse," Alonzo said.

"A killer simply kills someone. Robbers take valuables at gun or knife point. You're far worse, in my estimation. You prey on the gullibility of others, on their good natures. You're devious, Mr. Pratt. Much as Satan was when he preyed on Eve's gullibility in the Garden of Eden."

"The Garden of Eden?" Alonzo repeated. He didn't understand how the Bible had gotten into it. Not that he knew much about it, except from Sunday services at the orphanage and the little he remembered from his ma reading to his pa and him on occasion.

"To be perfectly honest, Mr. Pratt, I think you're a wretched human being."

"I can give some of the money back," Alonzo offered, thinking that would show he wasn't as vile as the man seemed to think. "I haven't spent all of it."

"And the people you fleeced whom you can't reimburse?" Worthington said, and shook his head. "No, returning some of the money is only a partial solution. You can be of much more use than that."

Owlsley, who had been silent a while, spoke up with, "I beg you to reconsider, Mr. Worthington."

"Who works for whom?" Worthington said. "You mentioned your objections earlier, when we discussed it. I am firm in my resolve."

"He's just a boy," Owlsley said.

"Nonsense," Worthington said, and fixed his flinty eyes on Alonzo. "How old are you, Mr. Pratt? The truth, if you please."

"Twenty."

"There? You see?" Worthington said to Owlsley. "He's a grown man. An adult. As such, the consequences of his actions are on his shoulders and his alone."

"But to do *that*, sir," Owlsley said. "The law would take a dim view."

"What law?" Worthington spat. "Crime is rampant.

Corruption widespread. Vermin and vice are everywhere, and it's high time we put a stop to it. That's why I helped form the Law and Order League."

Alonzo stiffened. He hadn't been in Denver all that long, but he was well aware of the vigilance movement. For years now, the League had taken it on itself to "arrest" suspected criminals and put them on trial. Upwards of twenty men had been hung.

"I see that caught your attention," Worthington said. "As well it should. You see, the League is always in need of examples, and you would be excellent in that regard."

"Excellent how?" Alonzo asked in confusion.

"To those who might be inclined to follow in your footsteps," Worthington said. "Who might be tempted to fleece honest souls as you've been doing." He smiled and nodded. "Yes, you will do nicely. We'll arrest you and hold a trial and then hang you from a streetlamp as a warning to others."

"You wouldn't!" Alonzo gasped.

"Oh, I assure you, we certainly would," Ebidiah Worthington said, and he uttered a cold, spiteful laugh.

6

———•◦•———

Alonzo Pratt never anticipated anything like this. He never imagined he'd become a target of the vigilantes. Not for the petty crimes he committed. He wasn't a murderer. He didn't even rob people. He swindled them, yes, but he saw that as different, and less apt to result in harm to them or him.

He thought about that as the burly underlings of Ebidiah Worthington forcefully guided him out the rear of the club. Each had hold of an arm, and their grips were like twin vises. Behind them, Worthington's cane clacked on the hardwood floor.

"Behave yourself, now, boy," the rich man said, "and you won't be hurt. Well, until we get around to hanging you." He chuckled.

Alonzo didn't find it the least bit humorous. And he'd be damned if he'd let the old buzzard use him as an example. His mind fairly flew as he racked his wits for a way out of his predicament. "This is wrong, Mr. Worthington. Terribly wrong."

"You're a fine one to lecture somebody on rightness and wrongness," the great worthy responded. "You're a cheat, and you deserve to be punished."

"Don't you think stringing me up is overdoing it?"

"Ah. You believe the punishment should fit the crime? That is the current rationale behind jurisprudence in our country, but the League doesn't subscribe to that namby-pamby notion."

"Ah, yourself," Alonzo said.

"Keep a civil tone, Mr. Pratt," Worthington warned. "I understand you must be feeling outraged right about now, which is perfectly normal. But don't let your temper get the better of your tongue."

They were almost to the rear door. The hallway was in deep shadow, and Alonzo couldn't see the faces of either of the hulks restraining him. He could see their necks, though.

"You have only yourself to blame for how you will shortly leave this world," Worthington prattled on. "You chose the life you live. No one forced you to go around duping honest souls out of their hard-earned money."

"I never hurt anyone."

"That's not the point," Worthington said. "The point is the principle of the thing. Without principles, Mr. Pratt, we're no better than animals. Without principles, civilized society becomes no more than forced civility."

Alonzo didn't know what that meant but he did know something. "You take a lot on yourself, you and your vigilante friends."

"And if we don't deal with lawbreakers, who will? Crime is rampant in Denver, so much so, people clamor for something to be done. Well, the Law and Order League does something. We send misfits like you to your just reward."

"I'm a misfit now?"

"Anyone who breaks the law refuses to fit in. Laws are instituted for a reason, and should be diligently followed."

"You're breaking the law right now."

"Grasp at straws all you want. It won't help you."

They reached the door, and the burly underling on the right opened it and led the way through, hauling on Alonzo's arm. The other pushed. Not hard, but enough that to resist would be futile.

Alonzo was startled to see a carriage waiting, a driver up on the seat. Once inside, his doom was practically sealed.

Twilight had fallen and was giving way to the growing dark of night. Stars had blossomed, sparkling like faraway jewels.

There were two short steps. The man in the lead didn't bother glancing down. He was looking at the carriage. Thus, he didn't see Alonzo suddenly thrust out a foot, catching the man about the ankles. With a snort of surprise, the man tripped and fell, and lost his grip on Alonzo's arm. Quick as lightning, Alonzo spun and punched his other captor in the neck. He didn't use all his strength. Even now, he refused to kill if he could help it. But he hit the man hard enough that he staggered back, gurgling, and clutched his throat.

Alonzo bolted. He was out the door and down the steps before either could stop him. The driver yelled something but he didn't catch what it was. Like a buck fleeing ravening wolves, he raced to a gap between the club and the next building and shot up it toward the street.

"Stop him!" Ebidiah Worthington bawled. "Don't let him get away!"

Alonzo ran for all he was worth, his legs flying. He

glanced back as he came to the far end and saw one of
the men after him, but well back. Plunging out into the
street, he sprinted into the growing night. Curious
stares were cast his way. He didn't care. He didn't stop.
He had to put as much distance as he could between
him and his would-be abductors.

Only when he had put several blocks behind him
and there was no sign of pursuit did he slow to a walk
to catch his breath. And to ponder. He was in a fix, and
he saw only one way out.

Ebidiah Worthington wasn't about to give up. The
word would go out. The other members of the League
would be alerted, and every vigilante in the city would
be on the lookout for him.

Alonzo figured to hide out in his room at the Carlton
for a while, and then realized that was the worst mistake he could make. Worthington had had him investigated. The vigilantes must know he was staying there.
The Carlton was the first place they'd look.

There should be time to collect his things, Alonzo
reckoned. He would dash in, throw them in his bag,
and be gone long before the vigilantes showed up. And
then what? He shook his head. He would work that out
later. The important thing was to get shed of Denver as
quickly as possible.

It was ten blocks to his hotel. Ten long blocks. He
passed scores of pedestrians and those on horseback
and a few in wagons. Every glance thrown his way
caused his nerves to jangle. He never knew, but one of
them might be a vigilante.

He tried to calm himself, to tell himself it was too
soon, they couldn't possibly be looking for him yet. It
did little good.

The Carlton was lit up, the lobby as bright as ever.

Crossing it, he felt terribly exposed. He saw a few faces he recognized but others he didn't, and each of them was a potential threat.

The desk clerk looked up and nodded in greeting. "Mr. Grant," he said.

Alonzo nodded back. He took the stairs two at a stride. Once in his room, he grabbed his carpetbag from under the bed. His possessions were few: the clothes on his back, a couple of extra shirts, a pair of everyday pants, suspenders, and his toiletries. And his pouch of money, which he'd hidden in the chamber pot he never used. He didn't own any weapons. Until now, he hadn't seen the need. That might change.

Since the clerk might wonder why he was leaving when he was paid up until the end of the week, Alonzo went out the back. The dark alley was empty, and he was about to head down it when a pair of silhouettes appeared at the far end. Hoping they hadn't seen him, he ducked around a refuse barrel and crouched.

Footsteps crunched as the pair hurried in his direction.

Coincidence, Alonzo hoped. Two men using the alley as a shortcut, nothing more, he told himself.

"Do we go in or stay out?" a gruff voice said.

"Our orders are to watch the back and make sure he doesn't get away," the second man replied.

"You have your billy club?"

"Of course."

"Use it if you have to. Mr. Worthington is most insistent. He wants this one. He wants him badly."

They came to the rear door and stopped.

Alonzo scarcely breathed. The vigilantes must be incredibly well-organized to have gotten there so soon. He was only yards away, and if they spotted him, from the sound of things they would beat him senseless.

"What's this one's name, anyhow?"

"They didn't tell me."

"Then how will we know him?"

"He's young and he'll be on the run. He has black hair and blue eyes and is well-built. That's all I know."

They fell silent.

Alonzo wished they would go in. He couldn't stay there forever. Other vigilantes might show up, or they might decide to look around. Even worse, the rest of the Law and Order League was probably spreading throughout the city, searching for him. He'd be hard-pressed to get away undetected.

"I don't like this waiting around," one of the men complained.

"We do as we're told."

"Why not go in and see if he's in there?"

"Someone else will attend to that. We're to cut off his escape."

"Then you stay here and I'll go in. For all we know, he's already gone and we're wasting our time."

"We were told to plant ourselves and wait."

Alonzo risked a peek around the barrel. A short, square-jawed man was pacing back and forth, the other, tall and sallow, had leaned against the wall with his arms folded. Their clothes were store-bought and plain, not the expensive kind that Worthington wore. Neither appeared as formidable as the pair at the Businessman's Club. Still, he imagined they were armed.

The man who was pacing stopped. "I'm going in."

"Damn it, Luke. You'll get us in trouble with the big man."

"I didn't join the League to please him, Campbell," Luke said. "I did it because I believe in law and order."

"Same here," Campbell said.

"Then stay here while I go inside and check. If he's flown the coop, we need to know right away."

"I suppose that makes sense," Campbell begrudgingly said.

Luke wasted no time going in.

"Damn him," Campbell said, straightening. Sliding a hand under his jacket, he moved so he faced the door and could see both ends of the alley. He didn't pay particular attention to the barrel.

Firming his grip on his carpetbag, Alonzo waited for his chance. It came when a loud noise out in the street caused Campbell to turn with his back to the barrel. Stepping out, Alonzo said, "Hey." Campbell jumped and turned, and Alonzo struck him full in the face. Bleating in surprise, Campbell stumbled back, at the same time drawing a Remington pocket pistol from under his jacket. Alonzo hit him again and sent him sprawling against the wall. In order to keep from falling, Campbell thrust out both hands and dropped the pistol.

In a twinkling, Alonzo snatched it up and pointed it.

"Don't!" Campbell cried. He shook his head to clear it while pressing as far back as he could.

Alonzo didn't shoot. For one thing, it would bring the other one on the run, and who knew how many more. For another, he wasn't a killer. He'd never shot anyone in his life and didn't intend to start. "You leave me be!" he said. "I won't be hung for stealing a few dollars."

"Wait. What?" Campbell said.

Holding the Remington steady, Alonzo backed away. "Don't come after me or I'll shoot," he warned.

"Mister, you'd better run like Hades," Campbell said. "We'll have thirty men out after you inside the hour."

"You do that," Alonzo blustered, and wheeling on a heel, he raced to the street. A glance over his shoulder showed Campbell darting into the Carlton. He went to move to the middle of the street, the light from a window spilling over him, and the woman he was about to pass recoiled in fright.

"My word! What are you up to, waving that thing around?"

Alonzo realized he still held the Remington. "Sorry," he said, and shoved the pistol into a pants pocket. It was heavier than he thought it might be and dragged at his pants, but it couldn't be helped. He'd hang on to it. Better to have a revolver and hope he didn't have to use it, he reasoned, than to not have one should he need it to preserve his life.

He smiled at the woman to reassure her, and hurried off. He must leave Denver without delay. He recollected that Eastabrook's Livery and Boarding Stable wasn't far, and they'd have horses for sale.

The city's nightlife was coming alive, and a lot of people were out and about. Some were enjoying the cool night air. Others were bound for the theater or making the rounds of Denver's saloons and taverns, or perhaps on their way to visit a bordello.

Normally, Alonzo would hardly pay them any mind. Tonight, every passerby drew his gaze. He saw no flash of recognition, saw nothing to indicate the League was closing in.

Lanterns hung on pegs glowed in the stable. An elderly man in overalls and a straw hat was shoving horse manure into a wheelbarrow and looked up as Alonzo came over.

"What can I do for you, sonny?"

Struggling not to give away the urgency that clawed at his insides, Alonzo said, "I'd like a horse. The best you have."

"To rent or to buy?"

"Buy," Alonzo said. "And I mean it about the best."

"Best how?"

"I want an animal that can go fast and far."

"In a hurry, are you?" the man said, and chuckled. When Alonzo didn't smile or grin, he set the shovel across the wheelbarrow. "Yes, I can see you are. Come out back. There's a bay that might suit you. I call him Archibald."

"You name the horses you sell?"

"Why not? We have names, don't we? Do you want to see him or not?"

To Alonzo it was silly, but who was he to quibble with the prospect of a noose being thrown around his neck? "I surely do," he said.

7

THE PRESENT

Four years. That was how long ago Alonzo had escaped from Denver with his hide intact. Since then, he'd wandered where whim took him, into the mountains now and then, out over the plains at other times. On his packhorse were a dozen sets of clothes.

Outfits that let him impersonate a wide range of people.

There was his Civil War outfit, which he'd just used to help himself to the farmer's poke. There was his gambler outfit, his minister's outfit, his own farmer's outfit, his cowpoke outfit, and others.

On this particular morning, encamped along the Platte River, Alonzo sat enjoying his first coffee of the day and listening to the birds sing in the trees. The river flowed peacefully past not a stone's throw away. It was one of those moments when all was right with the world.

Alonzo sipped, and smiled. He had over a thousand

dollars in his saddlebags. He should take it easy. Go somewhere and just relax for a spell. Make the rounds of the saloons. Maybe visit a house of ill repute, as some called them. Although, truth to tell, he'd always felt uncomfortable doing that. Which was a bit peculiar, he reckoned, in that while fleecing others didn't bother him one bit, paying for a night with a woman he didn't know somehow embarrassed him.

Chuckling at his own silliness, Alonzo pondered which outfit he should change into. He'd been using the soldier outfit for a while, and it was time to switch. After thinking about it and thinking about it he decided to don his lawman's outfit. It was one of his favorites. He could do pretty much as he pleased and no one ever questioned him, thanks to the real, honest-to-goodness badge he'd come across.

It had been only a couple of years ago. He was coming down out of the mountains below Leadville when he'd heard shots. He'd lain low a while, until he was sure the shooting had stopped, then warily gone on. When he came to a clearing and spied a body lying on its belly he'd almost gone around. Curious, he'd dismounted and cautiously ventured nearer. Whoever shot the man had appeared to be long gone.

Alonzo rolled the body over and received a shock. Pinned on the man's vest was a badge. A six-point tin star that read UNITED STATES DEPUTY MARSHAL. He'd recoiled in shock and almost run to Archibald and got the Hades out of there.

A couple of bullet holes close to the vest showed how the law officer had met his demise.

Alonzo had sat and debated what to do. He should report it. But he was many miles from a town or settlement. And whomever he reported it to might insist he bring them back to see the body for themselves. Worse, they might pry into who he was and what he was doing when he found the body. His background couldn't stand much scrutiny. For all he knew, there were circulars on him.

He'd finally made up his mind to bury the poor marshal—and to help himself to the marshal's badge. It was a harmless thing with great possibilities. He'd never impersonated a lawman, and the prospects it offered filled him with excitement.

The next general store he came to, he'd bought a shirt and pants and a brown broad-brimmed hat along with a matching leather vest to pin the badge to. The first settlement he came to after he'd donned the new outfit, the people there were so happy to see a lawman that they gave him free food and drink, and treated him grand. Later, he'd impersonated a lawman down in Kansas to collect "emigrant taxes" from settlers. There was no such thing, but the settlers didn't know that and his badge lent him authority.

Yes, Alonzo now decided, it was time for his lawman outfit. He finished his coffee and set about the "transformation," as he liked to call it. Stripping out of his army uniform, he folded it and placed it in one of his packs. From another he took his lawman's duds, but he went for a dip in the river before putting them on. He always tried to bathe at least once a week. And, too, he wanted to try to wash some of the gray dye out of his hair.

Not much did, so he used his bottle of brown dye to change the color. He had a whole collection of dyes. Anytime he wanted, he could change his hair to blond or red or black or about any color he pleased.

He shaved his mustache. He never much liked them, and only grew one now and again as part of a disguise.

Donning the outfit, he jammed on the hat, shrugged

into the leather vest, and pinned on the badge. Grinning, he rubbed it a few times, then bent and picked up his gun belt. The only part of the lawman impersonation he didn't like was having to always wear a six-shooter. Lawmen never went anywhere unarmed.

Alonzo still had an aversion to guns. He'd still rather rely on his wits than sling lead.

He had a well-worn gun belt and Colt he'd purchased at a pawn shop years ago, but hadn't yet fired the thing. His pocket pistol was in one of his packs, and he hardly every took it out.

Now, patting the Colt on his hip, he examined himself in his hand mirror and liked what he saw. He looked every inch the young lawman.

His stomach growled, reminding him he hadn't eaten breakfast yet. He got his frying pan and some bacon and soon had the strips sizzling in their own fat. He was out of eggs, unfortunately, and aimed to remedy that at the next town he came to.

He had flour, though, and some sugar, and he was a fair hand at whipping up biscuits. When they were done, he sliced them down the middle, placed pieces of bacon between the halves, and had a feast fit for a king.

Yes, sir, Alonzo reflected as he happily ate, his life was fine. He got to roam where he pleased and do as he pleased. He had money, he had his health. He had just about everything a man could ask for, he reckoned. Except for a companion. A pard, say, or better yet, a woman.

Alonzo stopped that train of thought right there. *No, no, no,* he told himself. Sure, he got to feeling lonely now and then. Awful lonely, if the truth be told. But there was no place for a wife in the life of a professional impersonator. He was a loner. He had to be, whether he liked it or not.

No sooner did the thought enter his head than a horse nickered. And not one of his own.

Alonzo glanced over, then leaped to his feet. He hadn't heard anyone come up, but two riders weren't thirty feet away to the east, staring.

They seemed as surprised to see him as he was to see them. The man on the right had a face that made Alonzo think of a rat he'd seen once. The man's clothes were rumpled, and greasy hair poked from under a dirty hat. On his left hip, worn butt-aslant for a cross-draw, was a Smith & Wesson. He had prominent buck teeth that made his upper lip protrude. "What do we have here?" he said.

The other rider was as different from the first as day from night. His clothes and hat were clean. He was taller and broader and strapped around his waist were a pair of matching pearl-handled Colts. He had piercing blue eyes and was the sort of handsome fella the ladies would cotton to. Those piercing eyes fixed on Alonzo, on his vest. "We have us a lawman, Wease."

"What?" Wease said. He, too, saw the badge, and gave a mild start. "Why, hell," he exclaimed, straightening. "Look at that."

"Calm yourself," the two-gun man said.

With a visible effort, Wease slouched back. "Sure thing, Burt."

Burt gigged his palomino, and Wease followed. They came within a few yards of the fire, Wease's dark eyes darting every which way. Burt only looked around once, but Alonzo had the impression those blue eyes didn't miss a thing.

"Fellas," Alonzo said. His nerves were jangling, as they always did when trouble presented itself.

"How do you do, Marshal?" Burt said.

"Deputy," Alonzo said, for want of anything else. He hoped the pair would simply be on their way.

"Yes, you would be," Burt said. "As young as you are." He leaned on his saddle horn. "You must be new to the territory."

"Don't you mean the state?" Alonzo said. Nebraska had become the thirty-sixth or the thirty-seventh years ago, as he recalled.

"You're sure a stickler for facts," Burt remarked, not unkindly. "But then, tin stars have that kind of disposition."

"What kind?" Alonzo said in confusion.

"The facts and only the facts. It must have somethin' to do with why you take up the work you do."

"Maybe they just like to ride roughshod over folks," Wease said. "Them and the airs they put on."

Burt glanced sharply at him. "Is that any way to talk to a minion of the law?"

"A min-what?" Wease said.

Burt smiled at Alonzo. "You have to forgive my partner, Deputy. He got arrested years back and he's held a grudge ever since."

"It's not just that," Wease said. "It's lawmen goin' around tellin' us what we can and can't do."

"All a lawman does is enforce the law," Alonzo felt compelled to say. "It's not personal or anything. It's just a job."

"It's personal to me," Wease said.

"Yes, well," Burt said, and his tone became as hard as steel. "I reckon we've heard enough out of you. If you can't keep a civil tongue, shut the hell up."

"Civil tongue?" Wease said in amazement.

Burt placed his right hand on the Colt on his right hip. He did so slowly, almost casually, yet the effect it had on Wease was remarkable. The rat-faced man reacted as if he'd been stabbed, and recoiled in his saddle.

"Now hold on."

"You're not listenin'," Burt said. "Shut. The. Hell. Up."

Wease swallowed, and nodded.

Alonzo sensed that the man was deathly afraid of his companion. Yet nothing about Burt suggested he was particularly vicious. To the contrary, the man seemed downright friendly. "No need for harsh words," he said.

Both Burt and Wease looked at him as if he might not be in his right mind.

"I'll be damned," Burt said, and laughed.

"What?" Alonzo said.

"Nothin'," Burt said. He made a show of sniffing a few times. "That coffee sure smells good. Arbuckles'?"

Alonzo nodded.

"Mind if I join you?" Burt asked, and before Alonzo could answer, he swung down as lithely as a cougar.

"Sure," Alonzo said. "I have plenty."

Burt opened a saddlebag and produced a tin cup. Coming to the fire, he bent, picked up the pot, and filled his cup to the brim. "I'm obliged."

"How about your friend?"

"He stays on his horse."

"I do?" Wease said.

"You do," Burt said. Taking a sip, he smacked his lips, then set the pot down. "I didn't catch your handle, Deputy."

Without thinking, Alonzo replied, "Deputy Pratt," then wanted to kick himself for being so reckless. He should have made up a name, as he'd done so many times before.

"Deputy Pratt," Burt said. "I'll remember that." Instead of taking a seat, he drank his coffee standing, his left thumb hooked in his gun belt.

Alonzo was unsure what to say or do. He sensed the man was studying him without being obvious. To make small talk, he said, "Where are you two bound, if you don't mind my askin'?"

"We're on our way to meet up with some friends."

"Do you live in Nebraska?"

Burt chuckled. "We go where the wind blows us."

Alonzo wondered why the man thought that was funny. "You must get around a lot. Hear a lot of things. Are there many lawbreakers in these parts?"

"Now that you mention it," Burt said, and chuckled anew, "I do believe I've heard tell of a few. There's the Cal Grissom bunch. Cal is short for California, which is where he's from. Six curly wolves ride with him, the most notorious outlaws between the Mississippi River and the Rockies. They range all over, from the Dakotas on down to Oklahoma."

"I'll keep my eyes and ears peeled for them," Alonzo said. And go the other way if he heard they were in his vicinity.

"There's Rufus Tanner," Burt said. "He was a trapper years back, and one day he got into an argument with a sodbuster and opened him up with a bowie knife. The law has been lookin' for Rufus ever since. If he was smart he'd head for the mountains and make himself scarce, but he's a stubborn one, old Rufus is. He likes Nebraska so he stays and plays cat and mouse with tin-toters like you."

"You don't say."

Burt wasn't done. "There's also Harvey Odom. Now there's a mean one. Him and his boys prey on pilgrims who don't have more sense than to be travelin' alone through these parts."

Alonzo reflected that *he* was traveling alone. "That's sure a lot of outlaws."

"Oh, there are more," Burt said, "but those are the ones everybody knows about. I'm surprised you haven't heard of them, but then, you did say you're new to the territory."

"That I am," Alonzo said.

Chuckling, Burt drained his cup in a couple of gulps. "Thanks again," he said. Turning, he replaced the cup in his saddlebags, swung onto his fine palomino, and touched his hat brim. "You take care, Deputy Pratt. Nebraska ain't Texas, but it ain't civilized yet, either. It's no place for amateurs."

"I'll be on my guard."

Burt motioned at Wease and tapped his spurs. Wease followed, glaring spite.

Alonzo was glad to see them go. He'd had no idea Nebraska was such a hotbed of hard cases. It set him to thinking that maybe he should impersonate someone else. A minister, perhaps. Or a patent medicine salesman. He'd have to change clothes, though, and that seemed like a lot of bother to go to. He decided to wear his lawman's outfit the rest of the day and pick a different one the next morning.

"What can one day hurt?" Alonzo said out loud.

8

Since Burt and Wease had gone east, Alonzo headed west. He wanted nothing more to do with them. And since water and game were to be had along the Platte, he stuck to the river. He knew that somewhere up ahead it divided into the North Platte and the South Platte, which were fed with runoff from the far distant mountains and a number of tributaries.

Alonzo reckoned that the next town he came to would, in fact, be North Platte. He didn't know much about it other than it was a railroad town, and reputed to be on the wild side. He couldn't remember if he'd heard it had a marshal or not, and hoped it didn't. The less law, the freer he could operate.

Alonzo took his time. He enjoyed the cool air close to the water, and the breeze out of the northwest. He liked the wildlife. He wasn't a country boy, by any means. Give him a city or town any day. But on occasions like this, when he didn't have to worry about dying of thirst or hunger, he could relax and enjoy the scenery.

He was so absorbed in nature that when something began to nip at the back of his mind, he ignored it. Only when a pair of jays took raucous flight behind him did he recall that earlier several crows had done the same. He hadn't thought much of it. Birds were always being spooked by one thing or another.

Now he wondered if maybe someone was following him.

Shifting in his saddle, Alonzo probed the woodland. He mustn't forget he was in Indian country. The Sioux, or Dakotas as some called them, were particularly hostile to whites, and would scalp and kill any white man they caught. They could be brazen, too, in how close they'd venture to towns and forts.

Alonzo swallowed. The last thing he wanted was to tangle with hostiles. He was no Indian-fighter. For that matter, he wasn't much of a fighter of any kind. He relied on his wits to get him out of scrapes, like that time in Denver with the Law and Order League. But they were tame compared to the Sioux, who could sneak up on a man as silently as ghosts.

Alonzo rode a little faster. He kept his hand on his Colt, which wouldn't do him much good if he was attacked. He wasn't much of a shot, either. When he thought about it, the only thing in the whole world he was really good at was impersonating others.

It was too bad he couldn't do it for a living. A legal living, that was.

The river's many bends and turns added to his unease. If someone was back there, they could close in at their leisure with little risk of being spotted.

Suddenly the natural wonders of the Platte weren't so appealing.

The woods were thick, too, which complicated things. Alonzo's woodcraft consisted of being able to start a fire—provided he had Lucifers or the old-fashioned way of starting a fire with steel and flint—and being able to tell north from south and east from west, provided he knew where the sun had risen or was setting. Daniel Boone, he wasn't.

Spooky times like this, Alonzo reflected, would sometimes make him think of doing something else for a living. Something he wouldn't be arrested for, like a store clerk or a bank teller. The problem was, the mere notion of spending the rest of his days in drudgery and boredom held as much appeal as being scalped.

Alonzo never had understood how so many folks stood such dull lives. Each and every of their days was the same as the one before. They got up at the same time, they went to work at the same time, they spent eight or ten hours at a job that had all the excitement of watching grass grow, and then they'd go home and eat their supper at the same time and go to bed at the same time, and the next day, start the same thing all over again.

It would drive him mad.

He supposed there were jobs that didn't do that, but if so, he hadn't heard of any that appealed to him. Being rich would be nice. The rich got to do howsoever they pleased. But rich called for a lot of money, and it was rare for him to have more than a thousand dollars in his poke.

He could try to save more, but he'd have to scrimp on how he liked to live. Namely, after each fleecing, when he was flush, he'd treat himself to a stay at a nice hotel and spend nights at a nice saloon, drinking fine liquor and playing cards.

His impersonations let him live high on the hog for a while. Not real high, but enough that the simple pleasures outweighed the risks of his profession. Except for moments like this.

Another bend came up, the river on his right gurgling quietly. Out on the water a fish leaped.

Simultaneously, there was the boom of a shot and the smack of lead striking the cottonwood that he was going around. Using his spurs, he hauled on the lead rope and plunged Archibald and the packhorse into a thick patch of timber. He only went a short way and drew rein. Palming the Colt, he waited breathlessly for some sign of the bushwhacker.

Alonzo's skin prickled. That had been close. The shot sounded like a rifle. He wasn't savvy enough about guns to tell, say, whether it was a repeater or one of the old buffalo guns.

The minutes crawled. As much as Alonzo wanted to get out of there, he held his impatience in check. Careless could get him killed.

Over half an hour must have gone by when Alonzo finally shoved his Colt into its holster and lifted his reins. There hadn't been a hint of the shooter. Not so much as the snap of a twig or a bush moving when it shouldn't. He figured—he hoped—that whoever took the shot at him had decided to go elsewhere.

His mouth going dry, Alonzo made for the trail. When sparrows erupted out of a thicket, his heart leaped into his throat.

Despite the screaming of the tiny voice in his mind to ride like hell, Alonzo held Archibald to a walk. He couldn't hear much when going at a gallop, and he needed to rely on his ears as much as his eyes.

Another half an hour went by, and Alonzo was just beginning to relax again when an acrid scent tingled his nose. *Smoke*. His first thought was that it must be Indians, but no, they wouldn't give themselves away like that. It must be whites, then. Eager for the company, since it might discourage his stalker if the killer was still back there, he brought his horse and the pack animal to a trot.

Pounding around yet another turn in the river, Alonzo abruptly had to drew rein.

Before him spread a wide clearing. In the middle a campfire burned, and beside it lay a man on his back, resting.

Alonzo thought that was strange. The man had to have heard him. Why hadn't he sat up? Then he saw that the man's shoulder was bandaged, and handcuffs were clamped to his wrists.

Before the significance could sink in, another man stepped out of the trees, holding a leveled Winchester.

Deputy Marshal Jacob Stone had been up at the crack of dawn, as was his custom, but he couldn't get the early start he wanted. Loudon was the problem. Despite Stone's best effort, Loudon's wound had become infected and the man was doing poorly. Loudon had a high fever and was as weak as a newborn kitten.

Reluctantly, Stone stayed put. He was camped by the Platte River, and put water on to boil to clean Loudon's wound. Yet again. It was all he could do. He didn't have any medicine. There was a sawbones in North Platte, but they were three days out, by his reckoning.

Stone was sitting by the fire, drinking coffee and waiting for the pot to boil, when he heard the distant crack of a rifle. He was immediately on his feet, his own rifle in hand.

Moving to the east edge of the clearing, he listened. There was only the one shot. It could be a hunter, he reasoned. Or it could be trouble.

If there was one thing Stone had learned in his many years of wearing a badge, it was to never, ever, take anything for granted. Moving into the trees, he knelt and waited. Patience was one of his long suits, and he had knelt there he knew not how long when hoofbeats brought him off his knees into a crouch. To say he was surprised by the rider who came around the bend was an understatement. When the man on the bay drew rein, Stone stepped into the open. "Another deputy, by God."

The man's face was a blank slate. "What?"

"Your badge," Stone said.

"What?" the man said again for some reason.

Stone tapped his own star. "What's the matter with you? I'm a deputy marshal, like you."

The man looked down at his vest. "Oh."

Stone moved closer. He saw that the other deputy was young, his clothes remarkably clean. And plainly upset. "Are you all right?"

"I was shot at," the young deputy said. His voice had changed, and he used a drawl a lot like Stone's own.

Stone thought he understood. Being shot at would rattle anyone. Concerned, he looked back the way the deputy had come. "By who?"

"Don't know. Could have been Injuns."

Stone hadn't seen any recent Indian sign. But that meant nothing. "I'm Jacob Stone," he introduced himself. "Who might you be?"

The younger man seemed to collect himself. "Grant," he said. "Robert Grant."

"Well, Deputy Robert Grant, it's a pleasure to meet you," Stone said warmly, and sobered. "Do you think whoever took that shot is after you?"

"No," Grant said. "Leastwise, there hasn't been any sign of anyone, and it's been a while."

"Come join me by the fire, then. I have coffee on, and you can tell me all about yourself."

"There's not much to tell," Grant said a bit guard-edly. Dismounting, he led his roan and his pack animal over. "What happened to that gent?" he asked, with a nod at Loudon.

Stone related the incident in Hebron, ending with, "He's doin' poorly, and I hope to get him to the doc in North Platte in time to save his life." He paused. "Is that where you're bound?"

"It's closest," Grant said.

"Let me have your cup," Stone said, and when his new acquaintance produced it from a saddlebag, he filled it and indicated Grant should take a seat. It puzzled him that Grant appeared somewhat unhappy about the turn of events. Turning so he faced the east edge of the clearing, he sank down, placed his Winchester across his lap, and said, "I'm all ears."

"I told you there's not much to tell," Grant said. "I'm a deputy, like you."

Stone smiled. "You're kind of prickly. Not that I blame you, bein' shot at and all. But who appointed you?" It was customary for the marshals in each district to appoint their own deputies. In districts where lawlessness was rampant, there could be dozens, if not scores. "Hodder? It couldn't be the marshal before him, Clyde Smith. You don't look old enough to have known him."

"I'm older than I look," Grant said. "But it was Hodder."

"How long ago?"

"What?" Grant said.

"How long ago were you appointed? Don't take offense, but you look new to the badge."

"It was, oh, two months ago, I guess," Grant replied in a strange tone.

"Are you askin' me or tellin' me?" Stone said, and

laughed. He remembered being green once. "What's your assignment?"

Grant appeared confused by the question. "I don't rightly have one. I'm just sort of wanderin' around, learnin' the territory."

"That sounds like Hodder. Learn as you go," Stone said. The marshal was a big believer in the old saying that experience was the best teacher. "It's lucky you ran in to me."

"How so?" Grant said. He hadn't touched his coffee.

"We can partner up, and I can learn you the ropes," Stone proposed. "You see these wrinkles?" he said, and pointed at his own face. "I'm not braggin' when I say I know just about all there is to know about bein' a marshal. I've been at it more years than anyone in the district."

"I don't know," Grant said.

"Why wouldn't you?" Stone said. "Hodder, himself, would say it's for your own good. Come with me to North Platte, and after that, who knows?"

"I don't know," Grant repeated himself. "Maybe I should go back and try to find whoever shot at me."

"What made you think it was Indians?"

"This is Sioux country, isn't it?" Grant said. "Although it could have been one of those men I met this mornin'."

"Who?"

"One called himself Burt and the other was named Wease. Burt was friendly enough, but I didn't trust that Wease."

Stone sat up, all interest. "Describe them, the best you can." After the younger deputy complied, he nodded and said, "Grant, you're about the luckiest lawman alive. That two-gun hombre was none other than Burt Alacord. His pard was Weasel Ginty. Everyone calls him Wease."

"Should I know of them?"

"They ride with Cal Grissom. Alacord is quick as anything. Wease is a backstabber. Alacord would come at you straight-up, but Wease is just the sort of no-account to take a potshot and then skedaddle."

Grant touched his badge. "All because I'm wearin' this?"

"Sonny, that badge makes you a target for every badman there is," Stone warned him. "Never let your guard down."

"I won't."

"You know," Stone said. "This is a stroke of luck in more ways than one. Grissom and his bunch must be close by. Once I get Loudon, here, to the sawbones, you and me should go after them."

"Just the two of us?"

"Why not?" Stone said. "It gives us somethin' to do, and I can teach you as we go."

"Just so we don't wind up dead," Grant said.

9

———◆———

Alonzo was so taken aback by this latest development,
he didn't know what to do.

What were the odds that he'd run in to a real lawman way out in the middle of nowhere? That the lawman took him as genuine surprised him no end, but
then, he'd always been good at his impersonations.

One of his secrets was to always say as little as possible about whatever profession he was pretending to
follow. When he impersonated a minister, he hardly
ever referred to the Good Book. He didn't know enough
of the Bible. But that was all right so long as he smiled
a lot and treated people like a real parson would.

Now he must do the same with his lawman role. He
must only talk about the law when Jacob Stone asked
him a direct question, and then keep his answers short.
He might give away his ignorance otherwise.

So now, as they wound along the slowly flowing
river toward North Platte, he didn't speak unless spo-
ken to. It helped considerably that Stone didn't like to

gab. He was one of those old-timers who thought that talking was something you did for a reason and not just to hear yourself talk.

As they rode, Alonzo racked his brain for all he could recollect about Federal law. He'd known that each deputy marshal had a territory they roamed, or "district," as Stone called it. He got the impression that they could do pretty much as they pleased, but he might be wrong about that.

It was another gorgeous day along the river. Any other time, he'd have admired the bright sunshine, the soft sounds the water made, the abundant wildlife. But he was too worried to admire much at the moment.

Alonzo needed to be shed of Stone. How to go about it without raising the lawman's suspicions, that was the question. He needed an excuse to part ways, but a believable one. Finally he decided he would play it by ear. Maybe events would give him the way.

They had been on the go about an hour when Stone looked back and smiled. "You're not much of a talker, son. I like that."

"You do?" Alonzo said.

"I've had partners who talked my ears off," Stone said. "One in particular—his name was Fred—used to jabber like there was no tomorrow. Used to drive me loco. I was glad when we parted company."

"How often do you work with other deputies?"

"Oh, about half the time, or a little less, I'd reckon," Stone said. "Marshal Hodder knows I like bein' on my own. He'll be plumb surprised when he hears I took you under my wing."

Alonzo saw his chance. "You don't have to if you don't want to. I can get by on my own."

"Nonsense," Stone declared. "I'd be failin' in my

duty if I didn't give you the benefit of my years. I've been at this a long while, and I can teach you things."

"I'm obliged," Alonzo said with little enthusiasm.

Stone chuckled. "I know what you're thinkin'."

"You do?"

"That I'm an old goat who should mind his own business. You'd rather learn as you go. That's how I was when I was your age. But as folks say, there's nothin' like experience to burn the fat off a brain."

That was a new one on Alonzo. "Where do they say that?"

"Down in Texas, where I was born and bred. Texans have a lot of savvy sayin's. We take pride in who we are."

"If you like Texas so much," Alonzo said, "what are you doin' in Nebraska?"

"I have asked myself that very thing many a time. I ended up here because they were short of deputies up this way, and I volunteered. Must have been out of my mind."

Stone laughed. "Lookin' back, I think the change in scenery appealed to me. I wanted somethin' different for a spell. Figured to give it a try for a year or two and then return to Texas. But it's been a lot longer and I'm still here."

"Why do you stay on?"

"I don't rightly know," Stone said. "There are days I could kick myself. But I do like the state. And I like the people. For the most part, they're the salt of the earth, as good and decent as you'll find anywhere. Plus, I've gotten used to it, and we tend to stick with what we're used to."

"You're quite the"—Alonzo had to think to remember the word—"philosopher."

"All old men are," Stone said. "We've lived so long, we feel we have to share what we've learned with everybody else."

"I hope I live as long as you," Alonzo said, for want of anything better.

"You just might, if you're a quick learner like I was. Use your head more than your guns, and you might live to retire someday."

"I've always believed in usin' my head," Alonzo admitted.

"That's a good start, a smart start."

Just then Alonzo noticed that Stone's prisoner, Loudon, was starting to slide off his horse. The man had recovered enough that they were able to get him on his animal, but Loudon rode hunched over and groaned every so often. Now he was quaking and sliding, and Alonzo quickly brought Archibald up next to him. "Stone!" he said. He grabbed at Loudon just as the man went to pitch from his saddle.

Reining around, Jacob Stone lent a hand. "Consarn it all. I was afraid of this. He's gettin' worse every mile."

They stopped, and Stone carefully lowered Loudon and placed him on his back in grass close to the river. Loudon had passed out. Stone placed a palm to the man's forehead, and frowned. "He's burnin' up."

"What can I do?"

"Get a fire goin'," Stone said. "I'll clean his wound again, although that's not doin' much good. Once infection sets in, it's hard to stop."

So Alonzo had heard, which was why he made it a point not to be shot. He busied himself gathering firewood and kindling a fire. Stone, meanwhile, filled his coffeepot and set it on to boil, saying, "For him, not for us."

"I don't need any coffee," Alonzo said.

Stone glanced at his packhorse. "You must need somethin'. What's all that on your pack animal? Most deputies travel a lot lighter."

Alonzo said the first thing that popped into his head. "I'm new at the job, remember? That there is everything I own in the world."

"You tote it all with you?" Stone said in astonishment. "I'm surprised Marshal Hodder didn't say somethin'. Deputies have to travel light."

"Now I know," Alonzo said.

"When we get to North Platte we'll find somewhere you can store most of it," Stone proposed.

"If that's what needs doin'," Alonzo said. Although he'd rather cut off his arm. His outfits were his livelihood. Without them, he'd be stuck in the role he was playing.

"That's the spirit," Stone complimented him, and bent to Loudon.

Alonzo watched the river flowing by, and sulked. Running into the old deputy had taught him a lesson. Never again would he pretend to be a lawman. The risks were more than he'd imagined.

"This ain't good," Stone said.

Loudon's breathing had become labored. He was as pale as a sheet and sweat poured from every pore.

Alonzo had an inspiration. "I can ride on to North Platte for the doc." Only he wouldn't return with him. He'd switch to another outfit and head for parts unknown.

"We're still days out," Stone said. "It'll be over sooner than that."

Alonzo had never seen anyone die. He'd seen bodies—his own parents, at their funerals. And others. But he'd never been by someone's side when they passed on. It was unsettling.

Loudon lingered for another couple of hours. His body seemed to slowly deflate, like a water skin drained until it was empty, and he shuddered a lot as if cold despite the heat of the day. The only sounds he made were low groans. Once, half-startling Alonzo out of his wits, Loudon opened his eyes wide and raised his head a few inches, gaping at the heavens. "I see you!" he cried. "I see you!" Then his eyes closed and he sank back, spent.

"What was that about?" Alonzo breathlessly asked.

Deputy Marshal Stone shrugged. "Who knows? People say strange things when they're at death's door. One time I had a man grab me and call me God and ask my forgiveness for his wicked deeds. Another time, an outlaw thought I was his ma and kept beggin' me to burp him because he had an awful bellyache."

"No," Alonzo said.

"Yes. He had the ache because he'd tried to shoot me and I put lead in his gut. I was goin' for his chest but he moved just as I shot."

That gave Alonzo something to ponder. "How many men have you shot, altogether?"

"*Had* to shoot," Stone amended. "I never do if I can help it."

Alonzo liked that, and said so.

"I'm not one of those who is always on the prod," Stone said. "And to answer your question, I've had to shoot four, countin' Loudon."

"That's not so many."

"Compared to what?" Stone said. "I know a lot of lawmen who go their whole careers and never shoot anybody."

"I'd like to not shoot anyone," Alonzo said.

"I'm pleased to hear that," Stone said in earnest. "But don't let that slow you when it shouldn't."

"How do you mean?"

"Always be on your toes. You never know when a drunk or somebody might go for their gun or try to stick you with a knife. Myself, I'm always friendly to everyone—but I never trust anyone until I'm sure I can."

Alonzo had little interest in learning the dos and don'ts of being a lawman. He figured, though, he should show some interest or it might make the older man wonder.

So he asked, "How can you be sure?"

"It comes with that experience we've been talkin' about," Stone said. "You learn to read folks like some read a book. It's in how they act, how they look at you, what they do and don't say. Trust me. It will come to you with time. The trick is to live long enough to learn it."

Loudon opened his eyes again. He gazed skyward as if searching for something, then said in a level, calm tone, "These are my last moments."

Stone leaned over him and placed a hand on his shoulder. "Do you want me to get word to any of your kin?"

"There's no one," Loudon said.

"How about your ma and pa?"

"I left home twenty years ago. I don't even know where they are." Loudon tore his gaze from the sky. "I want you to know I don't blame you, Deputy. You did what you had to. After you bury me, you're welcome to my things."

"I wish we could get you to a doc," Stone said.

"Too late." Loudon weakly smiled, let out a long breath, and became completely still.

"Well, hell," Stone said. "He died fine. No fuss at all."

Alonzo marveled that the man had gone so peacefully. Were it him, he might rail at the heavens for the injustice of it all. "I'll help you dig a grave. Or would you rather take the body in to North Platte?"

"What for? It'd be ripe by then, and the dirt here is as good as the dirt there." Stone shook his head while slowly rising. "No, I'll file a report on him, when I can. Let's plant him quick. I want to get after Burt Alacord and Weasel Ginty. With any luck, they'll lead us to Cal Grissom and we can put an end to his wild bunch."

"How many are we talkin' about?"

"I can't rightly say. It changes from time to time. Six or seven at the least, I expect."

The whole time he was digging, using a broken branch to break the earth and his hands to scoop it away, Alonzo was thinking that to go after the Grissom gang was plumb loco. It would be Stone and him against six or seven killers. He couldn't come right out and refuse to help. No real lawman would. But he could raise enough of a doubt to give the older man pause. Or so he hoped. Clearing his throat, he said, "Is it wise? The two of us tanglin' with that many?"

"Bothers you, does it?" Stone said as he shoved dirt aside. "Long odds come with the badge. We could telegraph for help, but by the time other deputies got to North Platte, Grissom will be long gone."

Alonzo tried to come up with a different argument.

"It's just you and me," Stone went on. "That's the way these things happen sometimes. We just have to make the best of it."

Alonzo dug slower. He was in no hurry to go after the outlaws. The best thing for him to do was to give the old man the slip as soon as a chance presented itself. Engrossed in debating whether to do it that night when the lawman was asleep, he didn't quite hear something Stone said. "What was that?"

"I wonder if the girl will be with them."

Alonzo looked up. "What girl?"

"There have been reports of a girl ridin' with Grissom and his crew. A stage driver swore a girl was with them when they robbed his stage, and the citizens over in Unionville claim a girl held their horses when they struck the Unionville Bank."

Just when Alonzo thought he'd heard everything. "Then it must be true. A girl outlaw! Who would have thought it? What do we do if we come across her? Arrest her and bring her in?"

"Didn't you just hear me say she helped to rob a stage and a bank? Females break laws the same as men. We treat them the same. Yes, we arrest her. Unless you'd rather fall in love and marry her." And Stone snorted and laughed.

10

Jacob Stone had taken a shine to Robert Grant. The younger man had a friendly disposition that would come in handy when he dealt with others, and Grant was so green behind the ears, Stone couldn't help but want to take him under his wing and teach him important things about their job, things that might keep Grant alive and let him reach the same ripe age as him. Which might be stretching things. Few lawmen stayed at it as long as he had. By rights, he should have gone off to pasture long ago.

As they rode eastward along the Platte, searching for sign of the outlaws, Stone tried to find out a little more about his new companion. He soon discovered it was like trying to pour whiskey from an unopened bottle. Grant refused to open up. He was so reticent that Stone began to wonder if there was something in the younger man's past that he was embarrassed about, or a tragedy of some kind. People were often reluctant to gab about the bad things that had happened to them.

Stone didn't press him too hard. The boy was new to his job, and it wouldn't do to badger him. Besides, Stone didn't go around talking about his own past much, either. It was personal. No one's business but his own.

Their search proved fruitless until the third day after they buried Loudon. Along about the middle of the morning they came on the charred remains of a campfire. The tracks told Stone that two riders had camped at the spot and gone off to the north, crossing the river at a gravel ford.

"This might be them," Stone announced as he gazed at the green wall of vegetation on the other side.

"It could be anyone," Grant said.

"We haven't seen sign of anyone else, and you told me they were headin' this way," Stone said.

"What's north of here?" Grant wanted to know.

"Not much," Stone said. About thirty miles or so was the Loup River. And then there were the Sandhills. Which were exactly as their name implied—hills and ridges, some miles long and hundreds of feet high, made mostly of sand. But it wasn't a desert. Far from it. Something about the sandy soil let it hold water really well, with the result that the Sandhills were some of the best grassland in the state. Farms and ranches were few so far, but Stone imagined that as word spread about the fine grass to be had and the plentiful water, more and more would spring up. For now, though, the Sandhills were largely the haunt of buffalo and other game. To say nothing of hostiles and those who lived on the shady side of the law, like Cal Grissom.

Stone led across the river and Grant followed, tugging on the rope to his pack animal, which for some reason balked. Stone intended to have a talk with him about getting shed of the packhorse at the first opportunity. Deputies needed to travel fast and light. A pack-horse was like an extra leg, and of no use whatsoever.

Stone reminded himself that Grant was young and had a lot to learn, and bound to make mistakes.

He looked for tracks on the other side and found some in the soft earth of the woods. The two riders had gone north. Soon the country became more open and more hilly, and the ground became harder. There was less sign. In another half mile there wasn't any at all. He figured a thunderstorm the night before was to blame.

Stone kept watch on the horizon like a hawk. He was concerned about the Sioux. There were reports they were mighty riled because gold had been found in the Black Hills up in the Dakotas, and whites were streaming in. The Sioux wouldn't abide that. The Black Hills were sacred to them. The Cheyenne, too, were re-ported to be causing trouble.

They had gone only a few miles when plumes of smoke drew Stone to the crest of a spine of grassy ground. He'd hoped it might be Burt Alacord and Wea-sel Ginty but the smoke came from a low building. "A soddy, by heaven."

"Way out here?" Grant said.

"Sodbusters are poppin' up everywhere," Stone said. And why not, when land was easy to come by and houses made of sod were easy to build? Most sodbusters were dirt poor, but that didn't stop them from dreamin' of better days once their farm turned a profit. "We'll go say howdy." He gigged his roan.

In addition to the sod house, there was a corral and an outhouse. That was all. A vegetable garden had been planted, and about five acres had been turned by a plow and corn planted.

"Not much, is it?" Grant said.

"To them it's everything."

Grant shook his head and said, "I don't understand how people can live this way. Out here all by themselves."

"Where's your pioneer spirit?" Stone joked, and chuckled.

"I reckon I must not have much," Grant said. "I'd never do what these people are doin'. It makes no sense to me. The risks involved, and for what?"

"They do it to have a place of their own, where they can do as they please."

"Still," Grant said.

A lanky man in overalls came out of the soddy. He was holding a Sharps rifle and raised it to his shoulder but didn't point it at them. "Who are you?" he hollered. "And what do you want?"

"Deputy Marshal Jacob Stone and fellow deputy Robert Grant," Stone yelled. "We're only passin' through."

The farmer smiled, and beckoned. "Come on in, then."

A lean woman emerged, with a pair of young'uns. The children clung to her legs, their eyes wide with fright. "Who is it, Hiram?" she said.

"You heard him," her husband answered. "They're lawmen."

"Are you sure?" she anxiously asked.

"You can see their badges, can't you?"

Smiling to put the woman at ease, Stone drew rein and leaned on his saddle horn.

"We're lawmen, all right, ma'am," he assured her. "After some outlaws who might have come this way."

"Outlaws!" she exclaimed.

"Calm yourself, Hortense," Hiram said. "Outlaws ain't about to bother us. We don't have anything they'd want."

Stone could have pointed out that the farmer was mistaken, that the farmer's wife was lure enough, but he held his tongue. "Have a couple of men been by here recently?"

Hiram placed the Sharps' stock on the ground. "Deputy, you're the first souls we've seen in a coon's age. You're welcome to light and sit a spell. We hardly ever have company."

"Hardly ever," Hortense sadly echoed.

"As much as I'd like to—" Stone started to say.

"I can make coffee or tea," Hortense said. "It won't take but a few minutes. We'd be ever so grateful."

The woman, Stone realized, was a bundle of nerves. She was probably one of those who fretted every minute—about Indians, about the weather, about her family's health. It wouldn't surprise him if she didn't want to be here, and all this was her husband's idea.

"Please, Deputy."

Stone changed his mind. The appeal in her eyes touched him. "I reckon we can spare an hour or so. And coffee will do us fine."

Grant glanced at him as if surprised.

"Oh, thank you so much," Hortense said. "Give me a few minutes. I was putting water on to heat when you rode up and it should be hot by now." Beaming, she turned and whisked into the soddy, her offspring half-hidden in the folds of her dress.

"You've done us a big favor, Deputy," Hiram said. "My missus is starved for company." He stepped to the dark doorway. "I'll be right back."

Stone became aware that Grant was staring at him. "What?"

"Why?" Grant said. "I thought you were in an all-fired hurry to find those outlaws."

"You heard them."

"You're doin' it to be nice?"

"Part of bein' a lawman. We don't just enforce laws

and arrest those who break them." Stone dismounted and stretched. "I make it a point to be as friendly as I can to folks like these. They're the reason we wear these badges."

"I don't know as I can be as nice as you."

"It takes practice, I'll admit," Stone said. "The thing to remember is that little things go a long way. A smile. A handshake. Always bein' polite."

"You missed your calling," Grant said, grinning. "You should have been a parson."

"I'm serious, son," Stone said. "A good lawman has a duty to put on his best face and always treat others with respect. Someone once said we are our brother's keeper, and I believe that, heart and soul."

"You're the most peculiar lawman I've ever met."

"You'll understand more as time goes by," Stone predicted. When he had been Grant's age, he hadn't appreciated the effect a lawman had on people. Back then, all he cared about was finding lawbreakers and bringing them in. It took a number of years before he caught on that how he acted made a big difference in how folks reacted, not just to him but to lawmen in general.

As if to prove his point, Hiram came back out with a plate of biscuits his wife had made for the entire family the day before, and offered to share them. Not ten minutes later the lady, herself, emerged with a pot of coffee.

Stone let himself relax for an hour. The couple were starved for news of the outside world. In particular, they were eager to learn whether the Sioux would break from the reservation. Stone was honest with them. He thought there was a good chance the Sioux might. He'd often thought that if the Sioux ever joined forces with other tribes, they could push the white man from the central plains. He didn't mention that to Hiram and

Hortense. But he did advise them that if anything suspicious happened around their place, if a horse or a cow disappeared or they saw moccasin tracks, they should hightail it to North Platte. "You can never be too cautious."

Deputy Grant hardly said anything the whole time. He listened intently, though, and at one point, after Hiram mentioned that they had every cent they'd owned tied up in their farm, the young deputy looked around, then asked, "And you reckon this is worth it?"

"It's *ours*," Hiram said proudly, and put an arm around his wife, who mustered a thin smile.

"But is it worth dyin' for?"

Stone frowned at his partner's lack of tact. "No one is goin' to die," he cut in. "Hiram and his missus are too sensible to let it come to that."

The harm had been done. The rest of their visit, Hortense chewed on her bottom lip and cast anxious glances at the hills to the northwest.

Stone hated to leave in the state she was in. He did his best to assure her that her family would be fine, but he could tell it had little effect. When the time came to leave, he took Hiram aside and suggested he take his family into North Platte anyway for a few days, "just to put your missus at ease."

Hiram said he would.

Once the farm was behind them, Stone vented his annoyance. "That was damned rude of you, Deputy Grant. Scarin' that lady like you did."

Grant seemed genuinely bewildered. "What did I do?"

"You shouldn't have brought up dyin'."

"They have kids, for God's sake," Grant said. "Don't tell me you aren't as worried about them as I am."

"You are?"

"They're decent folks, but they don't have a lick of

brains. I don't care what Hiram says, they have no business bein' there." Grant muttered something. "I never gave much thought to homesteaders before. Not those who live in soddies, anyhow. They have it pretty hard, don't they?"

"It's not a life for the faint of heart."

"They don't even have anything worth stealin'."

"What made you think of that?"

"I don't know," Grant said, rather angrily, Stone thought. "There are robbers everywhere, aren't there?"

"I do come across them from time to time," Stone acknowledged. "Arrested more than my share. Nothin' galls me more than someone who takes what ain't theirs. It's so low, it's despicable."

"There are robbers and there are thieves," Grant said.

"I fail to see the difference."

"A robber is someone like Cal Grissom. He takes from stagecoaches and banks."

"He's robbed people, too," Stone said.

"At gunpoint, I'd wager," Grant said.

"What else would he use?"

"A thief doesn't do that. He uses his wits, not a gun. He doesn't scare people."

"Stealin' is stealin'."

"That's how the law sees it," Grant said. "But to me it matters *how* the stealin' is done. A thief has more scruples than a common robber. More—I don't know what to call it—class."

Stone laughed. "And you called me peculiar? That's like sayin' a man who stabs somebody isn't as bad as a man who shoots somebody. A lawbreaker is a lawbreaker. It doesn't matter how they break it."

"If you say so," the other said, although he didn't sound convinced.

They came to the first hill and started up. Midway,

Stone's roan raised its head and pricked its ears. The horse had heard something he didn't. Out of habit, Stone placed his hand on his Colt. "What is it, fella?" he said quietly.

The answer presented itself as they neared the crest.

A bull buffalo lumbered into view, lowered its huge head, and snorted.

11

———◆———

Alonzo Pratt heard Deputy Marshal Jacob Stone quietly say, "Don't move and don't make any loud sounds."

As if Alonzo would. He was so shocked, he was speechless. He froze in his saddle and prayed Archibald wouldn't do anything dumb. Alonzo had never been this close to a buffalo before. He saw them from time to time in his travels but nearly always at a safe distance. This one wasn't thirty feet above them.

The brute stared at them and tossed its wicked curved horns from side to side.

Alonzo was afraid it was about to charge. He wasn't sure he could get out of the way in time. Archibald had a lot of stamina but wasn't especially quick.

Stone had frozen, too, with his hand on his Colt, and Alonzo hoped the deputy wouldn't draw. A revolver wouldn't do much good against a monster that size. Buffalo skulls, he had heard, were inches thick, and hard for a slug to penetrate unless a high-caliber rifle was used, like that homesteader's Sharps. Buffalo hearts and lungs were protected by a lot of muscle and fat. Alonzo knew that Indians killed them all the time using bows and arrows, although how they managed to penetrate deep enough to inflict a killing wound was beyond him.

The bull pawed the ground and did more tossing.

Alonzo didn't know much about the beasts. Only that they roamed all over, eating grass. And that to rile one was to invite an early grave. This one appeared riled. It tore a clod from the soil with its hoof and vigorously shook its head. Alonzo's mouth went so dry, it hurt to swallow.

The thing was so close, Alonzo could smell it. A sort of musty scent, unlike that of, say, a dog or a horse. He felt Archibald tremble under him and didn't blame his horse for being as scared as he was.

Suddenly the buffalo wheeled to the left and went about twenty feet, then started down the hill. It was leaving without attacking them. It looked back every now and then and snorted a few times.

"Thank you, Lord," Jacob Stone breathed.

"We could have been killed," Alonzo said.

"But we weren't." Stone smiled at him. "Always look at the bright side of things. You're better off that way."

Alonzo failed to see a bright side to any of this. Hunting a pack of killers was bound to get him or both of them killed. This whole law business had no bright side whatsoever, and he'd made up his mind he'd never impersonate a lawman again for as long as he lived.

"Don't look so miserable," Stone said. "We're still breathin', aren't we?"

The lawman seemed to think it was funny. Alonzo didn't. He needed to be shed of Stone, and soon. He decided to slip away that very night. He refused to take any more of this. That eased his worries enough that he smiled.

Stone noticed. "That's the spirit," he said, and gigged his mount.

Reluctantly, Alonzo followed. He hardly noticed the sea of grass or the occasional wildflowers. Hawks soared on high, but he didn't care. Deer bounded away. He hardly gave them a glance. He was focused on one thing and one thing only. Getting the blazes away from Jacob Stone.

The lawman kept scouring for sign. Apparently he had considerable experience as a tracker because he saw things Alonzo didn't. About the middle of the afternoon, Stone turned in his saddle and said, "We could be in luck. I think I know where Burt Alacord and Weasel Ginty are headed."

"Do you, now?" Alonzo said.

"I've been through here once before. About five miles on there's a spring in the woods. They'd likely stop there to water their horses."

"And still be there?" Alonzo said skeptically. It had been days since he ran into them.

"You never know," Stone said. "It could be where they were meetin' up with Cal Grissom and the rest."

"You're guessin'."

"So? Law work involves a lot of guesses," Stone said. "You have to use your brain all the time."

Alonzo almost remarked that going after known killers struck him as downright brainless.

"Yes, sir," Stone said excitedly. "I hope we are in luck. We can put an end to these outlaws, one way or the other."

Before Alonzo could stop himself, he said, "If they don't put an end to us."

"There you go again. Always lookin' at the worst that can happen. You need to learn to relax, son."

"That's another thing," Alonzo said, his ire up. "I'm not your 'son' and I'd be obliged if you'd stop callin' me that."

"What's gotten into you?" Stone asked, and didn't wait for an answer. "But if that's how you want it, sure."

Alonzo fell into another sulk. He shouldn't have done that, shouldn't have prodded the old man. Now Stone might be less friendly, and more suspicious. To try to cover himself, he said, "I lost my pa when I was young. Every time you say it, it makes me think of him."

"Oh," Stone said. "I'm sorry. That never would have occurred to me."

The old man sounded so sincere that Alonzo felt a twinge of guilt. That was another thing. Stone kept bringing out feelings in him he hadn't ever had. It was unsettling to think he might have a streak of decency buried deep down inside himself. That would never do. How could he go around breaking the law if he took to feeling guilty about it? Guilt was for saps. He'd learned long ago that the world was dog-eat-dog, that you took what you wanted and everyone else could be hanged.

"How did you lose your pa?" Stone asked.

"I'd rather not talk about it," Alonzo said.

"Someone sure is in a mood today."

Deputy Jacob Stone was commencing to wonder about his new companion. Something wasn't quite right about Robert Grant, but he couldn't put his finger on exactly what.

Being green didn't explain Grant's frequent moodiness. It could just be his natural disposition. Stone had met others who he'd swear were born with sour milk in their veins and went through life grumpy about everything.

Stone put it from his mind for the time being. He had more important worries. Namely, Cal Grissom's wild bunch.

Grissom had been terrorizing Nebraska and several other states for eight or nine years now. Someone, the Pinkertons, probably, had discovered that Grissom robbed so many stages in California, the governor authorized a special posse to hunt him down. Grissom prudently left for less threatening pastures. The next anyone heard of him, he held up a stagecoach in Kansas. It was the start of a spree that to this day made him the most notorious outlaw in all of prairie country.

Grissom's men—but not Grissom, himself, oddly enough—were reputed to be snake-mean. When they robbed a stage or a bank, if anyone resisted, one of the other outlaws would shoot them down without compunction. Cross the Grissom gang, common parlance had it, and you ate lead.

The exception was Burt Alacord. Burt was a genuine two-gun man, as adept with his left-hand Colt as his right. He was ungodly quick, too. Strangely enough, he was rumored to be an easygoing sort who never killed unless he absolutely had to. Stage passengers he'd held up and bank customers he'd held at gunpoint all claimed that Alacord was the "nicest" of the outlaws.

Not Weasel Ginty. Weasel had an even sourer disposition than Robert Grant. He was cowardly, and a backshooter. His only redeeming trait, if you could call it that, was his devotion to Burt Alacord. He had been part of Grissom's gang in California. Reports had it the pair were childhood friends, or close in some other way.

Four others were known to ride with Grissom.

Spike Davis got his name from the strange hat he wore, although calling it a hat was wrong. It was a helmet with a spike on top. Davis was Prussian. Rumor had it he'd been an officer in the Prussian military and was drummed out in disgrace over a scandal involving another officer's wife. His real name was supposed to be Ladislaus Dowid. Or so the circular on him claimed. "Dowid" was Prussian for "David," which might explain where the "Davis" came from.

Willy Boy Jenkins was the youngest of Grissom's gang. About Robert Grant's age. The law hadn't been able to determine much about him other than he was prone to violent fits. Once, during a bank robbery, a customer balked at handing over his own poke, and Willy Boy had pistol-whipped the man into a bloody pulp. Grissom had to pull Willy Boy off to stop him.

The last two owlhoots were pretty much cyphers. Ira Fletcher had done some lawbreaking up in Montana. An oldster, he favored a Dragoon Colt.

Thomas Kent, on the other hand, was a quiet killer who always stayed in the background. Word had it he was partial to knives.

And now there were new rumors of a girl riding with them.

Stone didn't know what to make of it. Female outlaws were rare, but they did crop up from time to time. This one was reputed to be young and pretty, which only added to the mystery. Why would any girl in her right mind ride with a despicable bunch like that?

Maybe the answer was in the question, Stone reflected. Maybe the girl wasn't *in* her right mind.

For Grant's benefit, Stone related everything he knew about the outlaws. Grant didn't show much interest until he got to the part about the girl.

"Do you believe it's true?"

"That she's part of their gang?" Stone rubbed his stubble. "Who can say? People do a lot of things you'd never think they would. Maybe Willy Boy has a girlfriend. They're about the same age."

"Cal Grissom. Burt Alacord. Weasel Ginty. Spike Davis. Willy Boy. Fletcher and Kent. And you expect the two of us to bring them in?"

"It's our job to try."

"You lawdogs sure are dedicated to your work."

"You're one, too," Stone reminded him.

Grant seemed to catch himself. "I just don't know if I'm cut out for this kind of work."

So that was it, Stone told himself. The youngster was having second thoughts about wearing tin. That was normal. A lot of lawmen went through the same thing at one time or another. Corralling badmen was dangerous work. It wasn't for the timid or the squeamish. "Give yourself some time. You might find you like it."

Time, Stone had discovered, was the cure for most ailments. Emotional ailments, that was. Give the boy a year or so, let him get over the worst of his jitters, and he might make a fine lawman.

The sun blazed red on the western horizon when a bluff rose in the distance to the north. At its base grew a crescent of timber.

"There's where we might find them," Stone said, pointing. "We'll lie low until dark, then sneak on in."

"I hope you know what you're doin'."

A gully offered concealment. Stone rode down in, swung down, and faced his fellow deputy. "You're beginnin' to worry me. This halfhearted attitude of yours."

Grant alighted and let the lead rope to his pack animal drop. "I can't help it if I feel we're makin' a mistake."

"That's just it. You can help it. You have to get your head right." Stone paused. "What goes on in here"—he tapped his own head—"can mean the difference between livin' and dyin'. You have to put everything from your mind and concentrate on what you're doin' and nothin' else. If you don't, sure as shootin' you'll get careless, and careless can plant us."

"You won't have to worry about me," Grant assured him.

An uncomfortable silence fell between them. Stone wanted to say more but figured it would only make Grant angrier. Hunkering, he marked the steadily graying sky and the advent of the first stars. Nightfall brought with it gusts of wind and the cry of a coyote.

Stone stood. "We'll leave our horses here and go on foot."

"Whatever you say."

The youngster's tone galled Stone. He had half a mind to tell him to stay there, but no, the experience would do him good. Shucking his six-shooter, he made toward the woods in a crouch. He saw no sign of a campfire, but the outlaws wouldn't be that obvious.

They were almost to the trees when a whiff of smoke brought Stone's head up. He stopped so abruptly that Grant bumped into him.

"Sorry," the younger deputy whispered.

"You smell that?"

Grant sniffed. "Yes."

"Not a peep from here on out," Stone cautioned.

The woods were black as pitch. There was no moon, and the starlight failed to penetrate. Conscious that the snap of a twig would give them away, Stone moved as if treading on glass. He placed each boot lightly and slowly applied his full weight.

Off through the cottonwoods and oaks, fingers of

flame appeared. The outlaws were keeping their fire small, which was smart of them. A lot of whites made their fires so big, they could be spotted from miles off.

Stone crouched lower. Any moment now, he should see the outlaws. He aimed to crawl the rest of the way and take them completely by surprise. They'd be less likely to resist, and he could avoid bloodshed.

Sinking onto his belly, Stone snaked forward. He was so intent on avoiding brush that might snag his clothes or knock off his hat that he didn't look at the figures ringing the fire until he was almost on top of them. Stopping cold, he smothered an oath. For all his talk to Grant about not making a blunder, he'd made one, himself.

Yes, someone was camped at the spring.

Only it wasn't the outlaws.

They were Sioux.

12

The shock Alonzo Pratt had felt on encountering the bull buffalo was nothing compared to the shock that spiked through him as he realized that the old lawman had led him to almost within spitting distance of half a dozen Sioux warriors. Alonzo went numb with disbelief, then flushed with anger at Stone. He could have hit the old man for being so careless.

A moment more, and one of the warriors gazed in their direction.

Alonzo forgot all about Stone. For a few harrowing seconds he feared the warrior had heard them or somehow spotted them, but the warrior turned back and went on talking with his friends.

All six, Alonzo noted, were young. All six were painted for war. It led Alonzo to reckon they had broken away from the reservation to go on the warpath against whites. Stone and he needed to get out of there.

One of the warriors said something that made the

others smile. They were at ease and showed no sign that they knew anyone else was within ten miles.

Alonzo nudged Stone. He wanted him to turn and start back. Stone did turn, but only to whisper, "Looks like we goofed."

Alonzo couldn't believe his ears. They were in danger of their lives, and the old man treated it as if it were nothing. He started to turn to get out of there himself, but Stone gripped his arm.

"Be still."

It took great effort for Alonzo not to scramble away in panic. He took a few deep breaths to steady his nerves and realized he was overreacting. They were at least forty feet from the fire, well hidden in the trees. Safe enough, for the time being. "What do we do?" he whispered.

"Look at the one on the other side of the fire," Stone whispered, "with his hair hangin' down over his right shoulder."

Alonzo did as instructed and was puzzled as to why until the warrior shifted slightly. A gasp nearly escaped him. A scalp hung from the warrior's waist. Several others, he realized, also had grisly trophies of recent kills.

"We can't let this stand," Stone whispered.

"What can we do?" Alonzo whispered. It was six to two, after all.

"What do you think?" Stone whispered. "Think of that family we spent time with today, and others like them."

Never, ever had Alonzo imagined a situation where he'd tangle with a pack of Sioux. His life had become one insane incident after another. "Do we shoot them where they sit?" That seemed the smart thing, to him.

"We'll try to take them alive," Stone said.

"Are you loco?"

"We give them the same chance we'd give anyone else," Stone whispered. "I'll crawl off in this direction," and he motioned to the right. "When I holler, jump out and cover them. If they come at us, shoot."

"There has to be a better way," Alonzo whispered.

"There isn't." Stone went to crawl off.

"This is a job for the army," Alonzo tried.

"The army's not here. We are," Stone said. "It's our duty to protect the settlers. Whether from outlaws or Injuns doesn't matter."

It mattered to Alonzo. He wasn't a lawman. He was only pretending to be. He should admit the truth, and if Stone arrested him, so be it.

"One of those scalps is a woman's," Stone whispered.

Alonzo looked and saw one that did, indeed, appear to be the long, lustrous hair of a female. He turned to tell Stone that it didn't matter, he wasn't about to fight any Sioux, but the lawman was already crawling off. He'd have to raise his voice, and the warriors might hear him.

The urge to flee became so strong, Alonzo half-twisted around. Something, he couldn't say what, stopped him. Maybe it was that he couldn't bring himself to run out on Stone. Maybe it was the thought of that poor woman. Maybe it was Hiram and Hortense and their kids.

Facing the fire, Alonzo drew his Colt. He wasn't used to using a revolver. It felt heavy and awkward in his hand. Holding it close to his chest to muffle the sound, he slowly thumbed back the hammer.

Alonzo's mouth went dry. *What am I doing?* he asked himself. He was going to get killed if he kept at this lawman nonsense. He would help Stone this once, and then either own up to the ruse he'd played or else take the first opportunity that came along to fan the breeze.

Enough was enough.

Jacob Stone was worried. Not about the Sioux so much as about his new partner. Robert Grant was scared. Stone supposed he shouldn't blame him. Grant was young and inexperienced. Stone had been young once. Although, thinking back, never as afraid as Grant sounded.

Stone could only hope that if things fell apart, the younger man showed some mettle. Grant must have some good qualities or Marshal Hodder wouldn't have made him a deputy.

Stone focused on the warriors. He'd fought Comanches once, years ago down in Texas. It wasn't an experience he'd ever care to repeat, yet it had taught him valuable lessons. The first was that Indians weren't invincible. In Texas, the Comanches were held in terror-struck awe. But they bled, and died, like anyone else.

The second lesson was that Indians were no different from whites in another regard. Some were brave, some weren't. When he and the other deputies sprang their ambush, some of the Comanches broke and ran. Others fought with incredible ferocity.

Stone suddenly stopped. He was about halfway to where he wanted to be, but one of the warriors had stood. The man moved toward the woods. Stone worried Grant had been seen, and tensed to spring to his feet.

The Sioux was only heeding nature's call. The yellow stream glistened in the firelight as he let out a contented grunt.

Stone was glad Grant didn't open fire. Stone stayed where he was until the warrior returned to the fire, then resumed crawling. When he was due east of it, he stopped, silently rose into a crouch, and moved to the edge of the clearing.

A horse raised its head and pricked its ears.

Stone froze again. If the animal whinnied, the warriors might grab their bows and lances and spring to investigate. He'd wait, so the element of surprise was on his side.

The horse was staring in his direction.

Stone doubted it could see him. Nor could it have caught his scent since the wind was blowing the other way. He exercised patience, and after a while the animal lowered its head again and went back to dozing.

Stone licked his lips. A long time ago he'd learned that when it came time to act, the thing to do was act quickly. Get it over with before he could have second thoughts. Especially when it put his life at risk.

Accordingly, Stone stood and boldly strode into the circle of firelight. His Colt leveled, he hollered, "Federal marshal. Stay where you are and you won't come to any harm."

Stone suspected that none of the young warriors spoke English. Few Sioux did. He had to try, though. Lawmen didn't gun people down without warning. Not even Indians.

He'd counted on surprise to rivet them long enough for him to get closer. The muzzle of his Colt should deter them from trying anything. It would certainly give outlaws second thoughts. But these weren't outlaws. They were haters of all things white, out to kill every white they came across. They had also been trained since childhood in the arts of war. Giving up wasn't in their nature.

Stone took one more step, and all hell broke loose.

Alonzo was incredulous when the old lawman moved into the open. The man took incredible chances. He heard Stone shout, and saw the six Sioux look up. Thinking that they wouldn't do anything rash if two revolvers were trained on them, he pushed erect and burst from the woods.

Half the Sioux were already rising. One grabbed a bow, another a lance. The bowman notched an arrow with lightning rapidity and pulled the sinew string to his cheek.

Stone shot him.

Now all the warriors were heaving erect. Another loosed a shaft at Stone, who threw himself flat.

Alonzo would have done the same except his arms and legs refused to move. A burly warrior was hurtling toward him with a tomahawk raised to bash his brains in.

"No!" Alonzo cried.

His countenance contorted in fury, the Sioux let out an unearthly howl. His whole body curled as he prepared to strike.

Alonzo shot him. He was holding his Colt down low, and his trigger finger tightened without him even thinking about it.

The slug caught the warrior in the gut. Clutching himself even as he staggered back, the warrior doubled over.

Alonzo heard Deputy Stone's six-shooter boom several times but he didn't look. He couldn't take his eyes off the Sioux in front of him. The man tottered, stopped dead, then looked up at Alonzo as if amazed that Alonzo had shot him. "You," Alonzo blurted. "I . . ."

Horror welled up in Alonzo's chest. He had shot another human being. He told himself it was justified, that the warrior had left him no choice, that if he hadn't fired, he'd be dead.

Then the warrior screeched and raised his tomahawk and sprang, his painted face a mask of pure hatred.

Alonzo shot him again. And a third time. And fourth. He couldn't seem to stop himself. His hand and arm shaking, he thumbed the hammer for another.

At each blast, the Sioux had been jolted. Now the warrior's eyes widened and glazed and his long legs gave out from under him. He fell to earth with his tomahawk not six inches from Alonzo's foot.

Aghast at what he had done, Alonzo shook even more. He'd killed a man. Killed a man. Killed a man. He almost threw the Colt down but reason reasserted itself. It had been him or the warrior. He must tell himself that over and over. Him or the warrior, and he was fond of breathing.

The shaking stopped.

Belatedly, Alonzo realized the clearing had gone quiet. Dreading that he would find his companion down and the other warriors about to pounce, he raised his head.

Three bodies lay in a line between the crackling fire and Jacob Stone, who was reloading. The nearest to Stone had been shot in the head, the others in the chest. Of the remaining pair, there was no sign. Sudden hoofbeats in the woods told where they had gone.

"Are you all right, son?"

Alonzo had to try twice to speak, his throat was so dry. "All right," he said, although he was anything but.

"You did fine," Stone complimented him.

"I only shot one of them," Alonzo said, when he would rather not have shot any.

"I've had more practice at this," Stone said, smiling encouragement. He took a step, limping, and pressed his left hand to his leg.

Only then did Alonzo see the shaft jutting from the lawman's thigh. "You took an arrow!" he exclaimed the obvious.

"And it hurts like hell," Stone said with a grimace. Bending, he gripped the wrist of the nearest warrior, feeling for a pulse. "I'll tend to it after we make sure these have gone to their Happy Hunting Ground."

"Their what?" Alonzo said in confusion.

"It's what some folks call the Lakota notion of heaven," Stone explained as he bent to the next body.

Alonzo checked the last one, his skin crawling as he touched the warrior's still-warm flesh. "This one is no more," he confirmed.

Shuffling to the fire, Stone slowly eased down, his left leg held as straight as a board. "We need to heat some water for when we take this out."

Alonzo thought of Loudon and how infected his wound had become. He also thought of something else. "What about the two who got away?"

"Long gone," Stone said, shoving his Colt into his holster.

"They might circle back."

"Unlikely. Indians aren't stupid. We have guns and they don't. And for all they know, we'll give chase." Stone shook his head. "No, they'll put as much distance as they can between us."

"If you say so."

"I can't do much walkin' with this leg," Stone said. "You'll have to fetch our horses yourself."

Alonzo thought of how far off they had left their animals, and swallowed. "By my lonesome?"

"What's the matter with you?" Stone testily demanded. "You need to get over this timid streak. Are you a lawman or aren't you?"

"*No, I'm not*," Alonzo almost said.

Stone arched an eyebrow. "Why are you still standin' there? Do I need to hold your hand for everything?"

Alonzo smarted at the deputy's tone. "Don't you

worry," he declared. "I can do what needs doin'." He turned to go and had taken a few steps when Stone said his name.

Stopping, he turned. "What now?"

"Be careful. Now that I think about it, you might be right about those two circlin' around. Could be they'll lie in wait for you."

"Wonderful," Alonzo said.

13

The night seemed darker than any night in Alonzo's life. He went slowly, the Colt cocked in his hand. Any sound, however slight, caused him to stop and listen until he assured himself it was nothing.

The two surviving Sioux hadn't fled. He was sure of it. They wouldn't just run off. Not Sioux warriors. They were out here somewhere.

More than ever, Alonzo regretted impersonating a lawman. He regretted it with every fiber of his being. That's what had gotten him into this fix. Once he was shed of Jacob Stone, he was going to take a rock and pound his badge into a shapeless wad of metal.

Stone. Alonzo couldn't for the life of him understand why the man had worn a badge for so long. Who in their right mind would take a job that could get them killed? And stay at it for year after year? Something had to be wrong with that old man, he told himself. Stone must have some kind of death wish.

The wind picked up, stirring the high grass, and the

rustling frayed at Alonzo's already strained nerves. How was he to hear the Sioux if they crept up on him? They wouldn't make much noise. Not those devils.

Alonzo had gone a considerable distance when it occurred to him that he might be going in the wrong direction. It was taking much too long to reach the horses. He studied the sky and spied the Big Dipper, but that was no help. He never could tell direction by stars. He wasn't a frontiersman or scout. It was part of why he always used a packhorse. If he tried to live off the land, he'd starve. To say nothing of always being lost.

Damn, I'm dumb, Alonzo almost said out loud. Talking to himself had become a habit, one he should break.

A gust struck him, a chill blast of wind, causing his skin to break out in goose bumps.

Alonzo scanned the grassland. He didn't see the horses. A glance back showed that the trees where Stone was waiting were a long way off. Farther than they should be.

Cautiously, he advanced. Soon the ground sloped upward. He was climbing a hill. But there hadn't been any hills between the horses and the Sioux camp. In frustration he stopped and stomped a foot, then froze. A stupid mistake like that could cost him his hair and his life.

Alonzo hated this. Hated it more than anything. If he did find the horses, he had half a mind to climb on and ride off, taking Stone's with him, and strand the old lawman afoot. It would serve Stone right.

Turning, he retraced his steps down the hill and bore more to his right. The horses were nowhere to be seen. He wondered if the two Sioux had taken them. Then both Stone and him would be stranded, a prospect that scared the hell out of him. He wouldn't last long in the wilderness on his own. He needed to keep Stone alive so Stone could keep him alive.

Alonzo just wanted to get it over with. Find their animals and get back. When he thought he had gone too far in the new direction, he changed course. Where, oh where, were the infernal horses?

A nicker brought him to a stop.

Alonzo brightened. He'd heard it as clear as anything. He peered hard into the night but still saw nothing. "Where are you?" he anxiously whispered. He remembered being told that things could be seen better at night when they were silhouetted against the sky so he crouched low to the ground.

A jolt of excitement coursed through him. Several large forms stood out against the stars not far off.

Elated, Alonzo hurried toward them. In his eagerness he threw all caution to the gusting wind. He broke into a run but had gone only a few yards when he thought he saw something move. Not one of the horses but something near them. It was a flash of motion, nothing more, but enough to cause him to dive flat with his breath caught in his throat.

He'd glimpsed a man, not an animal. He was certain. And the only other men around, besides Stone and him, were the two Sioux.

Alonzo had a terrible thought. What if the Sioux had found the horses and were waiting for someone to come for them so the Sioux could jump whoever came? It would be just like those crafty redskins.

This was the final straw. Then and there, Alonzo made up his mind to give up roaming the plains and stick to cities and towns from now on.

Another hint of movement made him stiffen. Was it

his imagination, or was someone slinking through the grass toward him. He stared so hard, his eyes hurt. But once again he saw nothing.

Alonzo smothered a groan of despair. No, he definitely didn't have what it took to be a lawman. He could impersonate with the best of them, and steal without a qualm, but put him in a situation like this and he went all to pieces.

Alonzo looked to his left, and his blood stopped in his veins. There was a shape in the grass that hadn't been there before. It could be a man, crouched low. One of the warriors. He raised the Colt but didn't shoot. He might miss, or only wound the man.

Then the unthinkable happened.

Something bumped his foot.

For about the tenth or eleventh time, Jacob Stone sat up and scoured the belt of woods south of the clearing. "Where the blazes is that boy?" he grumbled. It was taking Grant entirely too long.

Stone examined his wound. The pain had lessened a little and his leg wasn't bleeding as bad. He needed to get the arrow out, though, and soon. And he needed hot water to clean the wound and reduce the chance of infection.

It would be easier with Grant to lend a hand, but he couldn't wait forever.

Stone strained to hear hoofbeats and only heard the wind. He contemplated going to see if Grant was all right. But that might set his leg to bleeding more, and he'd lost too much blood already.

Stone had been wounded a few times in his career. Most were in his younger days, when he was green like Grant, and made more mistakes. Those mistakes. They bit you on the ass every time.

Stone recollected an incident down to the border country, in Texas. He and another deputy by the name of Whitehouse had gone to a village to look for a wanted man, a notorious pistolero by the name of Santiago who was quick with his temper and quick on the draw. Whitehouse and Stone had gone up to a hovel where an informant claimed Santiago was hiding.

Neither of them had much experience, and they stupidly stood in front of the door when Whitehouse knocked, instead of to either side. Santiago was in there, all right, and he cut loose with his pistols, shooting *through* the door. Whitehouse died where he stood, shot to pieces. Stone had taken lead in the shoulder, and fallen. He was lying in his own blood when Santiago made a mistake of his own; he opened the door to peer out. Stone shot him in the head.

The wound left a scar. So did another, from a time in Kansas when Stone rode into Salina intending to grab a bite to eat, and be on his way. But as he drew rein at a hitch rail, who should come ambling out of a general store but Floyd Banks, a desperado whose face was plastered on wanted circulars all over the territory. Banks saw Stone at the exact moment Stone saw him and they both went for their six-shooters. Banks, to Stone's embarrassment, was faster. Caught flat-footed, as it were, in his saddle, Stone was an easy target. A slug tore through his side. He'd answered with a shot that jarred Banks onto his bootheels. Both of them fired again. Banks missed. Stone didn't. Floyd Banks died with a third nostril.

Stone had a few other, smaller scars. On those rare occasions when he was naked, he sometimes traced his scars with his finger, remembering, remembering.

Now he would have a new one.

Stone scoured the trees once more. If he had to, he'd

take the arrow out himself. It would be a lot harder, but he could do it.

"Where *are* you?" Stone said to the empty air.

Alonzo Pratt twisted and looked up, and it was hard to say who was more astounded, him or the warrior who had almost stepped on him.

In a rush of insight, Alonzo realized the two Sioux had spotted him and one must have circled to come at him from behind while the other slunk toward him from the front. When he went to ground, they'd lost sight of him, and the warrior behind him had crept up and nearly stepped on him.

In the pale starlight, the warrior's expression was almost comical. It only lasted a few seconds. Then it changed to one of hate and wrath, and the warrior let out a war whoop and raised a knife to strike.

Without thinking, Alonzo shot him. His hand moved of its own accord, the Colt booming and bucking. The Sioux grabbed at his midsection but didn't go down. Instead, he growled deep in his throat and lunged.

Alonzo shot him again.

The warrior stopped and half-turned and took a couple of faltering steps to one side, then pitched face-down in the grass.

Alonzo had no time to savor his triumph. Moccasin-shod feed thudded. He whirled and scrambled to his knees, only to be slammed into by a battering ram driven by raw fury.

The last Sioux was beside himself. He shrieked as he attacked, the cry of a man on the brink of going berserk.

Alonzo barely got his left hand up and grabbed the warrior's wrist to keep a knife from being buried in his chest. For his part, the warrior grabbed Alonzo's wrist to prevent Alonzo from using the Colt. They struggled, thrashing and straining, each striving to break free and use his weapon.

For Alonzo, the whole thing seemed unreal. The warrior's swarthy, maniacal face was inches from his own. They were close in age, the two of them, and if not for the difference in their hair and their eyes, Alonzo would have thought he was looking at a mirror image of himself.

Hissing like a snake, the young warrior sought to sink the cold steel of his knife into Alonzo's neck. The tip drew ever closer. One cut, if it sliced a vein, would do the trick.

Alonzo had never fought so hard, so desperately. He exerted every sinew, his lungs working like a black-smith's bellows. He must prevail or he would die. It was that simple.

With a quick shift of his weight, the warrior was suddenly on top. His teeth showed white in a feral snarl as he bore down on his knife arm with all his weight. The blade was a whisker-width from Alonzo's throat.

Alonzo had only ever been in a few fights, most when he was a boy. He was about as skilled at fighting as he was at being a frontiersman. But he would be damned if he would let himself be slain.

Arching his body, Alonzo bucked. The warrior fell off him, and they rolled. Alonzo sought to get on top, but his adversary thwarted him. They rolled the other way. A knee caught Alonzo in the thigh. The warrior drove his forehead at Alonzo's face, and Alonzo jerked back.

Alonzo couldn't hold his own much longer. He would tire before the Sioux did, and the Sioux would finish it.

The warrior gave voice to an unearthly howl.

They rolled once more, and Alonzo drove his knee at the man's groin. He was surprised that he connected, surprised even more that the warrior partly doubled over and his grip slackened. Not much, but enough that Alonzo tore his right arm free and jammed the Colt's muzzle into the Sioux's cheek. They looked at one another, and for an instant, time froze. For an instant, they were just two men, one on the cusp of dying. Fear filled the warrior's eyes.

Alonzo fired.

Blood splattered his mouth and jaw, and Alonzo recoiled. Spitting and gasping, he heaved to his knees and shoved the body from him. Dizziness assailed him. He came close to passing out.

Fighting to stay conscious, weakness pervading his limbs, he was able to stand.

A gust of wind was a literal breath of fresh air. Alonzo drank in the cool feeling of the breeze on his sweat-soaked body. His hat was missing, his hair plastered to his head. He took a few stumbling steps, dumfounded at his deliverance.

They were dead. Both the warriors were dead. He had killed two Sioux all by himself. It didn't seem real. It was like a dream. Yet there they lay, as lifeless as those back at the clearing.

"Dear God," Alonzo said, and commenced to shake. This made three men he'd slain in the span of an hour. He could hardly believe it.

Alonzo held up his hand and stared at the Colt. He owed his life to it. He could never have beaten the Sioux without it.

A whinny brought him out of himself. He'd forgotten all about the horses, and about Deputy Marshal Jacob Stone with an arrow through his leg.

"I'm comin'," Alonzo said.

First he groped about until he found his hat. He still felt weak, but he stumbled to the horses, gathered up the reins to Stone's and the lead rope to his packhorse, and pulled himself up onto Archibald.

Archibald shied at the scent of blood, and Alonzo had to firm his hold. "Steady, fella," he said. "It's all right."

Alonzo headed toward the woods at a walk, drinking in deep breaths. He was grateful to be breathing; life had never been so precious to him as it was at that moment. He'd always taken it for granted.

It struck Alonzo that he need not go back. He had the horses. He could ride off, as he'd considered doing earlier, and be shed of Stone. All it would take was a jab of his spurs.

He couldn't do it. He didn't have it in him to desert someone, especially not someone who was wounded, and who had treated him decently. Against his better judgment, he entered the trees.

"I'm the biggest dunce there is," Alonzo said bitterly. It wouldn't surprise him a bit, if before this was over, he ended up dead.

14

When Deputy Marshal Jacob Stone heard shots, he was filled with alarm. It could only mean one thing: Robert Grant had run into trouble.

Stone placed his hands flat on the ground and tried to push to his feet. The young deputy would need help.

It was probably already too late, but Stone must try. He rose partway, only to have his thigh lance with agony. He bit his lip to keep from crying out and tried to keep rising; but his leg wouldn't support him, and he sank back down.

Refusing to give up, Stone gathered his strength and heaved erect. The effort cost him. He grew dizzy, and swayed. His leg nearly buckled. Getting his balance, he waited for the dizziness to pass, then shambled to where a fallen warrior lay, a lance half under him.

Stone girded himself. This would take some doing. Carefully bending but keeping his hurt leg straight, he pulled and tugged, moving the dead warrior enough that he could claim the lance. He'd never held one before. It was heavier than he reckoned, which was good. It could support him without breaking.

Using the lance as a crutch, Stone limped toward the woods. His leg refused to cooperate. He worried the arrow had sliced a tendon, and that his leg might not heal right. It would put an end to his lawman days, whether he wanted them to end or not.

Once in the trees, Stone was forced to go slowly. He'd take a step, slide his wounded leg forward while bracing himself on the lance, stop, then take another step. At this rate, it would take forever. He'd never reach Grant in time.

After only ten yards or so, Stone halted. He was caked with sweat, and close to exhausted. He attributed his weakness to loss of blood. It was too soon for infection to have set in.

Worried about Grant, Stone continued on. The lance bumped a log, and he tripped. More pain exploded up through him, but at least he didn't fall.

"What in the world are you tryin' to do, Deputy Stone? Kill yourself?"

Startled, Stone looked up. In his dazed state, he hadn't heard Grant come up, and with the horses, no less. "I was comin' to help you," he croaked.

"I didn't need any," Grant said, sounding surprised that he hadn't. He swung down. "Here. I'll get you on your horse and we'll take you back."

"What about the Sioux? Did they run off or are they dead?"

"They're no longer a worry."

"You killed both of them?" Stone said in some amazement.

"Believe it or not."

"Well, I'll be," Stone said. "You've done right fine, Deputy Grant."

"It doesn't feel fine," Grant replied. "I didn't want to do it, but it was them or me."

"That's usually how it goes," Stone said. Trouble, when it came, usually happened fast. Deputies learned to be quick with their wits and their guns, or died.

"Let me boost you onto your saddle," Grant offered, and slid his shoulder under Stone's arm.

"I'll be sure to tell Marshal Hodder how well you've done," Stone said. "He'll be pleased that you've justified his faith in you."

"Enough of that," Grant said. "If I never think about this night again for as long as I live, fine and dandy."

Stone frowned. Grant's attitude was still cause for concern, but he had a more pressing concern to contend with: his leg. Straddling the saddle nearly caused him to black out. Gripping the horn, he clung on as wave after black wave washed over him.

"Can you make it?" Grant asked.

"Watch me," Stone said. It wasn't in his nature to give up. He weakly clucked to his horse and winced when it moved. "Hold on to that lance. I might need it later on."

"I'll be right behind you."

Stone took a moment to give thanks for their deliverance. The two of them against six Sioux—the outcome could have been entirely different. As the saying went, someone "up there" was looking out for them.

As if Grant were reading his thoughts, he remarked, "We were lucky as can be, weren't we?"

"You can say that again," Stone said.

"And you do this law work day in and day out? I don't know as I can."

"Hold on, son," Stone said. "In all my career, I only ever fought redskins two times. Not countin' this. That's hardly a lot."

"Once was enough for me."

"Look on the bright side. This could be the only time you'll ever have to."

"You and your bright sides. I keep wearin' this tin star, it could be fifty times for all you know."

"So that's it," Stone said. He'd seen this before, in other young deputies. "You're goin' through a phase, is all. Where somethin' awful happens and you doubt you've made the right choice."

"My choices of late have been nothin' to crow about," Grant said.

"You're alive."

"Don't try to cheer me. I'm in a funk and I'll stay there a while, thank you very much."

"Just don't do anything rash," Stone advised. Like quit the marshal's service when he'd proven he had the mettle to make it as a lawman.

They reached the clearing, and even with the younger man's help, dismounting took a lot out of Stone. He was glad to sink onto his good side by the fire, and not have to move.

"Now we take that arrow out," Grant said.

"First put the water on," Stone said. "We'll need it good and hot." Wearily closing his eyes. he tried not to dwell on the ordeal to come. "I'm afraid you'll have to do most of the work. I won't be of much use."

"This has been some day," Robert Grant grumbled.

Stone didn't see what Grant had to complain about. Grant wasn't the one with the arrow in his leg.

Alonzo had never treated an arrow wound in his life, or any wound, for that matter. When it came to blood and the like, he'd always been squeamish. He'd always reckoned he'd have made a terrible sawbones.

Now he went about filling his coffeepot, then added

broken branches to the fire so the water would heat that much sooner.

Stone appeared to be asleep.

"You old goat," Alonzo muttered. This was all the old lawman's fault. They should have left the Sioux alone. So what if the warriors were on the warpath and would likely have added to their scalp collection?

Alonzo wrapped his arms around his legs and rested his chin on his knee. This was, without a doubt, the worst pickle he'd ever been in. Once he was rid of Stone, he would head for Denver and spend a month visiting saloons and bawdy houses, just to forget.

Closing his eyes, Alonzo imagined himself savoring a whiskey or indulging in a game of cards, or maybe with a warm, laughing dove on his lap. Life's little pleasures, that at the moment seemed like everything to him. He envisioned the dove leaning in close, her breath warm on his neck, about to say something about inviting him to her room.

With a start, Alonzo sat up. He'd almost fallen asleep. Stiffly rising, he checked the coffeepot. The water was steaming hot. Moving around the fire, he crouched next to Jacob Stone. "You awake?"

Stone didn't respond. His face was pale, and he was wet with sweat.

Alonzo examined the wound closely. The arrow had gone clean through, and the barbed tip jutted about an inch out the back of Stone's leg. He figured the best way to remove it was to break the tip off, then grip the feathered end and slide it out.

"How do I get into these things?" Alonzo said. Gripping the end below the tip, he felt his fingers grow sticky with blood. He tried to bend the arrow to see how easy it would be to break; he could barely bend it.

Whatever the Sioux made their arrows from, the wood was strong.

"Better and better," Alonzo groused. If he had a saw he could cut the arrow. Or if he had a big knife, perhaps. If, if, if.

The feathers were from a hawk, Alonzo suspected, and about five inches in length. As near as he could tell, they had been attached using a strand of animal sinew. Buffalo sinew, maybe, since Indians used buffalo parts for so much else.

At the other end, a notch appeared to have been cut, the arrowhead inserted, and then more sinew used to secure the arrowhead in place.

Arrows seemed so primitive compared to guns, and yet Indians used shafts just like these to kill bears and buffalo and their enemies all the time. He noticed a groove that ran the length of the arrow. A blood groove, he thought it was called. Appropriate, since it was filled with Stone's blood.

Alonzo pondered. Short of breaking the shaft, his best bet was to remove the barbed point and then pull the arrow out. With that in mind, he took a folding knife from his pocket, opened it, and proceeded to slice at the sinew. It proved hard to cut. He persisted for long minutes, and eventually the strands parted.

Stone stayed unconscious the whole while.

Alonzo felt a drop of sweat trickle into his eye, and wiped his brow with his sleeve. He didn't realize he was sweating so much. Carefully gripping the arrowhead, he pulled, but nothing happened. Changing tactics, he twisted and turned until the arrowhead came loose.

Once again, Stone remained out to the world.

Alonzo was growing anxious. The old man should

have woken up. He must hurry so he could clean the wound.

Shifting, Alonzo gripped the fletched end of the arrow, wrapped his fingers good and tight, placed his other palm against Stone's leg, and pulled. If he thought the arrow would slide right out, he was mistaken. It wouldn't budge. He wondered if it was lodged in Stone's thigh bone, in which case he might never get it out.

Frustrated, Alonzo pulled harder. The arrow moved, a smidgen. Stone groaned but didn't revive.

Taking a deep breath, Alonzo bunched his shoulder and pulled with all his might. The arrow was slow to move but it moved. A fraction at a time, but it came. His hand slipped, and he caused the leg to jerk. Jacob Stone groaned.

Alonzo wiped his palm on his pants and went at it again. His shoulder hurt but he stuck with it. The next instant, without any sign that it was coming loose, the arrow practically popped out of Stone's leg. It threw Alonzo off-balance, and he fell onto his backside so close to the fire that flames licked at his pants. He felt searing heat, and scrambled to his feet.

Smiling, Alonzo held the arrow up. He'd done it! Blood smeared his hand and was trickling down his wrist. Oddly, it didn't bother him at all. Setting the arrow down, he wiped his hand on the grass.

Jacob Stone stayed out to the world.

Something was clearly wrong. Alonzo put a hand to Stone's forehead. Stone might have a fever; he wasn't sure. "Deputy Stone?" he said, and lightly shook him.

At last the older man's eyes fluttered open. Licking his lips, he said thickly, "What is it, son?"

"I asked you to stop callin' me that," Alonzo reminded him, and gestured. "I got the arrow out."

Stone looked down. "I'll be switched."

"We need to clean the wound," Alonzo reminded him. "Do you take your britches off or do I cut them?"

"Cut," Stone said, and closed his eyes.

"Jacob?" Alonzo used his first name for the first time. "Talk to me. I don't like you passin' out like this."

Stone hadn't. "You can do it, son," he said so softly that Alonzo barely heard him.

"Damn it, Jacob. Please."

"Don't cuss. Cussin' is for folks who are too lazy to think of the right words to use."

Alonzo thought that was preposterous. "You're ramblin'. You need to stay awake while I work on you."

"Sure thing," Stone said, and slumped, unconscious.

Alonzo got to work cutting Stone's pant leg. He had a towel on his packhorse that he used to wash and clean the entry and exit holes. The flesh wasn't discolored, which was encouraging.

By his reckoning it was pushing two in the morning when Alonzo finished and sat back, tired as could be. Strips cut from the towel sufficed for bandages, and he hadn't done badly, if he said so, himself.

Alonzo added more firewood, then gratefully sank onto his back. Between the fight with the Sioux and now this, he was about done in. He supposed it would be wise to stand guard the rest of the night, but he didn't have it in him. He was exhausted. His eyes refused to stay open.

Alonzo let sleep claim him. If more Sioux came along, it was too bad. A man could only do so much.

Often during the night, Alonzo dreamed. Not this night. He slept the sleep of the dead, a sleep so deep and so black, he was aware of nothing at all until a slight sound roused him. He had the illusion of being at the bottom of a deep pit, and clawed toward a distant faint light.

The sound was repeated.

Puzzled, Alonzo felt his sluggish brain churn to life. He blinked in the harsh glare of the bright morning sun and rose onto his elbows, too befuddled to think straight. "What?" he said. "Jacob?"

"You shouldn't be here," a voice said.

Alonzo raised his head higher—and found himself staring into the muzzle of a rifle.

15

—————◆—————

Alonzo woke up in a rush, every sense alert. For a few harrowing moments he feared his head was about to be blown off.

"Didn't you hear me?"

Alonzo looked up. With all the shocks he'd had recently, he'd have thought he'd be used to another surprise, but no. His eyes widened and his jaw dropped, and he blurted, "It can't be."

"Can't be what?" demanded the person holding the rifle.

"You're female!" Alonzo exclaimed.

"Your eyes work. How about your brain?"

She was young, about his age, with a teardrop-shaped face, vivid green eyes, red lips formed in a perpetual pout, and high cheekbones. She appeared to be amused by his reaction, but there was nothing amusing about her Winchester, or the fact that the hammer had been cocked.

"You're dressed like a man!" Alonzo said. And she

was, in a man's shirt and man's pants, with suspenders instead of a belt. Her short-brimmed hat was the kind men wore and her boots, although uncommonly small, were the type men wore. She even wore spurs. A gun belt was strapped around her waist, and in her holster nestled a Colt.

"Nothing escapes you, does it?"

Alonzo could only stare. Her hair was as black as the night. At first he thought she'd had it cropped short, but no, he realized she'd tucked it up under her hat.

"Cat got your tongue?"

Alonzo found his voice. "Why are you pointin' that rifle at me?"

"So you'll behave. I know how men are, after what happened."

"How's that again?" Alonzo said.

"Plus, you're a lawman," she said, nodding at the tin star on his vest. "What a shame, you being so young and handsome and all."

"Wait? What?" Alonzo wondered if he was still asleep and dreaming. He couldn't remember a woman ever calling him handsome before.

"You need to catch up. They could show at any time, and there's no telling what they'd do to you and your hurt friend, except that it won't be pleasant."

"Who?"

"At last. An intelligent question," she said, and laughed.

Alonzo was more confused than he could ever recall being, and that took some doing. "Look. Can I sit up? And will you stop pointin' that thing at me? It makes me nervous."

"Where are you from?" the woman asked.

"I've been wanderin' all over," Alonzo began.

"No. I mean where were you born and raised," she clarified. "You have a cute Southern sound."

"Cute?" Alonzo said.

"Born," she repeated. "As in where your mother gave birth to you. You didn't hatch out of an egg, right?"

"God Almighty," Alonnzo said.

"Born," she said. "Where?"

"Missouri," Alonzo said, and stopped himself before he revealed more. He hadn't told anyone where he was really from since he took to impersonating to fill his poke. "As if it's any of your business."

"Prickly gent, aren't you? Here I am, trying to save your life, and you treat me like I'm a sister you can't get along with."

"I don't have a sister."

"Lucky her."

"How can she be lucky if I don't have one?"

"Slower than a turtle." She glanced at Jacob Stone. "Did you bandage him? You didn't do a very good job."

"Hold on," Alonzo said. "Forget about him for a moment."

"Forget that he's been hurt, apparently by one of the dead Indians lying about? Isn't he your friend? How can you forget about him?"

"I want to know about you."

"Call me Jenna." She smiled and dipped at the knees in a curtsey. "Get up and redo his bandage and we'll whisk you out of here before it's too late."

Alonzo was galled by her bossing him around. "We're not goin' anywhere until you explain a few things."

Jenna sighed. "Why do so many men act like they're ten years old?"

"I do not."

Her Winchester held steady, Jenna stepped back. "On your feet. They could be here any minute."

"Who are we talkin' about?"

"Since you're a lawman, I'd imagine you've heard of the Grissom gang?"

"Cal Grissom?"

"No, Sydney Perceival Grissom."

"Who's he?"

Jenna snickered. "You worry me, handsome. You truly do. Of *course* I mean Cal Grissom. Him, and his killers. You must have heard of them, too. That awful Weasel Ginty? Fletcher? Spike Davis? Kent?" She paused, and shuddered. "And last but worst, Willy Boy Jenkins."

"Why is he the worst?" Alonzo asked, and then thought of a better question. "And how is it you know so much about them?"

"Is there a brain between those ears?" Jenna replied.

"Quit insultin' me," Alonzo took umbrage. "My brain works just fine, I'll have you know."

"Says the gent who just tangled with the Sioux. There are safer ways to earn a living, you know."

Alonzo was about fit to burst with impatience. "You need to explain who you are and what you're doin' here."

"And you're like a dog worrying a bone, but there isn't time for that." Jenna pointed at Jacob Stone. "If you're not going to redo his bandage, then get him on his horse and you get on yours and ride like the wind. Please. Before it's too late."

Alonzo wasn't about to leave without learning more about her. "If you'll stop pointin' that rifle, I'll fix his bandage."

"And have you jump me and arrest me?" Jenna shook her head. "I think not. On your feet. You're leaving whether you want to or not."

"Whatever you say." Holding his hands out in front

of him to show he wouldn't do anything rash, Alonzo slowly rose and sidled to Stone. The bandage was, in fact, loose. "Sometime durin' the night it must have come undone," he mentioned as he knelt to retie it.

"What's your name?" Jenna asked.

The answer was out of his mouth before he could stop himself. "Alonzo."

"I like that. It has a nice, masculine sound," Jenna said. "Is it your first name or your last?"

Just then Jacob Stone groaned and mumbled and started to roll over, but Alonzo stopped him so Stone wouldn't get dirt in his wound. "Jacob? Can you hear me?"

The old lawman opened his eyes. "Robert? What's goin' on?"

"I'm fixin' your bandage," Alonzo said. "How do you feel?"

"Puny," Stone said. "And hot."

"You must have a fever. Don't worry. I'll take good care of you."

"Thank you, son." Stone smiled, and closed his eyes.

"He called you 'Robert,' " Jenna said.

"So?" Alonzo pried at the bandage to peer under it. The wound didn't look infected, but what did he know? He wasn't a doctor.

"You told me your name was Alonzo."

Alonzo thought quick. "That's my middle name," he fibbed. "I like it more than Robert. My last name is Grant."

"Robert Alonzo Grant," Jenna said, rolling the words on her tongue. "A good, strong name."

Examining the bandage, Alonzo said, "Why do names mean so much to you?"

"I suppose it's because I've never been very proud of my own."

"Why not?"

Jenna lowered her rifle, although not all the way. "We'll call it an accident of birth and let it go at that." She glanced into the woods to the north. "Less talk. You don't want to be here when the Grissom gang comes."

"You're on the run from those outlaws?"

Instead of answering, Jenna rebutted with, "Is your favorite food molasses, by any chance?"

"It's apple pie, if you must know." Alonzo looked at her. "Why are the outlaws after you? What can I do to help?"

"There's nothing anyone can do," Jenna said, rather sorrowfully. "Please. You really must hurry."

"This bandage is stiff with dry blood," Alonzo mentioned. "I need to clean it before I retie it."

"What are you waiting for? You'll be as dead as those Indians if you don't quit flapping your gums and finish up."

Rather than use the water from his canteen, Alonzo went to the spring. He dipped the bandage in and wrung it out but it didn't come clean so he dipped it in the water a second time.

Jenna had followed, and was watching and pacing. "Are you going this slow just to aggravate me?"

"You think awful highly of yourself."

"Hurry," Jenna said, and stamped a foot.

Returning to the fire, Alonzo rewrapped Stone's wound. The old man's skin was hot to the touch. If Alonzo had to guess, he'd say Stone's temperature must be a hundred, or more.

Since Stone couldn't ride, Alonzo had to tie him to his saddle. That took a while, Jenna fidgeting the whole time.

"Finally!" she exclaimed when he stepped back. "Now off you go."

"Not without you," Alonzo informed her. "Where's your horse?" He figured she had left it in the trees when she snuck up on them.

"I'm not going."

Alonzo thought of the things he'd heard about the Grissom gang. "You can't stay here. What if those outlaws get their hands on you?"

"I'll be fine."

"You're comin' with us," Alonzo declared, "and I won't take no for an answer."

"You can't force me to."

Alonzo had an inspiration. "Sure I can." He tapped his badge. "I'm the law. I can make you come for your own good."

"Listen," Jenna said, and to his surprise, she stepped up and placed her hand on his chest and looked him deep in the eyes. "I know what I'm about. Trust me when I say they won't harm a hair on my head. You and your friend, though, they'll do things to you. Unspeakable things. I once saw Willy Boy Jenkins cut off a man's nose and ears, and that was just the start. So please. Climb on your horse and light a shuck while you still can."

"Not without you."

"Damnation, you're stubborn."

"Deputy Stone, there, would tell you that ladies shouldn't cuss," Alonzo tried to make light of her annoyance.

"I'm no lady."

Alonzo looked her up and down. "I don't believe that for a minute. You don't dress like a lady but there's somethin' about you." Something that plucked at him in a way he'd never experienced.

"We can't stand here all day arguing."

"Then fetch your horse and we'll go."

"Men!" Jenna said. "If I don't go, your deaths will be on my head, and I don't want that. Wait here." Turning on a heel, she stomped toward the woods, her fist clenched in anger.

Alonzo smiled. He looked forward to her company, and to learning more about her. He did some pacing of his own until she reappeared leading a dappled mare with a star on its forehead. She had slid her rifle into the scabbard and now her right hand rested on her Colt.

"Are you sure I can't talk you out of this?" Jenna said.

"What kind of lawman do you take me for, that I'd let you fall into the clutches of those outlaws?"

"If this has to be, then let's get riding," Jenna said resignedly. She glanced to the north once more. "They're close. I feel it in my bones."

Alonzo asked her if she would lead his packhorse while he led Stone's mount, and she agreed. They headed south. As they emerged from the woods he spied buzzards circling above the grass not far away. The two dead Sioux, he reckoned, and reined wide to avoid the bodies.

Jenna hardly gave the buzzards any notice. She was more concerned about what was behind them. "Thank God we're out of there."

Alonzo debated where to take her. The sodbuster's was nearest, but if the Grissom gang was after her, it would go hard for Hiram and Hortense. The next logical place was North Platte. It shouldn't take more than five or six days if they pushed, and if Jacob Stone held up.

For over an hour they rode hard over pristine prairie.

Alonzo snuck glances at Jenna when he thought she

wasn't looking. He liked a lot about her; her face, her hair, those pouty lips, the way she carried herself.

They came to a ribbon of cottonwoods bordering an even smaller ribbon of water, and Alonzo drew rein to rest and water their mounts. He carefully lifted Jacob Stone down and laid him on his back.

Jenna joined them.

"Is there anything more you'd care to tell me about the Grissom gang and why they're after you?" Alonzo tried one more time.

"No."

Alonzo wouldn't let her off that easy. "For that matter, what are you doin' out here in the middle of nowhere all by your lonesome?"

"Who says I was?"

"What then?"

"You pry and you pry," Jenna said, and sighed. "Very well." She faced him. "The reason they're after me is because they want me back."

"They took you captive and you escaped?"

"No." Jenna's features grew dark with shadow. "I'm Cal Grissom's daughter."

16

Only then did Alonzo recollect Deputy Stone saying something about a girl being seen with the Grissom gang during their last couple of robberies. "That stage and the Unionville Bank? That was you?"

"You heard about those, did you?"

Alonzo absently gestured at Stone. "He told me. Most every lawman in these parts must know by now."

"They were bound to, I suppose." Jenna moved to the old lawman and stared down at him. "So he's your partner, is he?"

Alonzo realized she was trying to change the subject. "Sort of."

"What do you mean?"

"He is and he isn't." Alonzo refused to let her distract him and said, "Tell me more about how you helped rob a bank and a stage."

"All I did at the bank was hold the horses," Jenna said. "The stage, he made me tag along. To show me the kind of work he does. If you can call robbing and killing work."

"He bein' Cal Grissom, your pa?"

"Who else?" Jenna lightly nudged Stone with her toe. "I've never seen a lawman this old before. How old is he? Ninety?"

"Almost," Alonzo said, and got back to what interested him more. "What kind of father forces his daughter to break the law?"

"My pa has been breaking it since I can remember. It's all he knows how to do. His way of life, you might say."

"He can always stop," Alonzo said.

"Not him. To tell you the truth, I think he does it because he likes it. Sure, he could have taken an ordinary job anytime. But ordinary isn't for him. He likes the excitement, the thrill."

"Of bein' shot or hung?"

Jenna grinned halfheartedly. "He's the great Cal Grissom. He'll never be caught, or so he likes to say a lot." She sighed and turned. "As fathers go, he's next to useless."

"Then why were you with him?"

"Now you're getting personal," Jenna said, and walked off.

Alonzo would have gone after her but just then Deputy Stone groaned and stirred and opened his eyes. The old lawman looked about him as if confused, then focused on Alonzo.

"Deputy Grant? Where are we? What's goin' on?"

Alonzo hunkered. "You're sickly. Infection has set in, I reckon. I'm doin' the best I can but I'm no doc."

"Damn."

"I'm takin' you to North Platte," Alonzo informed him. "You did say they have a sawbones there?"

"They do, yes," Stone said. "Doc Haywood. I met him a couple of times. He's been around almost as long as me. Knows his stuff." Stone licked his lips. "I could go for a swallow of water right about now."

"Have as much as you want," Alonzo said, rising to get his canteen. He noticed Jenna watching him intently, and wondered why. She was still watching when he finished tilting the canteen to Stone's mouth and the old lawman had closed his eyes and drifted off again. "What?" Alonzo said.

"That was kind of you."

"He's hurt. He needs the help."

"Is that why you became a lawman? Because you like to help people?"

Alonzo hesitated. He didn't want to lie to her, but what choice did he have? He couldn't tell her the truth. She clearly didn't like outlaws much, and he was a lawbreaker. "Helpin' folks comes with the badge."

"A decent man is rare these days."

"There are a lot of decent folks around," Alonzo said, and almost laughed at how ironic it was for him, of all people, to say that.

"In California there were a few," Jenna said.

"Is that where you're from?" Alonzo guessed. Stone had told him that's where Cal Grissom got his nickname.

Jenna nodded.

"You're a far piece from home."

"Don't I know it. From home and my relations, such as they are, and everything else I've ever held dear."

"Then, again, why are you here?"

"I told you. That's personal."

Alonzo was growing impatient with her. "How am I to get to know you better if you won't open up a little?"

"Why would you even want to know?"

"You're pretty. You're smart. You have spunk. I like

you." The words were out of Alonzo's mouth before he could stop himself. Since no real lawman would say such a thing, he sought to cover his mistake by adding, "And it's as plain as the nose on your face that you're in trouble and need help."

"You really think so?"

"You said the Grissom gang is after you. Of course you need help."

"No. I meant, do you really think I'm pretty?" Jenna said, sounding incredulous that he could.

Alonzo answered honestly. "You're about the prettiest girl I've ever seen."

Her cheeks blossomed pink and a shy sort of smile curled her flower-petal mouth. "No one has ever called me that before except Willy Boy Jenkins, and he doesn't count."

Then and there, Alonzo felt a dislike sprout for someone he'd never even met.

"If you won't talk about yourself, tell me more about him."

Jenna's face darkened. "Willy Jenkins? He's about the same age as you and me. Beyond that I don't know a lot except that he has a dark soul. He hides it, the full darkness, but it's always there, lurking under the surface."

"I never heard anyone described that way." Alonzo sensed there was more she wasn't saying. "What else?"

"He took a shine to me. I did nothing to encourage him except be friendly, but he did anyway. He'd have forced himself on me, I suspect, except my father would have flown into a rage. Then there's Burt."

"Alacord?" Alonzo said. "How does he figure into this?"

"He's the nicest of the bunch," Jenna said. "And the only one I'd call a friend. If he thought Willy Boy was out to harm me, he'd shoot Willy dead without batting an eye."

"You sound fond of him."

"I suppose I am. He's easy to like." Jenna paused. "You'd have to meet him to understand. He's not like any outlaw you've ever met or heard of. He's easygoing, and laughs a lot. It's easy to be friends with him."

Alonzo recalled how Alacord had joked and grinned and generally treated him nicely.

"Burt Alacord would never harm me. I know that in my heart," Jenna had continued. "He'd let me go, I think, if I asked him, no matter what my father wanted." She bit her bottom lip, then said, "Willy Boy is another matter. If he caught us together, you and your partner would be dead and I'd face a fate worse than death."

Alonzo was taken aback. "A fate worse than death" meant only one thing. An act so vile, not even most outlaws would commit it. "He wouldn't."

"Haven't you been listening?" Jenna said. "If Willy Boy thought he could get away with it, he'd violate me in a heartbeat."

"I wouldn't let him," Alonzo declared.

Jenna smiled. "That's sweet of you. But I doubt you could stop him. When he puts his mind to something, he doesn't let anything stand in his way. That badge of yours? It's nothing to him except a target to shoot at, and believe me when I say he'd put the slug dead-center."

"He doesn't scare me."

"He should," Jenna Grissom said.

BACK THEN

William Bartholomew Jenkins was born on a cold and blustery winter's morning in Wyoming Territory. His mother liked to tell everyone that he came into the world wailing and fussing, and he had been complaining ever since.

From the earliest Willy could remember, there wasn't much about this world that he liked. Life was dull and pointless, a daily drudgery of chores and more chores. At night he'd fall into bed exhausted and sleep the sleep of the dead until the cock crowed and it was time to get up and do the same chores all over again.

Willy hated it. He hated that his folks were homesteaders. The land they'd chosen had a lot of trees, but little else. Clearing the land took forever. It was brutal, backbreaking work, and Willy loathed trees to this day.

He loathed chickens, too. Every morning it was his job to go to the coop and collect the eggs, and every morning one or another of the hens would peck him and squawk and raise such a fuss, he wanted to strangle it. His ma always said that was strange, the hens acting up like that, since they never acted up for her or his pa.

And don't get Willy started on cows. Day in and day out, he'd had to milk theirs before the sun came up, and then bring the pail inside so they'd have fresh milk for breakfast. Willy hated the critters. Cows were big and dumb and smelly. If he didn't squeeze their teats just right, they were prone to kick him. He'd have gladly shot them but he liked the pastries and puddings and cakes his ma sometimes made, and she needed milk for that.

By the time Willy was ten, he'd come to several conclusions. The first was that his pa was working himself to death, for nothing. Their small cabin and the land it sat on wasn't worth a life spent at hard toil. His father's only enjoyments consisted of their meals, and sitting in a rocking chair and smoking his pipe in the evening after all the work was done.

As for his ma, she worked just as hard at feeding them and washing and drying their clothes and whatnot. The high point of her life was their once a month visit to the nearest settlement where she'd spend hours paging through the catalogues at the general store, dreaming dreams that would never come true.

Willy's second decision was that he refused to waste his life the way they were wasting theirs. As soon as he was old enough, he'd go off and find a better way. There had to be more to life than drudgery.

Willy's third insight, he kept to himself. It had to do with what he'd learned about himself at an early age. One evening when he was six, he'd gone to the barn to feed their horse and heard mewing. One of their cats, a gray mouser, had a new litter of five kittens.

Puny things, and blind, to boot. He'd picked one up and seen how weak and helpless it was, and in disgust, had thrown it at the wall. The splat of its body and the smear of blood made him laugh. He'd laughed so hard, he picked up another and this time set it on one side, hiked his leg, and stomped it to death. The mother cat became agitated and caterwauled so he left the rest be and threw the bodies out in the brush. But it gave him food for thought.

Not a month later a hen pecked him as he was collecting eggs, and it infuriated him. Seizing hold of its neck, he'd strangled it to death, the hen flapping and thrashing all the while. A peculiar pleasure coursed through him. When the hen finally went limp, he stood there caked with sweat, and trembling. To cover his deed, he buried the body and told his parents he saw a coyote take her.

From then on, Willy couldn't get enough of killing things. He never did it quick if he could help it. He liked for the animals to suffer. The more he hurt them, the more pleasure he felt. It got so it became a need he couldn't resist.

Shortly after his fourteenth birthday, Willy decided enough was enough. His homesteading days were over. He bundled his few belongings into a blanket, tied the blanket to a pole, and in the middle of a warm summer's night, he slipped from their cabin and never looked back.

He was on his own, at last. He struck off for a town about twenty miles away, one his folks seldom visited. That he only had two dollars plus change to his name didn't worry him one bit.

Nor did the possibility he might run into hostiles or outlaws or wild beasts. If it happened, it happened. He never worried about what might be. All he cared about was what he was doing at any given moment. The here and now.

In the town Willy set eyes on his first saloon. It brought to mind the times he'd stolen a sip from his pa's whiskey bottle. Marching in, he smacked down a coin and demanded a glass. He half-thought the bartender would quibble about his age, but no.

The next day Willy took a room at a boardinghouse, and there went the rest of his money. He looked around for work but couldn't find any until he stumbled on a man who took pity on him. The man was heading up into the Tetons to hunt elk, and said he'd pay Willy to help handle the packhorses, and later to help carve the elk up and tote the meat down to the town butcher. The butcher paid five cents a pound for elk meat and then sold the meat to his customers for thirteen cents a pound.

Willy figured the work couldn't be any worse than back on the homestead. Since he didn't own a horse, the hunter let him ride one of his. In addition to the three pack animals and the horse he'd loaned to Willy, the man rode a fine bay with a handsome mane.

Willy liked that bay. He liked the man's rifle, too, a Winchester. And the man's skinning knife. And the man's saddle. By the time they'd reached the mountains, Willy couldn't stop thinking about how nice it would be if all of that were his. A daring notion crept over him. He fought it for a while, out of worry over being thrown into prison for the rest of his days.

Then came the night Willy lay staring at the stars. He remembered the hen he'd strangled and buried and no one ever found her. It had worked for a chicken, so why wouldn't it work for a man? The idea excited him so much that when he couldn't stand to lie there any longer, he got up, took a rock, and bashed in the brains of his unfortunate benefactor.

Willy spent the rest of the night by the body, marveling at what he'd done. With the break of day, he'd dragged the body into the woods and buried it good and deep. The digging took hours but it was worth the effort to ensure no one ever found it.

A week and a half later Willy rode into Cheyenne on the fine bay and sold the other horses. He was flush for the first time in his life, and went on a spree to celebrate.

Willy had found his calling. Some liked to farm and some liked to do clerk work or be barkeeps or carpenters or barbers.

Willy liked to kill.

17

Alonzo Pratt was unhappy. Several times during the long, hot afternoon he'd tried to get Jenna Grissom to open up to him, and she refused. When he asked what her life was like growing up with an outlaw for a father, she glared and snapped and said it was none of his affair. When he inquired as to why she was riding with a pack of notorious two-legged wolves, she growled that she was tired of his questions. He tried a couple of more times but she clammed up.

Now the sun was dipping toward the horizon and had set the western sky ablaze with bright splashes of red and orange. Birds were winging to their roost. It wouldn't be long before the deer came out to graze and the meat-eaters that fed on them would be on the prowl.

Alonzo was on the lookout for a place to camp. He preferred a place well hidden from unfriendly eyes, whether man or otherwise. Every few minutes he'd rise in the stirrups and scan the prairie. The sight of a string of hills to the southwest was promising. "We'll make for there," he announced, and pointed.

Jenna didn't respond.

Alonzo twisted in the saddle to look at Jacob Stone. The old man hadn't roused or let out a peep since they'd started out. Alonzo was growing concerned the lawman would die on him. Not that he should care. It wasn't as if they were friends or anything. A fluke of circumstance had thrown them together. That was all.

"You're worried about him, aren't you." Jenna broke her silence. It was a statement, not a question.

Oddly pleased at the throaty sound of her voice, Alonzo replied, "He's a good man, deep down. There aren't a lot like him around these days."

"Isn't that the truth," Jenna said. "But I'm surprised you'd say a thing like that."

To keep her talking, Alonzo asked, "Why?"

"Because you're a lawman, too. And I thought all lawmen have to be pretty decent at heart since they devote themselves to upholding the law."

"That they do," Alonzo said, feeling a flush of guilt at how he was deceiving her.

"I admire you for that."

His guilt deepening, Alonzo said, "I'm nothin' special."

"That's where you're wrong," Jenna said, gazing off across the plain. "I've seen how the other side lives. The lawless side. Those who don't care who they hurt. Who take what they want, and the rest of the world can go to Hades. And I have to tell you, I'm so sick of it, I could scream."

Alonzo was about to inquire as to why she rode with her father if that was how she felt, but he bit it off so as not to anger her by prying.

"When you've seen the dark side of human nature, you appreciate the good in us that much more," Jenna continued.

"That's awful . . ." Alonzo struggled for the right thing to say, "deep for someone so young."

"Posh and poppycock," Jenna said. "It's not how old we are. It's the things we've done. Or had done to us."

Alonzo wondered what she meant by that. He was holding their horses to a walk just so they could go on talking even though they might not reach the hills by dark. "I reckon that's true. The things that happened to me when I was young helped to make me who and what I am."

"Tell me a little about yourself," Jenna said. "Where are your folks?"

"Dead."

"Brothers? Sisters?"

"Just me."

"Same here," Jenna said. "I've often wished I had siblings. It would make the burden easier to bear."

"Burden?" Alonzo said, and hoped he hadn't made another mistake.

"Of being the daughter of one of the most ruthless men on the frontier," Jenna said with anguish in her voice.

"That's him, not you," Alonzo said.

"He's my father."

"So? He's the outlaw, not you. Why do you beat yourself over it when it's plain to me that you're as good a person as Deputy Stone, there?" Alonzo said. When she didn't answer, he glanced over and saw she was studying him with a peculiar expression on her face. "What?" he said. "Did I upset you again?"

"No, not at all."

Was it Alonzo's imagination, or had her cheeks flushed pink?

"That was a nice thing to say, given that you don't know me all that well."

Alonzo smiled and boldly said, "Whose fault is that?"

Jenna gave a mild start, and to his immense relief, she grinned. "I had that coming, I suppose. I haven't been very friendly, have I?" She didn't give him a chance to reply. "But if you were in my shoes, you'd understand. I've gone through, pardon my language, hell these past few months. I started out with the best of intentions but I was deluding myself. We do that, don't we? When we want something badly enough?"

Alonzo didn't have the slightest idea what she was talking about. "There's not a lot in life I've really cared about."

"Except the law, of course."

"Oh. Yes," Alonzo said.

"You're smart to put your trust in that and not in another person. The law doesn't let you down. It doesn't destroy those close to you. It doesn't take your heart and break it into little pieces."

More confused than ever, Alonzo said, "You sure talk fancy."

"Do I? I had a good education. I was sent to St. John's Grammar School for Girls when I was eleven and was there until I was eighteen. I might have gone on to a university but I needed to settle something first." Jenna paused. "Then there's the money issue."

"You've had a lot more schoolin' than me," Alonzo was embarrassed to admit.

"Bought with blood."

"How's that again?"

"I'd have gladly traded all my schooling for an ordinary life. A normal father, a mother, a home, friends."

"I never had much of that."

Jenna glanced at him sharply. "Me, either. That makes us kindred spirits, doesn't it?" And for the first time all day, she smiled at him.

Alonzo grew warm all over. It was silly, but he did. "It's nice we have somethin' in common."

"Yes, isn't it?" Jenna said.

After that, she grew silent. Alonzo was disappointed but he had made some headway in knowing her better and he looked forward to spending the night with her and perhaps learning more. It was funny that he only thought about talking to her. Were she a saloon dove, he'd have other things on his mind.

Alonzo derailed that train of thought before it could leave the station. She wasn't that kind of woman.

The sky faded from blue to gray. Somewhere a coyote yipped, and far off another replied.

They reached the hills just as darkness fell. Alonzo assumed the lead. There was scant cover, grass mostly, and no sign of water. Luck was with them, though, and they came on a small hollow between two of the hills. It would shelter them from the wind, and they'd be next to invisible in the night.

"We'll camp here."

Jenna offered to help, but Alonzo asked her to sit by Jacob Stone while he stripped and hobbled their horses, gathered brush, kindled a fire, and put a pot of coffee on. He hadn't thought to shoot anything for supper. Fortunately, he had plenty of supplies on his pack animal. Stone had joshed him about it, but he'd rather whip up corn biscuits than shoot and skin a rabbit. He was mixing flour with water from his canteen when he caught Jenna giving him another odd look. "What?"

"You can cook, too?"

"I have to eat, don't I?" Alonzo said. "And you haven't tasted it yet. I'm not the world's best."

"Who is?" Jenna stretched and tilted her head to the blossoming stars. "It's a beautiful night."

Alonzo hadn't noticed. He added salt to the pan and did more stirring, and tried not to think of how her bosom had pressed against her shirt.

"I can't believe we made it through the whole day," Jenna remarked. "I was sure they'd have caught up by now."

"They?"

"I told you. Willy Boy and whoever is with him. It could be all of them, for all I know."

"We're safe here," Alonzo assured her. "They can't see our fire."

"You picked the perfect spot."

Alonzo was going to tell her it was purely by accident, but didn't. What harm was there in her thinking he was good at this?

Extending her legs, Jenna crossed them, then leaned back. All day she had been as tense as a fiddle string but now she seemed to be relaxed and actually enjoying herself. "Can I ask you something, Deputy Grant?"

"Call me—" Alonzo was about to say "Alonzo," and caught himself. "Robert."

"What are your plans, Robert? For your future? Do you intend to be a lawman forever?"

"Not hardly," Alonzo said. As soon as he was shed of Jacob Stone, he'd impersonate someone else. Maybe a parson.

"Is that all the specific you can be?"

Alonzo shrugged. "I haven't ever planned my life out. I take each day as it comes, and survive the best I can."

"I had a plan but it hasn't worked out. I was foolish. I thought that deep down everyone is basically good at heart, and that if I appealed to that goodness, I could bring about a miracle." Jenna laughed coldly. "It's sad how we cling to hope when there isn't any. How we dream impossible dreams and delude ourselves into believing they can somehow become true."

"There you go with your fancy words again," Alonzo said. "Does this have to do with your pa?"

"I'm sorry for being so secretive," Jenna said, "but yes, it does."

"Ah," was all Alonzo said. He'd learned his lesson about prying.

Jenna drew her knees up to her chest, wrapped her arms around her legs, and rested her chin on her knee. "It's like this, Robert," she said softly. "My mother ran out on my father when I was seven. She just up and left him. For another man, no less. He was never the same after that. It twisted him, inside. Made him mad at the world and everyone in it. He lost his job and took to drinking, and the next thing, he held up a store for spending money."

"I'm sorry," Alonzo said when she paused, for lack of anything else to say. She didn't appear to hear him.

"It was all downhill from there. Some others joined up with him and they robbed a stagecoach and later a bank in Stockton. Suddenly half the lawmen in the state were after him, and he took me to live with his brother and his brother's wife in Sacramento.

"I was nine. I remember holding my aunt's hand and waving to my father as he rode off with Alacord and Ginty and some of the others, and wishing with all my heart that I could go with him. That was the last I saw of him until about a year ago."

Alonzo stayed quiet. He was afraid to interrupt for fear she would stop.

"My uncle and aunt are decent, hardworking people. She's a seamstress. He's a clerk. They never had any children of their own and treated me as if I were theirs. It was their idea to send me to St. John's Grammar School. I never thought to ask where they got the money. Or, for that matter, about how they paid for my clothes and whatnot over the years. I assumed it came out of their own pocket and purse. Then one day they came to visit and my aunt let it slip that nearly every penny they'd ever spent on me had come from my father."

Half a minute went by and she didn't go on. Eager to keep her talking, Alonzo said, "Did that surprise you?"

"It *shocked* me. I hadn't seen him or heard from him since that day he rode off. I'd assumed he'd forgotten all about me. That he'd left me to fend for myself and didn't want anything more to do with me. But no. He'd been providing for my upkeep the whole time." Jenna's voice dropped to a whisper. "I convinced myself he must truly care. That all those years, he was thinking about me and missed me as much as I missed him. I cried for joy, I was so happy."

Thinking of his own father, Alonzo said, "I always wished my pa thought more of me." Maybe then his pa wouldn't have drunk himself to death and left Alonzo alone in the world.

"Something else we have in common," Jenna said. "It explains why, as soon as I graduated, I set out to find him. By then he'd left California. My uncle and aunt didn't know where he was. They'd get a letter from time to time with money for me, but never a return address. All I had to go on were accounts I'd read in the newspaper."

"Yet you found him."

"Eventually. My aunt knew of a cousin's of Burt Alacord's. The cousin lives in Kearney. I sent him a letter and he wrote back that Burt paid him visits now and then, and he'd let Burt know that I wanted to see my father. Six whole months went by, and finally I heard from him. My father was willing to meet with me. I couldn't get to Nebraska fast enough, I tell you."

She would have gone on, but just then the horses raised their heads and pricked their ears. Alonzo heard the same thing they did; a guttural growl from out of the darkness. Placing his hand on his Colt, he turned— and an icy sensation rippled down his spine.

On the rim of the hollow, eyes gleamed.

18

BACK THEN

In Cheyenne Willy began to associate with what churchgoing folk would call "hard cases." In a seedy saloon, a scarred, foulmouthed and foul-smelling specimen of humanity struck up an acquaintance, and it turned out to be Three-Fingered Jack Barnes, an outlaw of some small repute, who made his living, if you could call it that, robbing homesteaders. It was Three-Fingered Jack who first called Willy "Willy Boy." Willy resented being called a "boy" but Jack was so unpredictably violent that he didn't make an issue of it, and before Willy knew it, everybody knew him as "Willy Boy."

Together with a man called Campton, they robbed and stole to their cruel hearts' delight.

Willy took to practicing with his Colt every chance he got, and discovered he had a knack as a shooter. He was quick and he was accurate. Not as quick as Burt Alacord, who he met later. But quick enough that he was talked about, and feared. It didn't hurt his reputation any that he gunned down two men in a span of two months.

The first shooting affray involved a loudmouth by the name of Zeke Evans. It happened in Coulton, Kansas. Zeke was Willy's age, and when he was drunk, which was often, he talked too much and too loudly and liked to push others around. He made the mistake of pushing Willy, and Willy told him to go for his six-shooter or shut the hell up. Evans went for his six-gun and never cleared leather.

The next gun affair was in Deadwood. Willy was playing cards and caught on that a gambler who went by the handle of Brodie was cheating. He called Brodie on it. The gambler flushed with anger, pushed his chair back, and stood. Parting his frock coat to reveal an ivory-handled Colt on his hip, he told Willy that he was a damn liar.

Willy pushed his own chair back as the other players and those nearby scrambled away. "If you're hankerin' to die, jerk that pistol, you son of a bitch."

Willy was surprised at how calm he felt. Brodie was supposed to be a bad hombre to tangle with.

"Take back what you said and I won't have to," the gambler told him.

"I saw you slip a card out of your sleeve. When you're dead, I'll pull that sleeve up and see what else is under there."

"You asked for it, boy," Brodie growled.

"That's Willy Boy, to you," Willy said.

For tense moments the two of them stood motionless. Then Brodie's hand flashed. Unlike Zeke Evans, he cleared leather, but his six-shooter wasn't quite level when Willy fanned a shot into Brodie's forehead, putting an end to his cardplaying days. And sure enough, when Willy peeled that sleeve back, he found an arm rig with several more cards. Some of the other players patted him on the back and thanked him for exposing the cheat.

Willy was more interested in that ivory-handled Colt. No one objected when he helped himself to it. And to the gambler's poke. And to a watch with a silver chain.

The body was hauled out and buried on Boot Hill.

After that, Willy was generally considered hell on wheels. He'd walk into a saloon and sometimes people would point and whisper. He ate it up with a spoon. The notorious Willy Boy Jenkins. That was him.

Then came the fateful day that Willy, Three-Fingered Jack, and Campton came upon a farm in eastern Nebraska.

"This one looks right prosperous," Three-Fingered Jack remarked as they sat in their saddles surveying the well-ordered fields and the white farmhouse and red barn.

"Let's go help ourselves to whatever they've got," Campton said, and scratched an armpit as he liked to do.

Willy hadn't cared one way or the other. It was just another robbery to him. He'd trailed after the other two as they approached the front porch.

Three-Fingered Jack had a trick he was fond of. He'd ride up to his intended victims, smiling and acting friendly, and when he had them off-guard, he'd throw down on them and do as he pleased.

A burly farmer came out and stood with a shotgun in the crook of an elbow. "Who are you and what do you want?" he demanded.

Drawing rein, Three-Fingered Jack went into his act. He smiled and held his hands out from his sides to show he meant no harm. "We were hopin' we could water our horses."

"There's a pump yonder," the farmer said, and nodded toward it. "Help yourselves."

"We're obliged, mister." Three-Fingered Jack rested the hand with three fingers on his saddle horn. "Nice place you have here."

"Thanks to hard work and the Lord's blessing," the farmer said.

Three-Fingered Jack rested his other hand on his hip above his holster. "Any chance we could get a meal as well as the water? We'd pay for some honest-to-goodness home cookin'."

"Pay or steal?" the farmer said.

"Beg your pardon?"

"You oughten to have spread your hands like you just did," the farmer said. "I could count your fingers."

Three-Fingered Jack stiffened. "So?"

"So my boys and me belong to the Farmer's Association, and the Association has sent out word about you to all its members. You've robbed a lot of farms and homesteads. They warned us to be on the lookout for anyone with three fingers. My boys and me figured the odds of you ever showing up at our place were slim, yet there you sit."

"You keep mentionin' your boys," Three-Fingered Jack said.

The farmer smiled and pointed at the overhang.

Willy looked up and did some stiffening of his own. Both of the second-floor windows were open, and at each crouched a young man with a double-barreled shotgun to his shoulder.

Three-Fingered Jack jerked as if he'd been slapped. "Now, you just hold on, mister. You have me mistook for someone else."

"I doubt that," the farmer said. "There aren't that many gents with only three fingers on their left hand.

Heard you got the other two chopped off in a bar fight."
He leveled his own shotgun at Jack. "We can do this
easy or we can do this bloody."

"The hell with this," Campton snarled.

"Behave yourself," Three-Fingered Jack said. "They
have us dead to rights."

"They're farmers," Campton said in contempt.

"Those hand-cannons don't care who squeezes their
triggers," Three-Fingered Jack remarked. "This close,
we'd be splattered to Kingdom Come."

"That you would," the farmer said.

"I won't be taken," Campton said. "I won't spend
time behind bars."

"You don't have a choice, outlaw," the farmer told
him.

"Like hell I don't."

"Campton, no, damn you," Three-Fingered Jack said.

Willy had never cottoned to Campton all that much.
The man was slow between the ears. Campton proved
exactly how slow by clawing for his six-shooter.

A shotgun in an upper window blasted, and half of
Campton's head exploded into fragments.

With an oath, Three-Fingered Jack went for his own
revolver.

The farmer and his son in the other window cut
loose simultaneously, each with both barrels. Their
buckshot caught Three-Fingered Jack in the chest and
blew him apart. The impact sent what was left of him
catapulting to the ground.

Willy did the only thing he could; he wheeled his
horse and fled. The thing that saved him was that the
farmer and both sons had emptied their shotguns and
needed to reload. Willy was at a full gallop, hunched
low, when the next shot boomed, and missed. Lashing

his reins, Willy Boy rode like a madman. Another shot was thrown his way and he heard the buzz of lead but was miraculously spared.

Willy didn't shed any tears over Three-Fingered Jack. Before the month was out, he had moved up in the world.

He became a member of the Grissom gang.

THE PRESENT

Alonzo Pratt wasn't much good at telling one set of eyes from another. The creature on the rim was big, that much was obvious from the size. That it was a meat-eater also became obvious when it uttered a great, rumbling growl that caused the horses to nicker in fright.

"What *is* that?" Jenna gasped.

Alonzo fumbled for his Colt. He was half-sitting on it and had to shift to draw. As he brought it up and thumbed back the hammer, a hand fell weakly on his forearm.

"No," Jacob Stone said.

Alonzo didn't take his gaze off those terrible eyes. He was relieved that the old lawman had come around at long last, but upset at his timing. "What are you doin'?" he said, shaking Stone's hand off. "It might attack us!"

"Don't shoot unless it does. And be sure when you squeeze. If you wound it, you'll only make it mad."

Alonzo could barely hear him, Stone spoke so quietly. "What if I fire into the air? Will it run off?"

"It might and it might not. You can't predict with cats."

"Cats?" Alonzo said.

"It's a cougar."

"Are you sure it's not a bear? Those eyes are awful big."

"You see how they slant?"

Now that the lawman mentioned it, Alonzo did. He'd never seen a mountain lion, or a bear, for that matter, this close before. He'd have to take Stone's word for it. "We do nothin', then?"

"The smell of our horses likely drew it in. Our fire will keep it away. Wait a minute and you'll see."

"I don't know," Alonzo said uncertainly. He still liked the idea of firing into the air.

"Listen to your partner," Jenna said. "He should know."

"Who in the world?" Stone said. Apparently he'd just noticed her.

Alonzo was only interested in the cougar. The thing crouched there, glaring and hissing. Was it making up its mind whether to attack? Cougars were supposed to be incredibly swift. If it rushed them, he doubted he could bring it down before it reached them. Better to wait, as Stone suggested.

Time crawled on claws of tension until the big cat uttered another growl. Then, with astounding speed, it spun and was gone, vanishing into the night as silently as it came.

Alonzo let out a breath he hadn't realized he was holding, and let down the hammer on his Colt. "Thank you, God."

"Don't blaspheme, son," Stone said.

"I was serious." Alonzo slid the Colt into his holster. Only then did he turn to Stone.

The old lawman lay on his back with his hands on his chest. He wasn't as pale as before, and had stopped sweating so profusely.

"Welcome back to the world of the livin'," Alonzo said, pressing his palm to Stone's brow. "Your fever's broke. You're on the mend."

"Let's hope," Stone said. He was staring at Jenna. "How long was I out?"

"A day or so," Alonzo said. "We're on our way to North Platte to have the sawbones tend to you."

"I'm still waitin' to hear who this young beauty is," Stone said, giving her a weak but friendly smile.

"Deputy Marshal Jacob Stone," Alonzo said with mock gravity, "I'd like you to meet Miss Jenna Grissom."

Stone blinked. "Grissom, you say? Are you any kin to an owlhoot by the name of Cal Grissom, young lady?"

"He's my father," Jenna said.

"The hell you say!" Stone exclaimed, then frowned. "Pardon my language, ma'am. I don't ordinarily cuss in front of women."

"That's perfectly all right," Jenna said. "I'm used to it after the months I've just spent in the company of those who ride with him. Their language at times was downright foul."

"You don't say." Stone looked at Alonzo. "You sure are somethin', do you know that?"

"What did I do?"

"I'm unconscious for a while and I wake up to find you in the company of a lovely gal who just happens to be the daughter of the very outlaw we're after. You must be one of those born to luck."

Alonzo thought of the loss of his parents, and the orphanage, and his years of impersonations. "If I am, it's news to me."

Stone turned back to Jenna. "I have a hundred questions for you, Miss Grissom. But they'll have to wait.

I'm as puny as a kitten, and could use somethin' to drink and some food."

"Leave that to me," Jenna said, moving to the fire. "I helped my aunt nurse my uncle when he was sick and know just what to do."

"Bein' shot with an arrow isn't the same as bein' sick," Alonzo said.

"Are you a doctor now?" Jenna said.

Jacob Stone chuckled.

Jenna commenced to fill her tin cup with water from Alonzo's canteen. "I know what I'm doing." Sliding on her knees over to Stone, she gently cradled his head in her hand and tilted the cup to his lips. "Here. Take it slow. Sip. Don't gulp."

"I'm in your debt, ma'am."

"You're not sipping."

Alonzo sat back. It bothered him, her treating him as if he were useless. It bothered him more that he cared what she thought.

"Has there been sign of more Sioux?" Stone asked between swallows.

"Not a lick," Alonzo was glad to report.

"It's not the savages you need to worry about," Jenna told the old lawman. "As I've been trying to impress on your partner, my father and his killers must be after me by now. And if they catch us, you two are as good as dead."

19

The way it happened was unexpected, and some folks would say, downright comical.

Willy was in Kansas. He'd decided to rob a stage out of Topeka, a run that usually carried a full load of passengers. He picked the crest of a steep hill the stage had to climb as the best spot. The stage had to slow for the grade, and when it reached the top it would be easy to stop. As added appeal, the stage rarely sent a shotgun messenger along. It would just be the driver.

So Willy pulled his bandanna up over the lower half of his face, drew his Colt, and waited behind a large boulder. He heard the stage from a ways off. As expected, it slowed for the grade.

Willy was ready when the stagecoach reached the top. He tapped his spurs to his mount and swept around the boulder, shouting, "Throw up your hands!"

At that selfsame moment, from amid a jumble of

boulders on the other side of the road, riders wearing bandannas over their faces swept out of hiding, and one of them roared, "Hands in the air or you die!"

Willy drew rein and the other outlaws drew rein, and they stared at one another in amazement.

The driver raised his arms, blurting, "What the hell?"

A skinny outlaw gestured angrily at Willy. "Why, that boy is robbin' the same stage we are!"

Willy would later learn the skinny one was Weasel Ginty. His attention was on an uncommonly handsome tall fella who held a pair of pearl-handled Colts, the same model as Willy's own, and who had trained them on Willy as quick as anything.

"Nice six-shooter you have," the handsome one said, and grinned.

Burt Alacord, Willy would discover, was the man's handle. He would also discover, to his considerable chagrin, that Alacord was living lightning on the shoot, quicker even than him.

The apparent leader of the gang, a broad-shouldered cuss, held up a callused hand and barked, "Hush." Ignoring the stagecoach driver and the faces of the passengers peering out the windows, he nudged his chestnut over to Willy and regarded him with eyes as green as new spring grass. "What have we here?" He wore a suit, of all things, and polished boots. His style of dress reminded Willy more of a banker or some other businessman than an outlaw. His revolver was a nickel-plated Smith & Wesson.

"This is my stage," Willy said. "You'll have to find another."

"Listen to you. Do you have any notion who I am? Or who they are?" The big man gestured at the rest of the outlaws.

Willy counted six, including the leader. "I appear to be outnumbered."

"You didn't answer my question."

"Mister, I don't know you from Adam. These others, neither. Wouldn't matter if I did. This is my stage."

"So you keep saying. How are you called, when you're not putting on airs?"

Angered at the slight, Willy pulled his bandanna down. "I'm Willy Boy Jenkins."

The big man in the suit studied him. "Heard of you."

"Have you, now?" Willy said with some pride.

"In a small way. Last I knew, you were riding with Three-Fingered Jack Barnes and another gent."

Willy didn't hide his surprise. "Who the hell are you, anyway?"

"Folks call me Cal Grissom. The Cal is short for California. My real first name is no one's business but my own."

Willy was impressed. Everyone had heard of the Grissom gang. They were the talk of the territory. "Why, you're half-famous, yourself."

"Only half?" Cal Grissom chuckled and blew out a breath.

The whiff of alcohol tingled Willy nose. He realized Grissom must have drank a lot of bug juice not that long ago, and he wondered what sort of man downed so much right before robbing a stage.

"Half-famous or famous all over," Grissom was saying, "a thousand years from now, no one will remember we were ever alive."

"What does that have to do with anything?" Willy asked. "We're alive now." His befuddlement grew when Grissom let out with a hearty laugh, a great peal of mirth that rumbled from a chest three times the size of his own.

"More's the pity," Grissom said.

"You've confused me," Willy admitted.

Grissom sobered and said, "Forget that for now." He wagged his Smith & Wesson at the stage. "We have to decide about the pickings. The way I see it, there are three ways this can go."

"I'm all ears," Willy said.

"You can ride off and leave the stage to us."

"Not goin' to happen," Willy informed him.

"Or we can gun you and rob it."

"I won't gun easy."

Grissom gestured at Burt Alacord. "You see that gentleman there? He can put two slugs into you before you squeeze your trigger."

"He can try."

Unruffled, Cal Grissom said, "Or we can do this the third way."

"Which is?"

"You join up with us and we rob the stage together."

"Me? Join the Grissom gang?"

"Why not? What's more natural than an outlaw joining other outlaws? And keep in mind I don't let just anybody ride with me. All my men are handpicked and have one trait in common. They're all killers, like you."

Willy was grappling with the suddenness of the invitation. "Why does that matter so much?"

"I want men at my back who won't flinch in a shootout. Men who won't break and run when the law or anyone else throws lead our way."

"That makes sense."

"So what will it be, Willy Boy Jenkins?" Cal Grissom asked. "Will you or won't you ride with me? You have a minute to decide."

"That long?" Willy said sarcastically.

"Someone could come along anytime," Grissom pointed out, "and we're not done with the stage."

It dawned on Willy that he was about to make one of the most important decisions of his life. Until now, he'd been what most would say was small potatoes. If he joined Grissom, his outlawry would be on a whole new level. He'd be up there with the likes of the Jameses and the Youngers.

"Yes or no?"

Willy grinned. "Let's rob us that stage."

THE PRESENT

Alonzo Pratt was happy as could be that Deputy Jacob Stone had recovered enough to be able to ride under his own power. Indeed, the old lawman was making a remarkable recovery now that his fever had broken.

Alonzo wasn't as happy that, as they made their way toward North Platte, Stone insisted on riding by Jenna Grissom's side and monopolizing her conversation. Alonzo wanted her attention for himself.

At the moment, Jenna was answering yet another of the lawman's many questions.

"I really don't know a lot about him, Deputy Stone."

"You must know somethin'. You've ridden with them for months, you told us."

Jenna sighed. "All I can tell you is that Spike Davis isn't his real name. Yes, he's Prussian. A disgraced nobleman, from what I can gather. He doesn't talk about it. In fact, he stays aloof from the others. They don't like him much and he doesn't like them, except for my father. For some reason, my father and him get along fine."

"Why would that be?"

Alonzo had listened to enough. Most of the morning was gone and he'd hardly gotten to say ten words to Jenna. "Why are you badgerin' her about the outlaws? Isn't it enough that she got away from them?"

"When I come across a gold mine, I tap the vein," Stone said.

Alonzo hadn't the slightest notion of what that meant, and said so.

"By Miss Grissom's own admission, she's a member of the Grissom gang. She helped rob a bank. She helped rob a stage. That makes her an outlaw, the same as them."

"Wait? What?" Jenna said.

"The law has been after Cal Grissom for years now," Stone went on to Alonzo. "It would help if we could learn more about them. Their backgrounds and their habits, and such." He nodded at Jenna. "This little lady knows things about them no one else does, and I aim to pick her brain. It could be she's the key to corralin' Grissom and his bunch once and for all." Stone paused. "I should think that you'd be as interested as me in learnin' all we can. You *are* a deputy, after all." He said that last almost mockingly.

Alonzo caught himself. He kept forgetting that he must act like a lawman, not as he normally would. "Of course I'm interested."

"You sure don't act it," Stone said, but then he grinned and winked. "I can savvy why, though."

"You do?"

"A pretty gal like her. I was young once, Deputy Grant."

"Hold on," Jenna broke in. "Get back to that business about my being an outlaw. I'm no such thing."

"Oh, really?" Stone said. "Did you or did you not take part in the robbery of the Unionville Bank?"

"I held the horses, but . . ."

"And did you or did you not take part in holding up the stage to—"

"I did," Jenna interrupted. "I've made no secret of it."

"Then, as I told my partner days ago, we're to put you under arrest. You'll be duly charged and put on trial, and who knows? The judge might feel kindly toward you and only give you five or six years."

"Years!" Jenna gasped.

Alonzo suspected that Stone was scaring her on purpose. Maybe to get her to open up about the outlaws.

"My partner never mentioned this to you, little lady?" Stone was telling her. "All the time I was out to the world?"

"He did not," Jenna said huffily.

"Awful lax of him," Stone said. "But now that I'm back on my feet, him and me can get on with the business at hand. Namely, puttin' a stop to your pa and his pack of man killers."

"I'm all for that," Jenna said.

"Your own pa?" Stone said skeptically.

"He was never much of a father," Jenna said. "He left my mother. He abandoned me." She stopped, and her eyes moistened. "When I learned he'd paid for my schooling, I had high hopes that maybe he really cared. I had this hope, this dream, that we might reconcile."

"Wishful thinkin'," Stone said.

"What a mean thing to say," Jenna snapped.

"I agree," Alonzo said. He keenly resented how the lawman was treating her.

"I'm only speakin' the truth, son," Stone said. "I heard missy, there, say she was eight when Grissom left her with her aunt and uncle. That's a lot of years between then and now. And Grissom never once looked her up. So what if he paid for her schoolin'? It's plain as can be that he wanted nothin' to do with her."

Alonzo could see that Jenna was close to tears. "Damn it, Stone. Quit upsettin' her."

"Who's the senior lawman here?" Stone countered. "I'll do as I please, and you'll back me because that's what you're supposed to do."

"I'm sorry," Alonzo said to Jenna, and frowned. "My partner doesn't give a lick about anything except the law."

"That's all right," Jenna said softly. "He has a point about my father. I'd hoped it wasn't the case. Hoped that, deep down, my father cared for me as much as I still cared for him."

"Even after he abandoned you?" Jacob Stone said.

"He's my *father*," Jenna said. "I had to be certain. I had to see with my own eyes. If I'd stayed in California, I'd have always wondered."

"Some doors are better left closed."

"I know that now," Jenna said sadly. "But you do what you must. If you feel you have to arrest me, go ahead. I don't care anymore. My dream has been crushed, and it doesn't matter what becomes of me."

"Don't talk like that," Alonzo said.

"Leave her be," Stone said. "It's sunk in, the trouble she's in. I feel sorry for her. I truly do. And I'd like to help her, if I could. But that depends on her."

"What would you have of me?" Jenna said, adding, "As if I can't guess."

"Information, missy," Stone said. "Anything and everything about your pa and those with him. In return, I'll put in a good word for you with the judge, and maybe get you off easy."

"Why don't I help you take them into custody while I'm at it?" Jenna said with obvious sarcasm.

"You know," Jacob Stone said, rubbing the stubble on his chin, "that's not a bad idea."

"You're joshing me," Jenna said, aghast.

Jacob Stone smiled broadly. "Not one little bit."

20

---◆---

BACK THEN

Within a month of joining the Grissom gang, Willy knew he'd made the right decision.

Cal Grissom had a lot to do with it. He used his head, for one thing. More than Three-Fingered Jack ever did, more than Willy, more than anyone Willy ever met. Cal planned every robbery out in fine detail, never leaving anything to chance. Willy was also pleased to find out that Grissom wasn't bossy by nature; he always asked for something to be done, and like the rest of their wild bunch, Willy came to like doing whatever Grissom wanted. Their leader had a way about him. Grissom was more refined than they were, and, Willy had to admit, more intelligent.

The only complaint Willy had, and he couldn't really call it that since Grissom never let it affect how he ran things, was Grissom's drinking. The man sucked down coffin varnish like there was no tomorrow. Cal would start in as soon as he woke up, with a few chugs of whiskey. By noon he'd have downed half a bottle. By nightfall, another half. Then he'd sit around their campfire, talking and drinking, until he turned in about midnight. At daybreak he'd start in all over again.

Willy had never seen anyone drink so much. Two bottles a day was more than most could handle. The incredible thing was, Grissom never showed it. He never passed out, never got tipsy, never so much as slurred his words. He drank and he drank and he drank some more, and it might as well be water for all the effect it had.

None of the others seemed to mind. They took it in stride, so Willy did, too. He did talk to Burt Alacord about it one day as they were crossing a prairie lush with wildflowers. Up ahead, Grissom tilted a bottle to his lips and gulped.

Without thinking, Willy said to himself, "I don't see how he does it."

Burt Alacord happened to be riding behind him and gigged his palomino alongside Willy's mount. "He's a marvel—that's for sure."

"How long has he been doin' that?"

"Drinkin'? Since I've known him," Burt said. "If you ask him, he'll say he likes his liquor. But he does it to forget."

"Forget what?"

"Not what. Who. He had a wife once, and he has a daughter in California he misses somethin' fierce. The booze numbs the pain."

"The pain of what?" Willy said.

"If you're ever a father, you'll understand."

Willy hadn't thought much more about it. He was having too grand a time.

Thanks to Grissom, his poke stayed fuller than it ever had.

As for the others, Willy would never admit it, but he liked Burt Alacord the best. Alacord was easy to get along with, which was peculiar, given that he was supposed to be a two-gun terror. The man went around grinning at the world and everyone in it, as if life were a private joke only he appreciated.

Weasel Ginty was the opposite. Weasel was as tightly strung as barbed wire, and had the disposition of his namesake. He grumped about everything. But he was a fair hand with a six-gun, he was fond of Cal Grissom, and he practically worshipped Burt Alacord.

Ira Fletcher was the oldest of them, by a good fifteen years. He wore a Dragoon revolver that he'd owned since he was old enough to tote a firearm. He refused to switch to a newer, lighter model, no matter how much he was teased. "When you find somethin' that works, you stick with it," was how he justified his obsession.

Tom Kent hailed from the northeast, from Maine or Connecticut or someplace like that. He'd worked on a whaling ship when he was young. The sea lost its luster when he'd nearly drowned, so Kent came west. Somehow or other he wound up on the wrong side of the law. He wore a revolver but he was partial to knives that he said were made in Italy. Double-edged and perfectly balanced, he favored them over his revolver.

Neither Fletcher nor Kent gave Willy any trouble. To them, Willy was a "brother wolf," as Fletcher liked to call everyone, and they accepted him as one of their own.

That left the Prussian.

On first meeting him, Willy thought Spike Davis was ridiculous. There was that metal helmet with the spike, for starters, and how the man went around as if he had a broom shoved up his backside; back straight, shoulders squared, stomach tucked in.

Alacord mentioned that Davis had once been an officer in the Prussian army but had to leave because of a scandal.

Spike Davis helped Grissom plan their robberies. That military background of his came in handy.

About a year to the day after Willy threw his lot in with them, trouble struck.

It started with Grissom announcing he was going off to visit a cousin, and he'd be back in a week. He took Burt Alacord and Weasel Ginty along, but no one else.

Grissom had visited his cousin before. Whenever they were anywhere near Kearney, Nebraska, off he'd go. Willy learned that the cousin sent money to Grissom's daughter somewhere in California. Curious, he'd tried to find out more and was warned by Ira Fletcher that it wasn't healthy to stick his nose into Grissom's private affairs.

"What will he do? Draw on me?" Willy scoffed.

"No, Cal will ask Burt to draw on you, and that will be that," the old outlaw replied, glaring. "Or the rest of us will jump you and stomp you into the dirt."

Willy became aware that Tom Kent and the Prussian were giving him hard looks. "Prickly much?" he tried to make light of it.

"You listen, boy, and you listen good," Fletcher said. "We have a great thing goin' with Cal. None of us amounted to much on our own. With him to lead us, everything always goes smooth. We live as we please, and we stay one step ahead of the law."

"I know all that."

"Then know this," Tom Kent said, fingering the hilt of one of the knives at his waist. "We won't let anyone spoil it. We look out for Cal. We make sure nothing ever happens to him."

"All I did was ask a damn question," Willy said.

"One too many," Fletcher said.

"*Ja,*" the Prussian chimed in.

Willy smiled and held up his hands. "Simmer down, for God's sake. For what it's worth, I agree. I never had it so good as I have with Cal."

"That's nice to hear," Fletcher said.

"He's the only one of us who matters," Kent said.

"*Ja,*" the Prussian said again.

Willy put Grissom and his daughter from his mind. For about six months all went well, then one day Cal and Burt and Weasel rode off to Kearney again, and when they returned, they weren't alone.

Jenna Grissom was with them.

Willy was astounded. So were the others. Cal introduced her and said she would be with them a spell, and they were to treat her like a proper lady, or else. Burt Alacord stressed that point by placing his hands on his Colts and declaring that anyone who gave her trouble would answer to him.

The threat notwithstanding, that was the last thing on Willy's mind. He wanted nothing to do with her. Women were trouble. Everybody knew that. Grissom was wrong to let her come. He wanted to say something, but like everyone else, out of respect for Cal, he held his tongue.

She was nearly always in her father's company. She ate when he ate, slept near him, rode beside him when they were on the trail. Hardly anyone except her father got to talk to her.

Which was why it surprised Willy considerably when he fell in love with her.

THE PRESENT

Alonzo Pratt was falling in love.

As the three of them wound toward North Platte,

Alonzo was stirred by feelings he'd never imagined he would feel. All his years of wandering, he'd had no interest in women. Now and then he'd dally with a dove in a saloon, but that was the extent of it.

Alonzo never hankered for a wife and a home. The life he led, marriage was out of the question. It was something other men did, normal men, not him. He had it settled in his mind that he'd never marry.

So it shocked him to his marrow when he began to feel things for Jenna Grissom, and after only a couple days of her company. It was little things at first. He liked sitting with her around the fire at night and talking for hours on end. He liked riding by her side during the day.

He found himself admiring how pretty she was—her sparkling eyes, her fine hair, her lithe grace when she moved. He especially liked a throaty purr that came into her voice now and then when she was most at ease. It tingled him down to his toes.

Alonzo tried to shrug it off. He told himself that he was being ridiculous. That the only reason he liked her so much was because he'd never been in the close company of a woman for so long. He sought to shut his feelings out, and couldn't. When he woke up in the morning and saw her, it was as if there was a second sun.

Alonzo thought he was doing a good job of hiding it. But one evening, as he was hobbling their horses toward sunset and Jenna was preparing their supper, a shadow fell over him and he looked up.

Deputy Jacob Stone had his hands on his hips and was slowly shaking his head. Except for a slight limp from his wound, the old lawman had fully recovered from the arrow in his thigh.

When Stone didn't say anything, Alonzo asked, "Why are you starin' at me like that?"

"I've never seen it to fail."

Alonzo had noticed the lawman giving him odd glances now and then but didn't know why. He finished with the hobble for his packhorse, and stood. "Is it a secret, or am I supposed to pry it out of you?"

"Put a young gal and a young fella together and it will happen every time," Stone said.

"You're takin' the long way around the bush."

"Don't play innocent," Stone said. "You're smitten. You're in love with her, and it wouldn't surprise me if you pop the question when we reach North Platte."

"You're loco," Alonzo said. "I hardly know her."

"That's your head talkin'," Stone said. "It's the heart that counts. And the heart wants what the heart wants."

"Where do you come up with this stuff?"

Stone glanced toward the fire, where Jenna was putting coffee on. "Listen, son. It's none of my affair but I need to have my say anyway. I don't blame you for fallin' for her. She's right pretty, and as sweet a gal as I ever came across. She has a good, practical head on her shoulders, and that's rare for anyone, male or female."

"Is this goin' somewhere?"

"Don't give me sass. It's you I'm lookin' out for."

"This should be good."

"Damn it. Hear me out." Stone realized he'd raised his voice and lowered it again. "You're a deputy federal marshal. You have a career ahead of you. A long one if you stick with it."

Of the few regrets in Alonzo's life, impersonating a lawman was now at the top of the list. Never, ever, *ever* again.

"The gal yonder is the daughter of the worst criminal in the territory. If you become involved with her, you risk your badge, your career, everything."

"*That's* what has you in a dither?" Alonzo said, and almost laughed.

"I had the same decision to make when I was about your age. Should I or shouldn't I hitch myself to a female. And do you know what I decided? That a lawman's life isn't any life for a gal who wants a husband and kids and all the rest. We're always on the go. The deputies I know who are married? Their wives hardly ever see them. Their kids grow up without fathers. Is that the kind of life you want to give her?"

"I'm not you," Alonzo said.

"You wear a tin star, the same as me," Stone countered. "Believe me when I say I know this law life inside-out, and I'd never inflict it on anyone I cared for."

"Is that all you have to say?" Alonzo wanted to go over by the fire and be with Jenna.

Stone did more head shaking. "I'm only tryin' to do you a favor. Spare you havin' your heart broke."

"I appreciate that. But what makes you think I'll stay a lawman forever? Given my druthers, if I have to make a choice between my badge and her, I'll pick her every time."

"Oh, son," Stone said.

"Don't take it personal," Alonzo said. "I'm not as devoted to the law as you are, is all."

"Oh, son," Stone said again.

"You must have known others who gave up their badge to take a wife," Alonzo said. For him it would be ridiculously easy since he wasn't even a lawman.

"I've known a few."

"There you go." Alonzo smiled to lessen the sting and clapped the old lawman on the arm.

"I can see I've wasted my breath," Stone said.

"Don't be like this, Jacob," Alonzo said. "I'm not you

and never will be." Going around him, Alonzo went over and hunkered across from Jenna.

"Is everything all right?" she asked. "You two looked so serious over there."

"I've never felt better," Alonzo said.

Stone joined them. To his credit, the old man plastered a smile on his face. "We were talkin' law stuff, missy. Don't fret yourself. Everything is fine."

They were camped in a clearing in a tract of woodland, ringed by tall trees and deep shadows. Just then, from out of those shadows, came a harsh command.

"You're surrounded! Throw up your hands or we'll shoot you to ribbons!"

21

---◆---

BACK THEN

The first month or so that Jenna Grissom rode with them, Willy hardly paid her any mind. She was always in her father's company and never had anything to do with the rest of them, except for Burt Alacord. She and Alacord talked a lot but there was never anything to it. Alacord was friendly to everybody. That, and Weasel Ginty let it drop that Cal Grissom had asked Burt to keep an eye on her, to serve as her bodyguard, as it were.

It led Willy to wonder who she needed guarding from. The answer hit him like a sock to the jaw. Cal had tasked Burt with guarding her from the rest of them, from his very own bunch.

Willy simmered at the insult. He didn't give a good damn about the girl or want anything to do with her.

At first.

As time passed, and Willy saw more of her, that changed. He was struck by how pretty she was, how her white teeth flashed when she smiled, how her laugh made him feel as if he wanted to laugh along. He grew to like how she moved, and particularly how she filled out the dresses she donned on occasion. Usually she wore men's clothes but not always.

Willy had been with enough sporting ladies to imagine how fine her body must be, and he'd daydream of him and her, doing the things he'd done with the pay-for-it tarts.

Willy took to drinking in the sight of her when he was sure no one was looking. He'd sit to one side or ride well back, and secretly admire her beauty. He yearned to talk to her, to get to know her better, but Grissom had made it clear none of them were to approach her without his say-so, and besides, Burt Alacord watched over her like a two-gun hawk.

Then fate intervened.

Cal Grissom had a certain stage in mind to rob, and they had made camp in a rocky gulch to rest for the robbery the next day. Their horses had been tethered and Ira Fletcher, as usual, was doing the cooking. The old outlaw was the best cook of any of them and probably could have made a living as one if he didn't like robbing and killing more.

Willy had just set down his bedroll and was stretching when he saw Jenna Grissom looking for a spot to spread her blankets. As she started past some rocks, there was a ripple of movement and a flash of reptilian scales. Without thinking, Willy's Colt was in his hand. A rattler reared, its tail rattling noisily, and bared its fangs to strike.

Jenna Grissom froze in horror, and Willy fanned three swift shots. His slugs smashed the snake to earth, where it writhed in its death throes.

Cal Grissom and Burt Alacord rushed over, and Cal

gripped his daughter by the shoulders. "Are you all right?" he cried.

"I'm fine," Jenna said calmly, "thanks to that young gentleman, there."

Willy's stomach fluttered. No one had ever called him a gentleman before. "Wasn't nothin'," he said, his throat constricted.

"On the contrary," Jenna said, "you very likely saved my life."

Burt Alacord had squatted by the rattlesnake. "That was some shootin', Willy Boy," he complimented him.

"I couldn't let it bite her, now, could I? She's Cal's little girl." Forcing himself to take his eyes off Jenna, Willy began to reload.

"I'm in your debt," Cal Grissom said. Visibly shaken, it was plain the incident had scared him half to death.

To Willy's astonishment, Jenna came over and placed her hand on his arm. He half-thought his shirt would catch on fire.

"So am I," she said. "I can't thank you enough."

Willy shrugged. "I'd have done it for anybody." She removed her hand but he swore he could still feel the pressure of her fingers.

Later on, when their supper was ready, Cal Grissom called Willy over to sit with him and Jenna and Burt Alacord. They usually ate apart from the rest.

"I'm honored," Willy joked as he eased down.

"It's my daughter's doing," Cal said.

Jenna nodded. "It's the least we can do, given what you did. Besides, I don't get to talk to anyone other than Burt."

"Am I that bad at it?" Alacord joked.

Jenna laughed and poked his arm. "No, you're absolutely precious. But it'd be nice to talk with someone else once in a while."

"Did she just call me 'precious'?" Burt said, looking stricken.

They all laughed, even Willy. But now that he was close to her, his mind had gone completely blank, like a slate wiped clean, and he couldn't think of anything to say. Panic set in, and he squirmed uncomfortably.

"Be at ease, Mr. Jenkins," Jenna said. "That is your name, correct?"

Willy's tongue felt as thick as his wrist. He nodded.

"The truth is, I've wanted to learn more about you and the others, but my father isn't keen on the idea." Jenna gave Cal a reproachful look.

"They're outlaws, girl," Cal said.

"So are you. So is Burt. But you let me talk to him."

"Burt is different. Him, I can—" Cal stopped and glanced at Willy and then at the rest, who were hungrily spooning stew into their mouths.

Willy might not be the smartest hombre who ever drew breath, but he wasn't dumb, either. "You don't trust us around her."

"She's my little girl," Cal Grissom said.

"I'm not so little," Jenna said, "and it seems to me that if you can depend on them when you're robbing stages and whatnot, you can depend on them not to molest me."

"Don't talk like that, daughter. About molesting, I mean."

"Good God, Cal," Willy said. He'd done a lot of bad things in his life. He'd stolen. He'd killed. But never *that*. Not that he hadn't thought about it once or twice when he saw a particularly fetching female. "What do you take us for?"

Cal opened his mouth, looked at Jenna, and closed it again.

"I'm glad this is out of the bag," Jenna said. "Maybe

now you won't be so upset when I want to talk to one of them."

Willy saw his chance and took it. "You can start with me, ma'am. I'd never harm a hair on your head, no matter what your pa thinks."

"Have a care," Burt Alacord said. "A father has to look after his own. And it's not as if we're Bible-toters."

"Tell me about yourself, Mr. Jenkins," Jenna said. "How did it come about that you live on the wrong side of the law? And ride with my father?"

Once he started, Willy babbled himself nearly hoarse, yet strangely enough, he couldn't recollect much of what he said afterward. All he could remember was her face, shimmering like a vision, and all he heard was her voice, music to his ears. He forgot her father and Alacord were there. There was just him and her and no one or anything else.

That night, Willy lay with his head cradled on his forearm, gazing at the host of twinkling stars without seeing them. Jenna filled his mind's eye; her lively, lovely eyes, her cheeks, her lips. A yearning came over him, a craving such as he'd never known. A craving a lot like he might have for food when he was hungry or for a stiff drink when he was thirsty. But this was for *her*. A yearning so strong, so potent, it made him ache inside.

He hardly slept a wink all night.

At daybreak Willy was the first up, and when Jenna eventually stirred and sat up, he made bold to greet her with a warm smile and a cheerful "Good mornin' to you, Miss Grissom."

Cal didn't object, which encouraged Willy to ride next to her for a while on their way to rob the stage. He mentioned how much he'd liked talking to her the night before and hoped they could do it again, real soon. She delighted him silly by inviting him to eat supper that evening with her pa and her.

Willy was careful not to betray how he felt about her. He acted friendly, nothing more. He sat a respectful arm's length away, and didn't stare at her, as much as he wanted to.

Later, after Jenna announced she was turning in, and got up and went over to her bedroll, Willy thanked Cal for letting him eat with them, and went to rise.

"Hold on," Cal said, almost harshly.

Racking his brain for what he could have done wrong, Willy sat back down. "Somethin' the matter?"

"You surprise me, boy," Cal said. "You treat her with respect. I like that."

"How else would I treat her?" Willy said. "Were you expectin' me to try and abuse her right before your eyes?"

"I don't rightly know what I expected," Cal Grissom said, and gazed with immense affection at Jenna. "You have to understand. She's my *daughter*. My own flesh and blood. The person in this world who means the most to me. I thought she was gone from my life forever, yet there she is. I—" He stopped, choked with emotion.

"You don't have to tell him any of it," Burt Alacord said.

"Yes," Cal said, and coughed. "Yes, I do. He's been nice to her. Damn nice. I was wrong about him. And I should probably give the others the benefit of the doubt, too."

"I'm glad we cleared this up," Willy said, and again went to stand.

"I'm not done." Cal reached for the coffeepot and refilled his cup. Sitting back, he sipped, then said quietly, "Her mother left me when she was little. She left me because I drink. You've seen how I am. I suck whiskey down from morning until night. I've tried to stop. God, I've tried to stop. And I can't. I don't have it in me."

"Some people are more fond of whiskey than others," Willy said.

"It's more than fondness. I can't live without it. But anyway, there I was, left to fend for her by my lonesome, and it worried me sick that I wasn't a good enough father. So I left her with my sister and her husband and rode off, never expecting to see her again."

"You did the right thing," Burt said.

"Did I?" Cal said dubiously. "Looking back, I have to wonder. But I did send money regularly, to help with her upkeep and schooling. I can't tell you how many times I wanted to write to her, to say I was sorry for what I'd done and I'd never stopped caring."

"You're gettin' awful personal," Willy said. It made him uncomfortable. No man should ever spill personal things to another.

"Sorry. Like I said, I want you to understand." Cal paused. "Her showing up out of the blue has been the wonderment of my life. She came to find me. *She* came to find *me*. Do you know what that means? She missed me all these years. Missed me as much as I've missed her. She tracked me down and came all this way just to be with me. It's a godsend."

Willy was startled to see Cal Grissom's eyes watering. He didn't say anything, but it was downright unmanly.

His voice thick with emotion, Cal said, "When she first got here, I made it clear the rest of you were to stay away from her—"

"As if we'd hurt her," Willy interrupted.

"I see that now," Cal said. "And I'm apologizing.

You were a perfect gentleman. From here on out, if you want to talk to her, you can."

Willy was about to ask if this was where he should bow down and kiss Cal's boots. Instead, he controlled his temper and remarked, "Thank you for the honor."

"You're about the same age. She'll find it easier to talk to you than, say, Fletcher or the Prussian."

Willy snickered. "That old goat and the foreigner? What do they have in common with her?"

"Exactly my point. So what do you say?"

"Will I be friendly to your girl?" Willy said. "Sure, so long as you don't make a fuss about it."

"I won't. I promise."

Willy thought it prudent to say, "You can be at ease, Cal. I'm not out to court her, and won't overstep myself."

That was a whooper of a lie, if ever there was one. Willy was smitten, and as the days and weeks passed and he was able to talk with her whenever he pleased and ride with her for hours on end, he became more than smitten. He fell in love.

Willy tried to keep it to himself, tried to bottle it up so none of the others would guess the truth, not even Jenna. Then one night his feelings got the better of him.

They were seated a little off from the others. By then, they'd been together so often, no one thought anything of it.

The night was gorgeous, with a full moon and the stars sparkling like gems. They were sitting shoulder to shoulder and staring at the sky when Willy turned and her beauty washed over him like a spring flood. He forgot himself, and placed his hand on hers.

Jenna glanced down, saying, "What's this?"

Willy knew he should put a lock on his mouth but he couldn't seem to help himself. Keeping his voice down so no one would overhear, he said, "I'm lettin' my feelin's show. You're the best thing that's ever happened to me, Jenna. You're pretty and smart and you always make me smile. I care for you like I've never cared for anybody."

"Willy . . ."

"Hear me out," Willy said. Now that the dam had broken, he had to say his piece.

"We should go off by ourselves, just the two of us, and start a life together. I may not amount to much now, but I will. For you, I'll amount to all I can. We'll have a place of our own, and kids someday if you want them, and live a good, happy life."

Jenna pulled her hand free and sat back. "Are you asking what I think you're asking?"

"I reckon so," Willy said, and cleared his throat. "Jenna Grissom, will you marry me?"

"No."

Willy was so taken aback, he was speechless.

"I like you as a friend, nothing more," Jenna said. "And I'd like to go on being friends if you can do that without making more of it than there is. Please. For my sake."

Willy was crushed. He mumbled that he would try, but it was hopeless. He wanted her, wanted her more than anything. Again and again he brought it up, to where she told him one day that if he didn't stop, she'd never speak to him again.

The next day, when she went for a stroll in some woods, Willy snuck away and caught up to her. She was annoyed, and told him to go back. In a rash moment, he pressed her against a tree and tried to kiss her.

Jenna slapped him and stalked off. The next morning she was gone.

Cal Grissom was beside himself. He stormed up to

Willy and demanded to know if she had said anything to him about intending to leave.

Willy said that no, she hadn't. He wasn't about to confess the truth. It would get him shot.

Cal roared at the others to saddle up, and set Fletcher, their best tracker, on her trail. For three days they stuck to her sign. Then, as night was falling, they spied a glimmer of light and closed in.

Willy was as surprised as the rest to find Jenna in the company of two strange men. When Cal gave the word to surround them, he drew his Colt and crept nearer. He was both eager and anxious about what would happen next. He was eager to see Jenna, and anxious she might tell her father about his proposal, and that kiss.

The next moment, Cal Grissom let out a shout.

"You're surrounded! Throw up your hands or we'll shoot you to ribbons!"

22

THE PRESENT

Alonzo Pratt reacted without thinking. Springing to his feet, he placed his hand on his Colt. It was a stupid thing to do; he was no gunhand. Fortunately, before he could do something even worse—draw the Colt—Deputy Stone grabbed hold of his wrist with both hands.

"Don't even try," the old lawman warned. "We're in the firelight and they're not." Realizing he could have been shot where he stood, Alonzo let go of the Colt, and when Stone released his wrist, thrust his arms at the stars.

Deputy Stone slowly raised his.

As for Jenna Grissom, she didn't do a thing other than sit there with her coffee cup in her hands, and frown.

The brush rustled and crackled and out of the woods strode seven armed men.

"Oh, hell," Stone said.

Alonzo recognized Burt Alacord and Weasel Ginty, and his gut balled into a knot. This was the Grissom gang, the most murderous pack of cutthroats in the territory. They'd come after Jenna, just as she'd said they would.

A big man in a suit, a Smith & Wesson on his hip, marched over to her. He was the only one who hadn't unlimbered his six-shooter. "Daughter," he said gruffly. "What did you think you were doing?"

"Father," Jenna said, and smiled sweetly. "Care for some coffee? We have plenty."

"How could you run off like that?" the man who must be Cal Grissom said. "You worried me sick."

Alonzo would have liked to hear more, but the youngest of the outlaws swaggered up to him and pointed a pearl-handled Colt at his face. "What do we have here? As I live and breathe, a tin star."

Staring into the muzzle, Alonzo broke out in gooseflesh. All it would take was a twitch of the young outlaw's trigger finger to send him into oblivion.

"Deputy Grant," Jacob Stone said, "meet Willy Boy Jenkins."

Willy Boy glanced at Stone. "Do I know you, old man?"

"We've never met," Stone said, "but I know a lot about you, and these others. Puttin' you behind bars or under the ground is my new ambition in life, you might say."

"Is that so, you old buzzard?" Willy Boy raised his revolver as if to bash Stone over the head.

"None of that," Burt Alacord intervened. He was several yards away, both pistols at waist level.

"Why the hell not?" Willy Boy demanded.

"Not unless Cal says to."

To Alonzo's vast relief, Willy Boy reluctantly lowered his arm, saying, "You heard this old coot. These are lawmen, out to take us in or bury us. We should plant them where they stand."

Burt Alacord grinned at Alonzo. "Do you remember me, boy?"

Alonzo nodded.

Weasel Ginty, grinning, turned to Willy Boy. "That one is so dumb, he let us ride right up to him and after jawin' a spell, we rode off without him suspectin' who we were."

"You don't say?" Willy Boy said in amusement, and then glowered. "I still think we should shoot the both of them and be done with it."

"That's not your decision," Burt Alacord said.

Cal Grissom had been talking in a low tone to Jenna, but now he spun. "Enough bickering, Willy. Burt is right. I decide what we'll do with them, not anyone else. Relieve them of their hardware and tie them, and we'll deal with them later. I have a more important matter to attend to."

Willy Boy appeared disposed to argue but he said, "Whatever you say, Cal. You're the boss."

"Don't you forget it," Burt Alacord said.

Alonzo stayed quiet. He submitted to having his Colt snatched from his holster, and to another of the outlaws coming over and binding his wrists. From the descriptions Jacob Stone had given him, it was the Prussian, Spike Davis.

A tug on the last knot, and Davis stepped back. "Dat should do, *ja*?" he said in a thick accent.

Weasel Ginty, meanwhile, tied Jacob Stone.

"Have a seat, gents," Burt Alacord said, coming up and twirling his Colts into their holsters. "Behave yourselves, and you'll live a little longer."

"Not if it was up to me," Willy Boy said.

Alonzo and Jacob eased down, and were promptly ignored. The other outlaws were more interested in their leader and his daughter.

"What do you have to say for yourself?" Cal Grissom was demanding. "Leaving like you did, without a word as to why. All by yourself, and us in the middle of Sioux country."

"The Sioux are the least of my dangers," Jenna said. "And before we go any further, I want to make something clear." She pointed at Alonzo and Deputy Stone. "Those two are not to be harmed. They've been nice to me, and if you hurt them, I'll never speak to you again for as long as I live."

"Hell, girl," Weasel Ginty said. "They're lawmen."

Cal Grissom glared at him.

"Sorry," Weasel said sheepishly, and took a step back.

"I mean it, Father," Jenna said. "I don't care who they are. I've put up with a lot to be with you but I won't abide you doing anything to them. If you care for me as much as you claim you do, you'll honor my request."

Ira Fletcher shifted his weight from one foot to the other and muttered, "Your gal is askin' a lot of us, Cal."

"Anyone wearing a badge is out to get us," Tom Kent said. "We need to get them first."

"Did I ask your opinions?" Grissom snapped.

Burt Alacord stepped close to Cal and swung to face the others. "We'll do whatever he decides, just like we always do. Anyone objects, speak up, and we'll settle things here and now."

Alonzo saw them glance at Alacord's Colts, and no one spoke. But they weren't happy about the turn of events.

Cal Grissom beckoned to Jenna. "Let's go off a ways and talk in private."

"Here will do," Jenna said.

"In front of everybody? What's gotten into you?"

"I have nothing to hide, Father," Jenna said. "So what if they hear us? If it's about why I left, let's just say I was tired of beating my head against a tree and let it go at that."

"Not that again," Cal Grissom said.

"I've asked you and I've asked you," Jenna said, and caught herself. "No. I've *begged* you to give up your outlaw ways. To go straight. So you and I can head off somewhere they've never heard of you and live a normal life. A peaceful life."

"What's this?" Burt Alacord said.

"She's been trying to convince me for weeks now," Cal told him.

"This is the first I've heard of it," Burt said.

"It's between my father and me," Jenna said. "It doesn't concern any of you in the least."

"That's what you think," Burt said.

"We'd follow Cal anywhere," Weasel Ginty declared. "To the gates of hell if we had to."

"*Ja*," the Prussian said.

"Don't you see?" Jenna said. "After all these years, he and I have a chance to make up for the time we've lost. We can be a family again. Can't you understand how important that is?"

"To you," Weasel Ginty said.

"Of course to me," Jenna said angrily. "Who else is there?"

"Us," Weasel said.

Jenna was confused, and it showed. "I'm his daughter. You're an outlaw who rides with him. I matter more than you do."

"That's just it, missy," Weasel said. "We're *his* gang. He picked each and every one of us. We do as he wants, and stick by him through thick and thin. He's as much ours as he is yours."

"That's the most preposterous thing I've ever heard," Jenna said. She motioned at Burt Alacord. "Tell your friend how ridiculous that is."

"I can't because it's not," Burt said. "In this Wease is right and you're wrong. We have as big a stake in your pa as you do. Maybe bigger."

Incredulous, Jenna turned to her father. "Will you please set them straight?" She waited, and when Cal Grissom looked away, she colored and set down her cup and stood.

"Is *this* why you've refused to go away with me and start over? Out of loyalty to *them*? You'd rather be with a bunch of man killers and highwaymen than your own daughter?"

Alonzo felt terribly sorry for Jenna. She loved her father very much—and he did this.

Cal Grissom took a deep breath. "Sweetheart, it's not as cut and dried as you make it out to be. I care for you. I truly do. I also have an obligation to these men. We have a bond."

"Now *you're* being preposterous," Jenna said. "What counts more than the bond between a father and his daughter?" Wheeling, she stalked off, her back as rigid as a board.

"Wonderful," Cal Grissom said. "The rest of you stay put. I need to go talk to her. Make her understand." He hurried in her wake.

"What do we do while they're gone?" Tom Kent said. "Twiddle our thumbs?"

As if they had all thought of it at the same instant, the six outlaws turned toward Alonzo and Deputy Stone.

"I know what I'd like to do," Willy Boy said. "Tom, lend me one of your knives and I'll carve on them some. Cut off an ear or maybe a nose."

"They're not to be touched until Cal says," Burt Alacord reminded him.

Willy Boy swore. "This outfit gets less fun by the day." He turned on a bootheel. "Since I have nothin' better to do, I'll fetch our horses."

"I go with you, *ja*?" Spike Davis offered.

"Sure, metal head, tag along," Willy Boy said. "You're worth a good laugh, if nothin' else."

Alonzo was glad to see Jenkins go. Willy Boy was a powder keg set to explode. If the others couldn't see it, he could.

Jacob Stone sat up. "Gentlemen. Permit me to introduce me and my friend. I'm Deputy Stone and this here is Deputy Grant. Harm us, and every lawman east of the Rockies will be after you."

"Spare us your bluster, old man," Weasel Ginty said. "We've been at this long enough, there isn't a tin star alive we're afraid of."

"One or two, I don't blame you," Stone said, "but how about ten or twenty? That's how many you'll have huntin' for you, all at once."

Burt Alacord chuckled. "You should be ashamed of yourself, old man, tellin' whoppers like that."

Alonzo wished they would all shut up so he could think. Most of his adult life, he'd gotten himself out of scrapes using his wits and his gift for gab. They could serve him in good stead here, if only he could think of how.

"What's wrong with the young lawdog?" Weasel Ginty said. "He doesn't say much."

"I'm behavin' myself," Alonzo said. "Isn't that what you want?"

"Are there any more of you hereabouts?" Burt Alacord asked Stone. "It would make me mad to be woken up in the middle of the night by more badges."

"There's just us," Stone said.

Alonzo would have kept that to himself. Or lied and said, yes, there were half a dozen deputies not far off, and the outlaws had better skedaddle. He glanced over toward the trees, where Jenna and her father were having their talk. Cal Grissom was angrily gesturing, and Jenna appeared to be on the verge of tears.

Burt Alacord came up and hefted the coffeepot. "There's enough for all of us. Who'd like some?"

"I would," Weasel said.

Ira Fletcher grunted and joined them.

Stone picked that moment to bend toward Alonzo and say, "So far, so good, eh?"

"We're at the mercy of the Grissom gang," Alonzo said. "If there's good in this, it's news to me."

"They didn't tie our legs," Stone said.

"So? Are you fixin' to kick them to death?"

Stone replied in a whisper. "We're goin' to hightail it into the woods. In the dark they won't find us."

"They won't have to," Alonzo said. "They'll shoot us before we get there."

"Grissom and Jenna are too busy arguin'. Willy Boy and that Prussian fella aren't back yet. And the other three are helpin' themselves to our coffee."

"No," Alonzo said.

"We might never have a better chance."

"No, I say."

"You'd rather stay here and be tortured and murdered? Because mark my words, they won't let us leave here alive, no matter what your lady friend wants."

"Don't call her that," Alonzo said, afraid the others might hear. "She doesn't even know how I feel."

"Don't kid yourself. Females always know." Stone rose to his knees and peered from under his hat at the nearest point of woodland. "I'll count to five and then we go."

"I'm not gettin'" myself shot."

"Then I'll go by myself."

"Jacob, please," Alonzo pleaded. If the old lawman were killed, he'd be on his own.

"I'm sorry, son," Stone said. "It's now or maybe never. Either you're with me or you're not, and if you're not, it was nice knowin' you." And with that, he exploded into motion.

23

In a heartbeat Alonzo was on his feet and sprinting after the old lawman. A voice in his head screamed at him to stop but he kept running. It was almost as if his body moved on its own.

"Look there!" Weasel Ginty hollered. "They're tryin' to get away!"

Alonzo expected to hear the boom of a gun and feel a slug core his body. He zigzagged so he'd be harder to hit. But no shots thundered, and to his amazement, he reached the woods unscathed.

A glance back showed Burt Alacord, Weasel, and Ira Fletcher in pursuit.

Grissom and Jenna had stopped arguing and were staring in surprise. There was no sign of Willy Boy and the Prussian.

Alonzo concentrated on running and nothing else. Jacob Stone had pulled ahead, even with his leg wound. For a man his age, he could really move. Alonzo sought to catch up but the brush and logs and other obstacles slowed him. He weaved, he ducked, he leaped, he tore loose from briars that hooked in his clothes.

His chest was hammering, his blood roared in his veins. He was positive that if the outlaws caught him, they would eventually kill him, no matter what Jenna wanted. *Jenna*. He felt guilty for abandoning her, but his life was at stake, not hers. Cal Grissom would never let harm befall his daughter.

A tree loomed.

Alonzo darted around it and almost collided with Stone, who had stopped and tilted his head, listening.

"Down!" the old lawman hissed, and dropped flat.

"What?" Alonzo said. To him it made more sense to keep running, to put as much distance as they could between them and the outlaws. He nearly yelped when Stone knocked his legs out from under him. The next he knew, he was flat on his back.

"Don't move," Stone said in his ear. "Don't make a sound."

Alonzo opened his mouth to protest being dumped on his backside but the crash of underbrush strangled the outburst in his throat.

From somewhere to their left, Weasel Ginty bawled, "Where are they? I've lost sight of them."

"Me, too!" Ira Fetcher shouted.

"Spread out!" Burt Alacord yelled. "They have to be around here somewhere."

Alonzo glimpsed movement in the trees, and scarcely breathed. A silhouette took shape, moving away.

From the direction of the clearing, Cal Grissom called out, "Did you catch them? What's going on?"

"Not yet," Burt Alacord replied.

Alonzo glanced at Stone but couldn't see his face in the dark.

The crackle of brush warned of another outlaw, coming close.

Alonzo was so mad at himself, he could spit nails. This latest impersonation of his had become one nightmare after another; Deputy Stone, the Sioux, the outlaws. The only good thing that had come of it was Jenna. Even there, his affection for her was one-sided. And once she found out he wasn't a lawman, that he'd deceived her this whole time, she'd want nothing more to do with him.

Hooves drummed, growing louder.

Alonzo tried to sink into the earth.

From the sounds, there were two horses. Willy Boy was on one of them because he hollered, "Where are they? Point us the way they went."

"We don't know," Weasel Ginty answered. "The ground up and swallowed them."

"I leave you alone for two minutes and you let them get away," Willy Boy said. "We should have shot them when I wanted to."

Burt Alacord piped up with, "Quit your damn gripin' and start searchin'. Swing west. Davis, you swing east. Circle wide, and we'll catch them between us."

"You're not our boss," Willy said.

"Boy, you're startin' to aggravate me," Burt Alacord said. "And that's the last thing you want to do."

"Fine," Willy spat.

The horses made a lot of noise as they separated.

Stealthy footsteps came near. Dry leaves crunched, and a shape materialized not a dozen feet away.

Alonzo tried to melt into the earth. He could feel eyes on him, or thought he could. He was mistaken, though, because presently the shape turned and crept in a different direction.

The next half-hour was one of the most terrible of his

life. The outlaws were determined to find them, and ceaselessly roved back and forth. Now and then one would come so close that Alonzo imagined he heard the man breathing.

Then someone came plowing through the woods, and Cal Grissom bawled, "Anything yet?"

"Not a sign," Burt Alacord replied, sounding disgusted that the outlaws had failed to find them.

"They got plumb away, Cal," Weasel said.

"I doubt that," Grissom said. "We'll look for them in the morning. For now, call everyone back."

A few shouts from Alacord, and the outlaws made off toward the clearing. A rider passed within a pebble-toss of Alonzo. Willy Boy, Alonzo suspected. Gradually the woods grew quiet, until the sigh of the breeze was all that broke the stillness.

"We did it," Jacob Stone whispered.

"Good for us," Alonzo said. He felt as if he'd aged ten years.

"We have a fightin' chance now," Stone said, and sat up.

"The two of us against all of them," Alonzo said, "and they have guns and we don't."

"A good lawman never gives up."

But that's just it, Alonzo thought to himself. He wasn't a lawman. He was a fake. He'd rather flee than fight. If it wasn't for Jenna, that's exactly what he'd do. Propping his elbows under him, he pushed up and sat with his head bowed in dismay.

"What's the matter with you?"

"Life couldn't be better," Alonzo said bitterly.

"You have to quit lookin' at the bad side of things. That will only get you down." Stone held out his arms. "Here. Untie me, and I'll untie you. Then the fun will commence."

"I'm almost afraid to ask," Alonzo said, "but what sort of 'fun' do you have in mind?"

"Tanglin' with those outlaws, of course."

Most of the others, including Jenna, had turned in, but not Willy Boy Jenkins. Not so long as Cal Grissom and Burt Alacord were still up. Willy wanted to hear what they had to say, so he nursed a cup of coffee and listened, while acting as if he wasn't the least bit interested.

". . . at my wit's end," Grissom was saying. "She has her mind set on going back to California."

"Don't take this wrong," Burt Alacord said, "but did you really expect her to go on robbin' banks and stages? Who ever heard of a female outlaw?"

"I didn't think that far ahead," Grissom said gloomily.

"You want my advice? You'll let her go. You can't force her to stay. Unless you're thinkin' of doin' as she wants and goin' straight."

"I'm tempted."

"Honest to God?" Alacord said in surprise.

"She's my daughter, damn it. I should try to make up for deserting her. To be the father she never had."

"If that's what you want."

"You heard her. It's what she wants."

"And you kept it from me. We've been friends for over twenty years, and you'll walk away on her account."

"I haven't made up my mind yet. I was waiting until I did to tell you. I knew how you'd take it."

Willy looked over at the sleeping form of Jenna Grissom. That girl was nothing but trouble. Without her pa to lead them, the gang would fall apart. They'd drift their separate ways, and likely never have it as good as they did now. He should be angry about it, but he wasn't. He was angry about something else.

Jenna had rejected him. He'd admitted his feelings for her, and she'd thrown them in his face. He vividly recollected the cold look that came over her when he'd tried to kiss her. One little kiss. That was all he'd wanted. She'd turned her face and twisted free, and given him a hurt look. "I thought I could trust you," she'd said. Then she had wheeled and gone off, and the next morning, she'd disappeared.

Willy was sure he was to blame, that when her pa caught up to her, she'd tell Cal what he'd done and Cal would be furious with him. But no. She hadn't said a word.

Why? Willy wondered. Could it be that maybe she cared for him, if only a little, and she didn't want to get him in trouble? If so, there was hope for him yet. He might win her over, given time. Time he wouldn't have if Cal and her went off to start a new life together.

Willy placed his hand on his Colt and drummed his fingers. He had a decision to make. A big decision. It depended on which was more important to him—riding with the Grissom gang, or Jenna. The father or the daughter. His thoughts were intruded on by Cal Grissom saying his name.

Willy looked up.

"We're turning in," Cal said. "Those lawdogs are still out there and might try something. I want someone keeping watch. Say, two hours each. Do you mind taking the first?"

"Fine by me," Willy said. It would give him time to think.

"Keep your eyes peeled," Burt Alacord said. "They'll want their horses, and their guns."

"They won't get either while I'm keepin' watch," Willy vowed.

Grissom and Alacord went to their respective bedrolls, spread their blankets, and made themselves comfortable.

Willy refilled his tin cup. Two hours wasn't very long. He'd have no trouble staying awake. He sipped, and stared at Jenna. She was curled on her side with her back to him.

In the distance a coyote yipped.

Willy scanned the woods. The firelight didn't spread that far, but it did bathe the horses in enough light that if the lawmen tried anything, he'd spot them right away.

Willy glanced over at Grissom and Alacord. They were lying still but might not be asleep yet. He'd give them a while.

The Prussian began snoring.

An owl hooted.

"What to do?" Willy said quietly. An idea had occurred to him. A loco idea. But the more he thought about it, the more it appealed to him. It was unlike anything he'd ever done, but there was a first time for everything.

Is she worth it? Willy asked himself. Only he could answer that. He checked on her father and Alacord again. They appeared to be asleep. Setting down the cup, he rose and moved around the fire. Jenna still had her back to him. He was almost to her when she suddenly rolled over. He stopped, fearing she'd open her eyes, but no.

She mumbled something, was all.

Willy hunkered, folded his arms across his knees, and watched her sleep. She was so beautiful it about took his breath away. Her smooth cheeks, those lips, her hair. It was all he could do not to reach out and stroke it. He'd never wanted anyone or anything as much as he craved Jenna Grissom at that particular moment.

Willy looked over at her father once more. He liked Cal. He truly did. He liked riding with him. But not enough to make him rethink his crazy notion.

Bending over Jenna, Willy listened to her breathe. Every soft breath was like a caress on his skin. He grew hot all over, and prickled as if he'd broken out in a rash. He could smell her, a scent like no other. His mouth went dry, and his need mounted.

Willy made up his mind. The consequences be damned, he would do what he had to. Rising, he quietly retraced his steps around the fire and over to their horses. He hadn't unsaddled his. Thankfully, Jenna's mare didn't shy when he threw her saddle blanket on, and then her saddle. He couldn't help making a little noise, but no one woke up. When he was done, he led both animals over to where Jenna lay.

This was the moment of truth. Willy could still change his mind. He could take the horses back and wait until the two hours were up and wake someone to relieve him.

Willy firmed his jaw. No, he wanted her too much. Taking his rope, he pulled his boot knife and cut a length long enough for his purpose. Replacing the rope on his saddle, he sank to a knee, untied his bandanna, and wadded it.

Just then Tom Kent rose on an elbow and gazed sleepily around. He saw Willy and gave a little wave. Apparently he didn't notice the rope or the bandanna.

Willy smiled and nodded.

Kent rolled onto his stomach and went back to sleep.

It was now or never, Willy told himself. Jenna's right arm lay flat beside her, her left across her bosom. Making a small loop at one end of the rope, he was about to slide it over her hand when she muttered and moved, placing both wrists side by side. He couldn't ask for better luck. Quickly, he gingerly lifted her right hand, slid the loop around her wrist, then pressed her right forearm against her left. It was the work of seconds to bind her.

Jenna stirred and blinked and raised her head. "What—"

Willy shoved his bandanna into her mouth. She recoiled and sputtered, and he put his mouth to her ear. "You wake anyone up, I'll gun them before they can get to their feet."

Jenna's eyes grew wide.

"Not a peep, or you pa is the first I'll shoot," Willy said. Scooping her into his arms, he threw her over her saddle, legs first. She clutched the saddle horn and looked at him in disbelief.

Quickly, Willy vaulted onto his horse, grabbed her reins, and rode off into the night with his prize.

24

———————

Alonzo Pratt couldn't believe his eyes. He and Deputy Stone had snuck to the south side of the clearing and were crouched behind a thicket. They were waiting for the outlaws to turn in. Then Stone aimed to get to their horses and get out of there.

"They'll be after us at daybreak," Stone had whispered, "and if they have a good tracker, we could be in trouble."

To Alonzo's way of thinking, they already were. It was loco, them going up against a pack of vicious killers who would shoot them dead as quick as look at them.

All the outlaws except Willy Boy Jenkins finally retired to their blankets.

Alonzo was perplexed when Willy went over and, for the longest while, stared at Jenna Grissom. When Willy Boy brought a pair of horses over, his puzzlement grew. Then Willy produced the rope and the gag, and Alonzo was lanced by alarm. "What is he up to?"

"He's goin' to snatch her, I bet," Stone said, sounding amazed.

"No." Alonzo forgot himself and raised his voice. Not loud enough for Willy to hear, but close to it.

"Hush, consarn you," Stone cautioned. "Grissom and those others will hear you if you're not careful."

Anything else Alonzo might have said was drowned out by the drumbeat of hooves as Willy spurred his mount to the west and took Jenna with him.

Brandishing their hardware, the other outlaws sprang up. They likely figured they were under attack by hostiles, or the law, or even Stone and Alonzo. Some rose in time to see Willy Boy and Jenna plunging into the trees.

"What the hell?" Cal Grissom roared. "Where's Willy going with my girl?"

Burt Alacord was the only one who had the presence of mind to try to stop him. Taking several swift steps, he drew his right-hand Colt in a blur of motion and fanned two shots into the trees after Willy.

"Don't!" Cal cried. "You might hit Jenna!"

"Did I just see right?" Weasel said. "Is that fool Willy Boy stealin' her?"

"Looks like it to me," Ira Fletcher said.

Cal Grissom started toward the woods, then must have realized the futility of giving chase on foot. Stopping, he looked at his men. "Why are you just standing there? Saddle our horses! We're going after them."

The outlaws scrambled to obey.

Alonzo looked at Stone, who returned the favor.

"Well, this is somethin'."

What does that even mean? Alonzo wondered. "That poor girl is in trouble."

"It's what Cal Grissom gets for lettin' her ride with men like those who ride with him," Stone said. "They were askin' for trouble."

"I bet he never expected anything like this," Alonzo said. "Her, neither."

"Then they're fools. Those are the worst outlaws in the territory. What did the Grissoms think, that Jenkins and those others would act like saints?"

"You know everything, don't you?" Alonzo said, irritated that the lawman wasn't more worried about Jenna.

"What did I do?"

The outlaws were experts at fanning the breeze quickly. They had to be, the lawless profession they'd chosen. They saddled their mounts in no time. When Cal Grissom swung onto his, the rest were already in the saddle, their reins poised.

"You saw with your own eyes, gents," Cal said savagely. "That son of a bitch took my girl!"

"I never did trust him," Weasel Ginty said.

Cal Grissom rose in his stirrups. "I want Willy Boy alive if possible so I can show him what I do to those who turn on me."

"What if he won't let us take him alive?" Tom Kent said.

"I won't be a stickler about it," Cal said. He made a fist and waved it over his head. "Now after them! And we don't stop till my daughter is safe. You hear me?"

With a chorus of angry yips and yells, the outlaws galloped to the chase.

"Will you look at that?" Jacob Stone said. "A gift horse, and then some." Grinning, he rose and strode from concealment.

In their haste to go save Jenna Grissom, the gang had forgotten about Archibald and the packhorse, and Stone's own animal.

"Hold on," Alonzo said, half-worried that one of the outlaws would glance back and see them.

Stone beckoned. "Come on, son. Time's a wastin'. The Good Lord has seen fit to lend us a hand, and we should take advantage of his generosity."

Nervous as a cat in a yard full of hounds, Alonzo stalked from hiding. "I never saw anything like this in all my born days," he marveled.

"Makes two of us."

The fire still blazed, the coffee and the remains of the outlaws' supper left untended.

"It was reckless of them leavin' our horses," Alonzo said.

Stone had stepped around the fire, and drew up short. Staring down, he grinned and said, "That's not all they left behind."

There, in a pile, sat the lawman's six-shooter and rifle and Alonzo's own six-shooter.

"We'll, I'll be," Alonzo said in delight.

Stone reclaimed his hardware. "I feel undressed without these." He brushed his rifle off, checked that his Colt was loaded, and nodded in satisfaction. "This is an omen, son."

Alonzo saw it as pure luck. He was glad to be armed again, but guns weren't as important to him as they were to the deputy. Shoving his Colt into his holster, he said, "If you say so."

"I do," Stone insisted. "It's the Almighty's way of sayin' we need to go after them. Nothin' has changed. We'll still put an end to the Grissom gang once and for all."

"All we've done so far is get ourselves caught," Alonzo reminded him.

"A setback," Stone said, "which has been set right. We're back where we started."

"Only without Jenna." Saying it filled Alonzo with dread. "Who knows what Jenkins will do to her?"

"We both know the answer to that."

"He'd better not," Alonzo said. The thought of Willy Boy's hands on her made him burn with fury.

Turning, Jacob Stone helped himself to a tin cup, lifted the pot, and poured.

"What in the name of heaven are you doin'?" Alonzo asked. "We don't have time to waste. We should be after them."

"In a minute," Stone said. "First we eat and drink to keep our strength up."

Alonzo fought an impulse to hit him. "How can you think of food with Jenna held captive? What on earth is wrong with you?"

"Nothin'," Stone said, treating himself to a bite of biscuit. "I'm not the one who's in love with her."

Forgetting himself, Alonzo said, "What if I am? Is that so bad? She's a fine gal, and you know it."

"I admit she is," Stone said, nodding and chewing. "She's also a bank and stage robber, and must be held to account."

"Over my dead body," Alonzo vowed.

"What a terrible thing for a lawman to say."

In a welter of emotion, Alonzo opened his mouth to tell Stone the truth.

The night wind was cool on Willy's face as he led Jenna Grissom across the prairie at a gallop. It was reckless to ride that fast at night. Prairie-dog holes and other dangers were all too common. But if he didn't spirit Jenna far away, and quick, he wouldn't live to see the dawn.

Now that he'd actually done it, Willy was a bit amazed. He'd stolen a woman! Cal Grissom's girl, no less.

Willy supposed he shouldn't be so surprised. He stole for a living, after all. Money. Valuables. Whatever he could get his hands on. Stealing a woman was no different. So what if she was a living, breathing person? Stealing was stealing.

And, too, Willy wanted her. Or a better word was "desired" her. Or "craved" her. He liked that one, craved. He was in love. There was no other explanation.

When over a mile of hard riding dropped behind them, Willy brought their animals to a stop.

Jenna was holding fast to her saddle horn with her bound hands. Either the gag had jiggled loose or she'd tried to spit it out, because one end dangled from her mouth.

"You probably want that out of there," Willy said, and reaching over, he yanked the bandanna out.

Jenna tried to spit a few times, and couldn't. "You miserable wretch."

"The thing you need to know," Willy said, "is that if you holler for them to hear, I'll hit you so hard, your teeth will rattle."

"I believe you would, you animal." Jenna raised her wrists toward him. "Untie me."

"Don't be stupid." Shifting in his saddle, Willy studied their backtrail. So far there was no sign of anyone. "Looks like we got clean away."

"Now who's being stupid?" Jenna said. "My father won't rest until he catches up to us."

"That'll take some doin'," Willy said. "I don't aim to make it easy."

"Why did you do this?" Jenna said. "Tell me that much, will you? We were getting along. I treated you nicely, even when you overstepped yourself."

"Is that what you call a man sayin' he loves you and wants to do right by you? He oversteps?"

"The woman has to want to, too."

"Not really," Willy said.

"What now?" Jenna scornfully asked. "You ravish me?"

"Hell, no," Willy said. "I aim to have you as my missus."

Jenna appeared thunderstruck.

"You heard me right," Willy said. "You and me will do well together. You've been on a few robberies. You know how it goes."

"Let me be sure I understand the full enormity of your stupidity. . . ."

"Hey, now," Willy said.

"You want me to be your wife?"

"Correct," Willy said, proud of the fancy word he used.

"And you want the two of us to rob banks and stagecoaches and whatever else strikes your fancy?"

"I do," Willy said, confirming it with a nod.

"And do you want us to have children, too?"

"Why not?" Willy said. "We could be a family. The family you never had but you've always hankered after."

"And we'll rob our days away in merry contentment, and live happily ever after? Is that how this goes?"

"You sure put it sweet," Willy flattered her. "I couldn't have said it better, myself."

"I've been abducted by a moron."

"Stop that," Willy said.

Jenna jabbed her thumbs toward his head. "What do you have between your ears? Rocks? You can't just take a woman and make her yours. That's not how it works."

"Sure it does. I bet I'm not the only man who's ever done this," Willy said. "You'll like it, in time. I'll treat you right. Give you all the things your pretty heart wants."

With deliberate slowness, accenting each word, Jenna growled, "I . . . don't . . . want . . . you."

"You're only sayin' that because the notion is so new," Willy said. "Give it time to sink in."

Jenna suddenly lunged at the reins to her mare, seeking to wrest them from his grasp, but he yanked them away.

"Behave," Willy said.

"If I had a gun, I'd shoot you," Jenna fumed. "And I've never shot a soul in my life."

"That's your anger talkin'. You'll get over it," Willy predicted. "A month from now, we'll be two peas in a pod."

"A month from now you'll be dead, courtesy of my father. Or if he doesn't kill you, Burt will."

"What's Alacord to you?"

"A friend. Which is more than I can say about you."

Willy had listened to enough. "Let's keep goin'. Remember what I told you about hollerin'. You ride, and you keep quiet, and everything will be fine."

Jenna raised her hands in appeal. "Wait. Please. I'm begging you, Willy. Don't do this. It can only end badly."

"I've made up my mind," Willy truculently declared. "I'm takin' you off to the Black Hills. There's not much law there, for one thing. For another, there's plenty of easy pickin's, what with the mines and boomtowns and such."

"There are also a million Sioux."

"We'll fight shy of those red devils." Willy used his spurs and tugged on her reins. "You'll see. You and me will be good together. We'll go to Deadwood first. I hear it's wide open. No marshal or nothin'. A place like that, a man like me can make somethin' of himself."

"All you'll have to do is kill everyone who stands in your way," Jenna said sarcastically.

"Exactly. That includes your pa and Burt Alacord and those lawmen, too, if they come after us."

"I hope they do," Jenna said.

25

Alonzo couldn't do it. He couldn't bring himself to admit that he was impersonating a lawman. Given how devoted Jacob Stone was to the law, the deputy might arrest him on the spot.

Instead, Alonzo squatted by the fire and drank coffee and tried not to think of how he'd rather be in the saddle, flying to the rescue of Jenna Grissom.

"What's wrong now, son?" Stone asked.

The way Alonzo saw it, everything that could go wrong already had. Willy Boy Jenkins abducting Jenna was just the latest in a long string.

"Cat got your tongue?" Stone said, smiling.

Alonzo's conscience pricked him. The old man was only trying to help. "It's nothin'."

"Then there is somethin'. And I reckon I know what it is."

"You're worried sick about that pretty gal you're sweet on. That must have been quite a shock, Willy Boy takin' her like he did."

"The outlaws were shocked, too," Alonzo said.

"Dumber than a stump, that Willy Boy," Stone said. "Cal Grissom will be out for his blood, and those others are as loyal to Grissom as we are to our badges. Burt Alacord in particular." Stone chuckled. "That'd be a sight to see, Alacord goin' up against Willy Boy. I know who I'd put my money on."

"Burt Alacord," Alonzo guessed.

"So long as they go at it straight up," Stone said. "Willy Boy's the kind who might decide it's smarter to back-shoot Burt and go on livin'."

"Poor Jenna," Alonzo said.

"I knew it."

"Leave it be. For my sake."

"Sure," Stone said.

Alonzo could only force down a little bit of stew, as worried as he was. He drank coffee instead.

Stone wasn't in any hurry. He took his time eating. When Alonzo remarked that molasses moved faster, Stone grinned. "You need to learn to relax more. I was a bundle when I was your age, and experience taught me that frettin' never does anyone any good."

"Easy for you to say," Alonzo grumbled. "You probably never loved anyone."

"That was cruel," Stone said. "I did, in fact. A gal down in Texas. I thought she was the prettiest female who ever drew breath, and I wanted her to be mine. I even got down on bended knee, like folks say men should do."

"And?" Alonzo said when the old lawman didn't go on. This was an unexpected side to Stone, and he'd like to learn more.

"Here I sit, an old bachelor."

"She said no?"

"She did," Stone said. "And yes, I asked her why."

Sadness etched his many wrinkles. "She told me that she cared for me a lot. Enough that she could have said yes if it weren't for the badge on my shirt."

"She didn't like lawmen?"

"Not as husband material, no. She said she'd spend every minute I was gone worryin' over whether I'd make it back. A lawman is a target for every badman out there. Her exact words. And she didn't want that, thank you very much. She wanted a husband who could walk out the door without bein' shot." Stone stopped. "It might do you to consider that, your own self. Could be your Jenna feels the same as my gal did."

"Jenna Grissom isn't mine," Alonzo admitted, as much as he'd like her to be. "And not all women are the same. A lot of lawmen have wives and families."

"The lucky ones."

They fell silent again. Alonzo stood and impatiently tapped his foot while Stone took his sweet time drinking the last of his coffee.

"You're doin' this to get my goat," Alonzo complained.

"I'm doin' this so we can ride all night and all day tomorrow if we have to," Stone said.

"Then let's *go*."

"You shouldn't let your emotions get the better of you," Stone advised. "Emotions lead to mistakes, and mistakes lead to dead."

"I swear," Alonzo said.

Stone swallowed, and sighed. "I could use more, but we'd best fan the breeze before you bust a gut." He stood. "Happy now?"

Alonzo started to turn toward their horses. "I'll be happy when . . ." He didn't get any further. Shock rooted him.

"Well, hell," Stone said.

Not twenty feet away stood Ira Fletcher, his big Dragoon revolver held firmly in both hands. He had already cocked it, and his finger was curled around the trigger. "Don't so much as twitch."

"I didn't expect this," Stone said.

"Hands in the air, both of you," Fletcher commanded.

Alonzo complied, but Stone raised his with all the speed of a tortoise while asking, "What are you doin' back here, Ira?"

"Cal's doin'," Fletcher said. "He realized he made a mistake not bringin' your horses. Can't blame him, though. He was too worried about his gal to think straight."

"So he sent you to fetch them," Stone guessed.

"Mister," Fletcher said, falling into a crouch. "If you don't get those hands up right quick, I'll put a hole in you as big as a dinner plate."

"Wouldn't want that," Stone said, and finally elevated his arms.

Fletcher sidled around behind them, that big Dragoon rock-steady. "Stay still, and I won't blow your spines in half."

"You're all heart," Stone said.

"You have a mouth on you, don't you, old man?"

"I'm annoyin' everybody tonight," Stone said.

Alonzo felt his Colt lifted from his holster and heard a thud when it was tossed to one side.

"Now it's your turn, oldster," Fletcher said, moving behind Stone.

"Who are you callin' old? You're not much younger than me."

Out of the corner of his eye, Alonzo saw Fletcher relieve Stone of his Colt and cast it away.

Fletcher came around in front of them once more, only now he was closer.

"What did you say your name was again, old man?"

"Stone," Stone said. "Deputy Jacob Stone."

"You're as old as Methuselah," Fletcher said. "What are you doin', runnin' around the countryside after outlaws like us when you should be whittlin' on a rockin' chair somewhere?"

"I'm so tired of hearin' about my age," Stone said wearily. "It's not how many years you've lived. It's how you've held up. It's what you can do. And I can still do my job."

"Not for much longer," Fletcher said in an ominous tone.

"Am I to gather you don't aim to take us alive?"

"Why bother?" Fletcher said. "We were fixin' to kill you both anyway. And you'd only slow me in catchin' up to the others." He bared a mouthful of splayed and uneven yellow teeth. "I ain't killed me any lawmen in a while. This will be fun."

Cal Grissom was a seething volcano of rage and worry. His daughter, his only child, his pride and joy, had been taken by a desperado who had no scruples about snuffing wicks. Burt Alacord was faster on the shoot, but Willy Boy Jenkins was the true killer of their bunch. When he wanted to, Willy could be downright vicious.

And now Jenna was at Willy's mercy.

As he led his men deeper into the night, Cal told himself that he should have known something like this would happen. His life never went smooth for long. Something always came along to spoil things.

His boyhood had been wretched. His pa was a beater; beat his ma, beat him, beat their dog and their cat. Sometimes Cal was beat for doing things he shouldn't. Other times, Cal suspected his father had beat him for the hell of it.

His pa was a drinker, and whenever his pa was deep in his cups, he'd get around to taking off his belt and give Cal a lashing. His ma, too, received her share, although not with the belt. His pa would slap her silly, smack her and smack her until she was on her knees sobbing, begging him to stop.

Later, his ma up and ran off, and that was the last they saw of her. Cal took that as a hint, and ran off when he was old enough to make it on his own. He met a woman and fell in love and married her. They had Jenna. All was right with his world, or would have been except for one thing.

Cal was as fond of liquor as his pa. He drank like the proverbial fish, and his wife didn't like that. One day he came home and found a note saying she'd had enough and gone off with another man, someone who hardly ever took a nip. A friend of his, the bastard.

That was bad enough. To make it worse, his wife had the audacity to leave Jenna with him. That never made any sense to Cal. Why leave their daughter with the man she accused of drinking himself into an early grave? Wouldn't it have made more sense for her to take Jenna with her?

After that, Cal drank even more. He went around in a perpetual stupor until one night, sitting at the kitchen table with a half-empty bottle in front of him, he looked over at Jenna, barely out of her swaddling clothes, and had a rush of insight that made him cover his mouth with his hand to keep from screaming.

Cal realized he wouldn't be any better for her than his pa had been for him. Not that he'd use his belt on her. He'd never do that, not in a million years. But he couldn't stop drinking, no matter how he tried. And it wouldn't do for his daughter to be raised by a lush.

The hardest thing Cal ever had to do was take Jenna to his sister and ask her to raise the one person in the world he truly loved. She and her husband balked until Cal assured them that he'd send them money, as regular as clockwork.

Riding off that night, Cal's heart broke anew. He drank and he drank, and ran out of money, so he robbed a store. He liked to think the alcohol made him do it. One thing led to another, and inside of a year he was a wanted outlaw.

Cal was never without a bottle yet somehow he continued to function where most men would have passed out. He got a reputation, ironically enough, for having a good head on his shoulders. Other outlaws were drawn to him, and looked up to him as their leader. Burt. Weasel. Ira. And others.

Cal knew he was a marked man. Sooner or later his luck would run out. The law would nab him or he'd be shot fleeing a bank, and that would be that. Outlaws seldom met peaceful ends.

Cal didn't care. He had nothing to live for. His life became an endless repeat of drinking, riding, and robbing. He drank half a bottle for breakfast and more throughout the day. He reckoned that eventually the liquor would kill him if nothing else did.

Then a miracle occurred. His little girl came back into his life. Jenna sought him out, all on her own. She wanted to be with him, wanted for them to be a father and daughter again. It was his innermost, most secret wish, come true.

As usual, though, his slice of heaven on earth didn't last. Jenna made it plain she'd like for him to give up the owlhoot life. She wanted the two of them to go off somewhere no one had ever heard of the Grissom gang.

They'd assume new names and start over. Have a whole new life. Together.

Most fathers, Cal figured, would leap at the chance. To his dismay, he found he couldn't. It should have been an easy decision. His daughter versus "a life of crime," as the newspapers called it. How could he *not* agree?

Jenna was terribly upset, and Cal didn't blame her. He'd wrestled with the issue for days, until, out of the blue, Jenna up and left. He shouldn't have been surprised. He'd crushed her dream. Ruined the whole reason she came to see him.

And now this.

Jenna, taken captive by Willy Boy Jenkins.

Cal recalled how friendly Willy Boy had been to her, how they'd talked and ridden together at times. He'd never once sensed there was more to it than friendship, especially on her part. Willy taking her had to be entirely Willy's idea. Burt said he'd seen ropes on her wrists as Willy Boy was leading her off, which was all the explanation Cal needed.

Jenna. His sweet, wonderful Jenna. Cal nearly choked on his rage. Rage so strong, it made his head hurt. Rage so potent, it smothered his need for drink. A feat nothing else had ever accomplished.

Cal didn't lose his head entirely. After a couple of hours of hard riding he slowed to a walk to give their horses a breather. When one of his men came up alongside him, he didn't need to look to know who it was.

"How are you holdin' up?" Burt Alacord asked.

"How do you think?"

"I always reckoned that boy might be trouble someday."

"Rub salt in the wound, why don't you?"

"Sorry," Burt said.

"No, I'm sorry," Cal said. "I shouldn't take it out on you. I trusted him, and I shouldn't have. My instincts failed me." His features hardened. "But do me a favor, if you can. Ask the others, too."

"Anything."

"When we catch up, I don't want him dead right away. If it's at all possible, take him alive."

"You'd like to whittle on him some? Maybe break a few bones? Make him die screamin' in pain?"

Cal smiled in pleasurable anticipation. "Would I ever."

26

———·———

Federal Deputy Marshal Jacob Stone had been held at gunpoint a few times before. Even once was one time too many. The worst had been a drunk who nicked his ear with a slug fired at his nose. Fortunately the jackass couldn't hold his revolver steady if his life had depended on it. Which it had.

To say it hadn't rattled him would be a lie. A drunk and a cocked pistol were a deadly combination. Drunks were like bears, unpredictable as could be.

Ira Fletcher wasn't drunk. He was stone sober, and his flinty eyes glittered at the prospect of doing them in. He couldn't seem to make up his mind which of them to shoot first. He pointed that big Dragoon at Stone and then at Robert Grant and then at Stone again.

"Shouldn't it be youth before age?" Stone said, earning a sharp look from young Grant.

"What's that?" Fletcher said, raising his head. "You want me to shoot your partner before I shoot you?"

"If you don't mind," Stone said.

"Well, I'll be," Fletcher said, and laughed. "You hear that, boy?"

"I heard," Grant said angrily.

"I reckon this old goat ain't ever heard of standin' by a friend through thick and thin," Fletcher said, and cackled.

"I'm surprised at you," Grant said to Stone.

"We do what we have to, son," Stone said.

"How many times do I have to tell you to quit callin' me that?" Grant exploded. "I'm not your son and never will be."

Fletcher cackled anew. "I could eat this up with a spoon. I never have liked tin-toters. Were it up to me, you'd all drop dead."

"So you could do as you please, robbin' and killin' folks to your heart's content," Stone said.

"What of it?" Fletcher said. "It's human nature to prey on those weaker than you. Animals do it all the time."

"We're not animals," Stone said.

"The hell we're not. Don't give me that Bible-thumper hogwash. This life is all there is, and this life, in case you ain't noticed, is dog-eat-dog."

"Listen to you," Stone said.

"But tell you what," Fletcher said, and he pointed the Dragoon at Robert Grant. "I'll do as you'd like and blow the top of his head off before I do you in."

"You son of a bitch," Grant said.

"Now, now, boy," Fletcher said. "If you aimed to die in bed, you shouldn't ought to have become a lawman."

Stone's chance had come. He was still holding the tin cup, half-filled with coffee; Fletcher hadn't made him let go of it when they raised their arms. Girding himself, he said, "You've been at this outlaw business a long time, haven't you?"

"As long as you've been a lawdog, I'd imagine," Fletcher said. "Why?"

"That Dragoon," Stone said. "You don't see many men usin' those old hand cannons these days."

"I like it," Fletcher said. "It kicks like a mule but it gets the job done."

"I had one once. They do put a hole in a man. They're also heavy and cumbersome. You can't move them as quick as a new Colt."

"I may not be Burt Alacord, but I'm quick enough," Fletcher declared.

"Let's find out," Stone said, and dashed the coffee into the old outlaw's face. Fletcher reacted as Stone hoped; he yelped and blinked and stepped back. In a twinkling Stone was on him, knocking Fletcher's gun arm aside even as he drove his other fist into Fletcher's jaw. But if he thought the outlaw would go down easily, he was mistaken.

Howling in rage, Fletcher swung the Dragoon like a club. Stone ducked and planted his other fist in Fletcher's gut. It had no more effect than his first punch. Fletcher was as tough as old rawhide.

Grabbing the outlaw's wrist to prevent him from using the Dragoon, Stone sought to trip him. He glimpsed Robert Grant, standing openmouthed, and hollered, "What are you waitin' for? Lend a hand!"

Stone got hold of Fletcher's other wrist, and wrenched, twisting Fletcher half around. Fletcher hissed like a struck snake and arced a knee at Stone's groin. Stone shifted and absorbed the blow on his thigh. Taking a gamble, he lowered his head and shoulders and slammed into Fletcher's chest, seeking to bowl him over. Fletcher staggered back but stayed on his feet.

"Your six-shooter!" Stone bawled at Grant. "Shoot him!"

Panic lit Fletcher, and he lowered his own head and rammed into Stone, going tit for tat. Stone was knocked back and nearly lost his hold. He saw Grant scoop up his revolver and point it, but the younger deputy seemed unsure and hesitated.

Ira Fletcher commenced to spin, hauling Stone with him, turning faster and faster to make it harder for Grant to hit him. Stone dug in his bootheels, to no avail. Fletcher weighed more than him, and although Stone was loath to admit it, Fletcher was stronger.

"Shoot!" Stone yelled.

There was method to Fletcher's spinning. He was whirling them away from Grant, and from the fire. Once out of the ring of light, he could break free and flee.

Stone clung on. He was bound and determined to either arrest Fletcher or end his outlaw days permanently. Fletcher wasn't some drunk on a spree; he was as hard-hearted as they came, a cold killer who thought no more of snuffing a human life than he would of squashing a fly.

"Damn you!" Fletcher roared, tugging and pulling. "Let the hell go of me!" He drove a boot at Stone's knee.

Sidestepping, Stone suddenly let go of Fletcher's left wrist, balled his fist, and swung at Fletcher's chin. In the act of pulling back, Fletcher jerked his head higher just as Stone swung, and Stone's fist struck Fletcher's throat, instead.

Fletcher came to a complete stop. A startled look came over him. He clutched at his throat and gurgled, then dropped like a sack of rocks.

Stone sprang aside, shouting, "Shoot before he can use that Dragoon!"

"No need," Grant said.

Fletcher had let go of the Dragoon and pressed both

hands to his throat. Thrashing wildly, he tried to say something, and couldn't. He flung clawed fingers at Stone as if he wanted to squeeze Stone's own neck. Then, uttering a loud whine, he stiffened, raised the whites of his eyes to the stars, and was still.

"What in blazes?" Stone said.

"You crushed his throat," Grant said.

Stone grunted in surprise. He'd never killed a man with his fist before. He'd heard of it happening, but it hadn't been his intent. Squatting, he felt for a pulse that wasn't there. "I'll be damned."

"Another person dead," Grant said.

"You have to get used to things like this," Stone advised him. He let Fletcher's arm fall, stood, and gazed in the direction the other outlaws had gone. "There's bound to be a heap more of it before we're done."

All Jenna Grissom ever wanted out of life was her father. Her mother was lost to her, since Jenna had no idea where to find her. But once she'd discovered her father had sent money all those years, reuniting with him became her life's ambition. It was all she thought about. All she dreamed about. Day and night, month in and month out. Finally came that glorious day when they met, the happiest day of her life.

Her aunt once asked Jenna why she was so anxious to see Cal again. After all, he'd abandoned her, hadn't he? Not really, Jenna said, because he'd provided for her upkeep and schooling, and that showed he cared. To Jenna, his caring mattered more than anything else in the whole world.

Her euphoria lasted about a month. Then her father announced that he planned to rob the Unionville Bank, and wouldn't it be wonderful if she went along and held the horses for them?

Jenna should have said no. She should have told him, flat-out, that she wanted no part of breaking the law. In fact, her heartfelt desire was that she could convince him to give up his lawless ways.

But she held the horses, and later went with the gang when they struck a stagecoach.

Her father was proud of her. He kept saying how wonderful she'd done, and gave the impression that he expected her to go on taking part in their robberies. Father and daughter, together again, living a life of crime.

It astounded Jenna that he'd think such a thing. What sort of father, what sort of human being, saw nothing wrong with involving their children in robbing and killing and all the rest? She began to wonder if he truly cared for her. He claimed he did, but words weren't enough. The proof was in the pudding, as the saying went, and in her father's case, the pudding was half-baked.

Jenna tried to persuade him to change his ways. She sat down with him one evening and explained how she would very much like for him to give up his outlawry, go away with her, and start a new life. They could be a normal father and daughter, and live a normal life.

When he balked, Jenna was crushed. He told her he'd think about it but the truth was in his eyes. He didn't want to give up his outlaw ways. He liked being who he was. Liked it more, apparently, than he liked her.

Now, being led across the benighted prairie, Jenna regretted ever believing she could change her father's ways. Between his refusal—and Willy's unwanted affections—she had decided enough was enough and struck off on her own for North Platte. From there it would be on to California.

Her dream had been dashed. But at least she'd tried.

She never counted on anything like this, though. On being taken against her will, with a fate worse than death in store. For long hours, now, she had stewed and simmered, and when, toward dawn, Willy drew rein to rest their horses and scan the rolling plain behind them, she made up her mind to do something. Her wrists were still bound, but that wouldn't stop her.

"The sun will be up soon," Jenna remarked.

Willy didn't respond.

"We've been at this all night. Can't we stop and eat and rest a while?"

"You'd like that," Willy said. "It'd give your pa a chance to catch up."

Jenna's horse was slightly behind his, and to one side. He had hold of the reins, and wasn't about to let go. Moving slowly so as not to alert him, she gave a slight tap of her heels to gig her mount alongside his. "Is there no way I can talk you out of this?"

"I've made up my mind," Willy said. "You're goin' to be mine, and that's that. You might as well get used to the idea. I don't want to hear anything more about it."

Jenna refused to let him browbeat her. "The woman doesn't have a say? Is that how it goes?"

"A man hankers after a woman, he should have the right to make her his own," Willy said while continuing to study their backtrail.

"I never suspected you felt this way," Jenna said. "You fooled me. I took you for more open-minded and fair."

"I'm not any different than most men."

Jenna laced her fingers together and balled both of her hands into a single fist, careful to hold them behind her saddle horn where he wouldn't notice. "You're wrong, Willy. Most men give their woman a choice.

They ask for her hand, and if she says no, they accept her decision. They don't drag the woman off against her will in the middle of the night."

"No doesn't always mean no."

"It sure as hell does."

Willy looked at her. "Don't cuss. It's not ladylike. You're mine now, and that's all there is to it."

Jenna shifted in her saddle toward him, and leaned slightly out so he was within arm's reach. "You can't force me to care for you."

"Sure I can. Once we've been together a while, you'll get used to it. But don't worry. Do as I say, and I'll treat you decent. I won't beat you unless you deserve it. That's a promise."

"A man should never beat a woman, period," Jenna said, and leaned a little farther. "My uncle never beat my aunt."

"So what? There are a lot of men who beat their women all the time. It's the only way to keep the woman in line."

Jenna was almost ready. "Did your father beat your mother? Is that where you get this from?"

"I got it on my own," Willy said. "From seein' how some men let their females ride roughshod over them."

"It's perfectly all right to hurt the one you say you love? Is that what you're trying to tell me?"

Willy turned to watch behind them again. "You hurt a dog, don't you, when it won't do as you want? A woman is no different."

"Remember you said that," Jenna said, and swung her balled hands with all her strength. She caught him on the jaw so hard it snapped his head around. He was nearly unhorsed, and clutched at his saddle horn to stay on. The next instant she'd grabbed her reins, torn them from his grasp, and slapped her legs against her mare.

Willy let out a roar of fury.

Bent low, Jenna rode for her life. Her only hope was to gain a quick lead and hold it.

"Stop!" Willy hollered.

As if Jenna would. She lashed her reins and slapped her legs some more. She was pulling ahead, and smiled. She'd show the smug son of a bitch.

It never occurred to her that he might try to shoot her.

Until his Colt boomed.

27

⸺⸺ ◆ ⸺⸺

Alonzo Pratt was accustomed to long hours in the saddle but not to riding hard for hours on end, and not at night. When he was on his own, he always made camp by sunset and spent the night the way a man should spend it, asleep. But now the woman he cared for, even if she didn't know it, was in peril. He'd ride all night and all the next day if he had to.

Deputy Stone was of a similar mind. He mentioned several times when they stopped to rest their horses that he was greatly concerned for Jenna's safety.

Alonzo wished Stone would stop bringing it up. He was worried enough as it was. Now, with dawn close to breaking, they'd drawn rein yet again and dismounted to stretch their legs.

"We won't overtake them before noon, if then," Stone mentioned.

"However long it takes," Alonzo said.

"Her pa and his killers will catch up to them before we do."

Alonzo had a disturbing thought. "How do we know we're still on their trail? You can't track in the dark."

"As near as I can tell, Willy Boy is headin' for the Black Hills country," Stone said, "and this is the likeliest way."

"What if you're wrong?"

"We'll backtrack and look for sign."

"That'll delay us even more," Alonzo said, alarmed.

"What do you want from me?" Stone said. "I'm only human." He regarded Alonzo a few moments, then said, "Don't take this personal, but the more I get to know you, the less I reckon you're cut out for this sort of work."

"Oh?"

"Your heart is in the right place, but you're too timid by half."

"I killed those Sioux, didn't I?" Alonzo replied, annoyed at the suggestion that he wasn't manly enough.

"Only because you had to," Stone said. "But you never wanted to go after Grissom and his gang. I could tell. Now you have to because you're smitten by his girl—not because they're outlaws, which should be reason enough."

"You think you know everything," Alonzo said. The truth was, the old lawman had him pegged.

"Don't fret about it," Stone said. "Some men are cut out for law work and some aren't. It's good you found out early."

"If you say so," Alonzo said grumpily, and then it struck him that he was arguing about how fit he was for a profession he had no interest in. He was impersonating a lawman, not the real article.

"Let's concentrate on Miss Grissom for now," Stone said. "She is in more danger than just from Willy Boy."

"How do you mean?"

Stone gestured in the direction they were going. "The closer we get to the Black Hills, the more Sioux there will be. The Hills are sacred to them. It's what the Custer fight was all about."

"Willy Boy is out of his mind to go there."

"No, he's smart like a fox," Stone said. "There's no law, for one thing. And there are hundreds of square miles to hide out in."

Alonzo was tired of talking. "Shouldn't we be on our way?"

They rode and they rode.

As dawn streaked the eastern sky with pink, Stone slowed and pointed at the ground ahead of them.

Alonzo was no tracker, but even he could see that the ground had been churned by a lot of hooves. About half a dozen, he would guess, riding hell bent for leather. "The outlaws."

"Cal Grissom will ride his animals into the ground if he's not careful."

"It's his daughter," Alonzo said.

"And your sweetheart."

"I doubt she knows I like her."

"Women always know."

They didn't speak again until the sun was well up and they came to a ribbon of a creek meandering through the grassland.

Alonzo was angry when Stone called yet another halt, but it had to be done. As their horses drank, he paced and smacked his right fist into his left palm.

"You have to learn patience," Stone said, "among other things."

"I've learned a lot already." Alonzo was tired of the lawman carping about his shortcomings.

Jacob Stone squatted, plucked a blade of grass, and

stuck the stem between his teeth. His brow knit in thought, he chewed the stem, then spit it out, and stood. "I've thought about it and thought about it and I've made up my mind."

"About what?" Alonzo absently asked.

"About you." Stone put his hand on his revolver. "Who are you really? Is Grant even your true name?"

Alonzo stopped cold.

"I've had my doubts about you for a while," Stone went on. "Somethin' about you didn't sit right with me. Your attitude, and all those clothes on your packhorse. Somethin' was off, and I couldn't put my finger on it. Now I have." He raised his left hand and pointed at Alonzo. "You're no lawman."

Tapping his badge, Alonzo said, "What's this, then? I wear it for decoration."

"That had me stumped," Stone said. "It's a real badge. An older one, and you claim to have only been a federal deputy a short while. The marshal would have given you a new one."

"Not if this was all he had handy."

"No," Stone said, shaking his head. "You're a fraud. And in case no one told you, pretendin' to be a lawman is a crime. So I'll thank you to hand me your six-shooter. I'm placin' you under arrest."

Jenna didn't draw rein. If Willy shot her, he shot her. She wouldn't put it past him, but she didn't care. She'd tolerated his abuse long enough. And she'd rather die than let him have his way with her. She hadn't saved herself all these years for the man who would one day claim her heart only to be violated by a vile specimen like Willy Boy Jenkins.

"Stop, damn you!"

Jenna lashed her reins harder. Ahead grew timber. If

she could reach it, she might be able to lose him. She glanced back only once, to see him in mad pursuit.

Once she'd escaped his clutches, she'd have a whole new problem. She was lost. She had no idea where she was in relation to North Platte. Should she go south? Southeast? Southwest?

Jenna was getting ahead of herself. First she had to lose Willy. She knuckled down to riding, and reaching that timber. Intent on getting away, she didn't realize the blunder she'd made until Willy Boy shouted.

"Look out! Prairie dogs!"

Jenna looked down, and gasped. All around her were the mounds and burrows of a prairie dog town. She'd ridden right in among them. No sooner did she awaken to her plight than her mare pitched forward, squealing in pain and fright. There was the loud, sharp *crack* of breaking bone.

Jenna sought to throw herself clear but only partially succeeded. A tremendous blow to her back sent her tumbling like a twig in a gale. She came down hard. The brutal thud of her impact caused her head to swim. The world seemed to have turned upside-down. Her mind darkened and she was on the verge of passing out when a strident whinny restored her jumbled senses. Dazed, her shoulder in excruciating pain, she raised her head.

Her mare had stepped into a prairie dog hole. The force had snapped its leg so violently, the shattered bone was exposed. Struggling and whinnying, the mare was trying to rise but her leg was jammed fast.

Jenna groaned. Not because of her shoulder, but for her mare. Rolling over, she made it to her hands and knees. Nothing seemed to be broken although her left shoulder hurt terribly. She pushed upright, swayed, and took a couple of unsteady steps.

"You dumb girl."

Jenna started to turn toward the sound of Willy's voice and received a jolting shock to her chin. He'd hit her. She staggered, her world spinning anew, and blurted, "No. Don't."

"You've killed your damn horse." Willy was glaring at the mare, his fists balled. "Now we'll have to ride double."

"I didn't—" Jenna began, and got no further. To her disbelief, he stormed into her, swinging. She tried to avoid him but she was too weak, too woozy. He punched her on the cheek, on the temple. Once again her mind darkened, and the next she knew, she was on her knees, blood trickling from a gash in her cheek, feeling new waves of pain.

Willy stood over her, his right fist cocked, his face red with rage. "I should bust your teeth!"

"Is this what you call love?" Jenna spat. She couldn't help herself. Fury rose in her gorge like lava in a volcano.

"You don't know nothin'," Willy said, and hit her again.

Jenna was knocked onto her side. She tasted blood in her mouth and knew one or both of her lips had been pulped. She wished she had a gun or a knife. "You miserable sack of scum."

More blows descended, and a boot caught her in the ribs. Then there was nothing, for how long, she knew not.

Suddenly Jenna's eyes were open, the sun hot on her face. Judging by the sun, she figured she couldn't have been out more than ten or fifteen minutes.

Willy was pacing and muttering to himself. He kept looking to the southeast.

Clearly, he was worried about their pursuers.

The mare had stopped thrashing and whinnying and breathed in great gulps, her nostrils flaring with each breath.

Jenna had to try twice to speak. She managed to wet her hurt lips, and swallow. "What are you waiting for? Put her out of her misery."

Willy stopped pacing and glowered. "Do you see what you've done to us?"

"My mare," Jenna said. "She's in pain."

"Whose fault is that?" Willy swore and looked away.

"You have to shoot her," Jenna said. It was all they could do. They had no means of setting the broken leg, and it wouldn't support the mare's weight if they did. Otherwise, the poor horse would die a lingering, agony-racked death that might take days.

"Like hell I do."

"Please." Jenna tried being reasonable. "You know you do. You can't let her suffer. It's inhumane."

"You'd better learn here and now that I only do what I want to do, not what you want me to."

"She's hurting!" Jenna cried.

"Not my doin'," Willy said, and jabbed a finger at her. "You hit me. Damn near broke my jaw. Then you tried to get away, and look."

"Don't take it out on my horse," Jenna said. "I'm begging you."

"Beg all you want. Why should I bother? I'm havin' second thoughts about you," Willy said. "You're not all I figured you were."

"Forget about me and deal with my horse."

"Shut up." Willy turned his back to her.

It took considerable effort but Jenna made it to her knees. "Give me your revolver. I'll do it."

Willy uttered a bark of a laugh. "Not likely."

"I promise I'll only use it for her," Jenna said. "I give

you my word I won't shoot you." As much as she yearned to, the mare was more important.

"No."

"You're despicable."

"I'm tired of your name-callin'," Willy said. "Not one more, or else."

Marshaling all her strength, Jenna stood. A sharp pang in her head caused her to bite her lip to keep from crying out. Taking a faltering step, she held out her hand. "I'm asking politely. Let me shoot her and I'll give your revolver right back."

"I don't trust you."

"Then take your rifle and cover me," Jenna suggested. "Stand behind me, and if I try anything, you can shoot me."

"You want her dead that much?"

"Haven't I made that plain?" Jenna looked at her poor horse. The mare was quaking as if she were cold.

"Listen," Willy said, "even if I let you, there's somethin' else. A shot can carry for miles."

"You're afraid my father might be close enough to hear?"

"I'm not afraid of anything," Willy snapped. "And it's the Sioux I'm thinkin' of. We don't want a war party breathin' down our necks. Not if we have to ride double."

Jenna saw there was no budging him. Not unless she did something drastic. "How about this. You shoot her for me, and from here on out, I'll do whatever you say, no arguments whatsoever."

"I don't believe you."

"You've been around me long enough to know that when I give my word, I keep it." Jenna took a deep breath. "As much as I hate saying this, I'll do whatever you want from here on out. I vow to you before God and all that's holy."

A wicked gleam lit Willy's face, and his mouth twisted in an ominous sneer. "Well, now. This horse of yours has done me a favor." Drawing his Colt, he turned to the mare and extended his arm. "I'm lookin' forward to tonight."

Jenna did some quaking of her own.

28

Just when Alonzo Pratt thought things couldn't get any worse, they did. The old lawman had seen through his impersonation. To be honest, Alonzo was surprised he'd been able to pull off the deception as long as he had. The prospect of being disarmed, though, didn't sit well with him. "I'm no threat to you."

"You admit it, then?" Deputy Jacob Stone said. "I'm right, and you're not a lawman?" He held out his left hand. "I'll have that pistol, if you please."

"Think about this," Alonzo said. "We're in the middle of Sioux country, and we're after the worst outlaws in the territory. What use can I be to you without my revolver?"

Stone wagged his hand.

"If I'd wanted to harm you, I had a million chances to do it," Alonzo reminded him. "I'm not Willy Boy Jenkins. I'm no killer."

"What *are* you, exactly?" Stone said.

"I pretend to be people I'm not in order to trick others out of their money," Alonzo confessed.

"A confidence man?" Stone said. "You're damn good at it. You had me fooled for the longest while."

"You've had other things on your mind," Alonzo said, "and you were shot with that arrow, besides."

"True," Stone said.

"And it was me who looked after you when you were out to the world," Alonzo reminded him. "I could easily have put a slug in you or slit your throat, but I didn't."

"That's true as well." Stone pursed his lips in thought. He looked at the revolver in his hand, then lowered it. "All right. You've made your point. It wouldn't do to have only one of us armed if hostiles jump us or we catch up to Cal Grissom's bunch."

"Thank you," Alonzo said sincerely.

"Don't think I've gone soft," Stone said gruffly. "I haven't. I'm bein' practical. Once we've rescued Miss Grissom and we get her to North Platte, I'm still arrestin' you. You have to answer for your crimes."

"If you say so."

About to turn to their horses, Stone paused. "Why do you do it, son? An intelligent hombre like you? Why not hold a real job? One that won't get you thrown behind bars?"

Alonzo shrugged. "I started doin' it almost by accident and stuck with it because I was good at it. And I never really hurt anyone. I'm not like Willy Boy Jenkins or those others."

"Still, it's stealin'."

"I admit it's wrong," Alonzo conceded. "But my conscience never bothered me enough that I considered quittin'."

"It's a shame," Stone said. "You're not a bad person. I'd sense it if you were. Seems to me you're misguided more than anything."

"What I am," Alonzo said, "is worried sick about Jenna."

"Makes two of us, so let's fan the breeze." Stone took a step, and stopped. "What's your real handle, anyhow? I doubt it's Robert Grant."

Alonzo told him.

"Well, Mr. Pratt, this is your lucky day. I usually clap handcuffs on lawbreakers." Stone grinned to show it was a joke.

As he climbed on Archibald, Alonzo gave silent thanks that the old lawman was being so reasonable. He liked Stone, he truly did, and he suspected that Stone liked him, as well. But he wouldn't let Stone arrest him. When the time came, he must find a way to thwart him.

Jacob Stone had a lot on his mind.

Saving the Grissom gal was his top priority. After that came dealing with her pa's gang. And after that came dealing with young Mr. Alonzo Pratt.

Pratt's gall amazed and amused him. To impersonate a lawman took sand. Not that Pratt had shown much grit in their clash with the war party. Yes, Pratt killed some of the Sioux, but only because it was them or him. Pratt didn't like violence, and went out of his way to avoid it.

Stone believed the younger man when he said he was no killer. It was one of the reasons Stone let him keep his six-shooter.

Over the course of his many years bringing lawbreakers to justice, Stone had learned a few things about human nature. One was that some folks were willing to break the law, but only to a certain point. There was a line they wouldn't cross. With a lot of them, that line was murder. They might rob, they might cheat, they might do a lot of illegal things, but they'd never, ever willfully take a life.

Alonzo Pratt was one of those.

Then there were the other kind. Those who never drew the line at anything. Those who regarded murdering someone as no different from stepping on a bug. They were the true killers. Men like Willy Boy Jenkins, Ira Fletcher, Tom Kent, and Weasel Ginty.

The Prussian was a bit of a mystery. Stone had heard tell that Spike Davis, or whatever his real name was, once shot a townsman when the gang was riding off after a bank robbery. But the Prussian had been returning fire.

That left Cal Grissom and Burt Alacord. Stone wouldn't categorize them as outright killers. Grissom and Alacord only shot someone when they had to, and in the former's case, if reports were to be believed, that had only been a couple of times in his entire lawless career.

Stone grinned. Here he was, making excuses for a notorious outlaw.

Next he'd take up knitting or join a sewing circle. He almost laughed at his silliness. Instead, he knuckled down to riding hard. Dawn found them still on the outlaws' trail, the tracks plain enough that a ten-year-old could follow them. With no rain in prospect, sticking to them posed no problem.

Stone found himself thinking about the girl. She'd broken the law, too, and had to be brought in. It was a shame, her being so young. And all because she wanted to be with her father after all those years apart.

Here I go, Stone thought, *making excuses again*.

He never had liked arresting women, though. It went against his grain. He'd been raised to regard females as special. As different from men. As better. It wasn't true, of course. There were bad women just as there were bad men.

Jenna Grissom wasn't a bad person. She was a victim of circumstance. Her love for her pa had led her to stray from the straight and narrow, and now look. She'd been taken captive by a gent with no more conscience than a rattler.

Stone felt sorry for her. And for Alonzo, too. The young ones these days did a lot of stupid things. They should know better. Or maybe the young were always scatterbrained, and he'd just never paid it any mind before.

One thing was certain.

The worst of this affair was yet to come.

Tom Kent was the quiet one of Cal Grissom's gang. The only one who spoke less was the Prussian.

Kent didn't talk much because he never had much to say. He didn't have opinions about everything, like some of the others. All he cared about in life was having money to spend, and his knives.

Kent bought them on a whim from an Italian merchant who set up shop in New London. They were throwing knives, and the Italian had taught Kent the basics. The rest Kent picked up on his own. He had a knack for it. The knives became as much a part of him as his arms and his hands.

The first man Kent killed was a drunken sailor, in a row. The sailor had pulled a derringer, and Kent put two knives into his chest before he could shoot. He'd had to flee New London one step ahead of the constabulary, which had proven to be a godsend in disguise. It brought Kent west, and to a way of life that fit him like a glove.

Kent never would have thought it. He'd lived near

the sea as a boy, and loved the sea so much that he signed on with a whaling vessel. Not to specifically hunt whales so much as to be at sea.

One terrible day Kent was washed overboard during a fierce storm. That his shipmates were able to haul him in and save him was little short of a miracle. He'd swallowed so much water, he came within a mouthful of drowning.

So much for the sea.

Kent had taken to spending his nights at waterfront dives, drinking more than he should. That's where he got into the fight with the sailor.

Kent didn't stop running until he was west of the Mississippi River. He joined a party of men heading for Denver and the distant Rocky Mountains, and they set off across the prairie. Along the way a strange thing happened. He fell in love with the vastness of it all. The prairie stretched on forever, a sea of grass as vast as the real seas he had sailed on whaling vessels. The wide open spaces, as they were called, appealed to him as much as the wide open ocean.

On reaching Denver, Kent lived pretty much hand to mouth. He took up with some rough characters, and one thing led to another. He never set out to become an outlaw, yet that was how events unfolded. And now here he was, a member of the Grissom gang.

Kent had never had it so good. He never wanted for money, and in fact, he'd saved over four thousand dollars from his share of the robberies they committed. A wad of bills thick enough to choke a dolphin was secreted in his bedroll.

Kent looked up to Grissom. He'd do anything for the man. So when they stopped to rest their animals and Burt Alacord mentioned that they were a couple of hours behind Willy Boy and Grissom's daughter, Kent stepped forward.

"I have an idea, Cal."

Cal Grissom had been a study in despair all day. He'd squatted and was glumly gazing off into the distance. "About what?"

Kent motioned at the setting sun. "It'll be dark in less than an hour. If we don't catch up to Willy before then, he might change course during the night and give us the slip."

"What do you propose?"

"I'm the smallest and lightest out of all of us," Kent brought up. He barely stood five feet in his stocking-feet and didn't weigh more than a hundred and ten pounds.

"You're damn near a midget," Burt Alacord said, and laughed.

Kent grinned. He was used to Alacord's good-natured ribbing. "Put me on the fastest horse we have and I'll overtake them before dark. We know they're riding double since we found that dead horse, and that will slow them."

"Jenna's mare," Cal said, frowning. "But just you alone?"

"You don't think I can take Willy Boy?" Kent said, and patted the knives at his waist. "You've seen me with my blades."

"All things being equal," Cal said, "a knife is no match for a six-shooter."

"Not if I was stupid enough to walk up to him and let him draw on me," Kent said. "I'm not that dumb. Once I've caught up, I'll wait for dark and slip in close and put my knives in him before he knows what's happening."

"It could work," Burt said to Cal.

"*Ja,*" the Prussian said.

"Better him try than me," Weasel Ginty said. "I'm no match for Willy Boy and I know it."

Cal gnawed on his bottom lip. "You think I should let him?" he said to Burt Alacord.

"We were lucky not to lose their trail in the dark last night," Burt said. "We might not be as lucky tonight." He nodded. "Yes. I reckon you should."

"You'd have to be careful as can be," Cal said to Kent. "It's my girl we're talking about. If anything happened to her . . ."

"It won't be on account of me," Kent assured him. "I won't do anything that will place her in harm. Trust me."

"If I didn't, you wouldn't be riding with me," Cal said, and stood. "All right. Take my bay. It's the fastest and doesn't tire easy."

"I'll take good care of it," Kent said.

Cal placed his hand on Kent's shoulder. "I'm counting on you, Tom, like I've never counted on anyone."

Kent coughed and declared, "I won't let you down."

The bay was several hands higher than Kent's sorrel. Once in the saddle, he had the illusion he could see for miles. He nodded grimly at the others, then said to Cal, "I'll fetch her back safe and sound." With that, he used his spurs.

Kent liked to ride. The rolling gait of a horse reminded him of the rolling pitch of a ship. And unlike some of the others, he could go all day and all night and not be bothered by stiffness or cramps. Maybe his size had something to do with it.

To the west, bands of red and yellow splashed the horizon. A flock of crows rose and were silhouetted against the sun.

Kent thought of Willy Jenkins, and how Willy had betrayed Cal's trust. He'd never liked Willy much. The boy put on airs and acted like he was the cat's meow. Kent had no compunctions about killing him. Not that he'd take any delight in it, as he had with a few others. It had to be done, was all, for Cal's sake.

The bay was superb. The horse flowed over the ground as if it had wings on its legs.

To the south Kent spied large dark shapes that might be buffalo. There had been no sign of a herd, so maybe it was only a few bulls. He understood that the males stayed to themselves until mating season.

Kent grinned, remembering the time he stood at the rail of a ship, watching a pod of porpoises swim by. How different his life was now.

Low hills appeared. Only a few had trees on them.

Kent rode to the top of the first hill he came to, and drew rein. From his vantage it was like standing in a crow's-nest. He really could see for miles. The sun was almost gone, and the red and yellow were giving way to the gray of encroaching twilight.

Kent saw something else, too. A stick horse with two stick figures on its back, going around a far hill.

"Got you!"

29

———◆———

Willy Boy Jenkins was fit to be tied. Things weren't going well. The stupid woman had gone and killed her horse by running it into a prairie dog town, and now his own animal was flagging from having to bear both of them. With sunset not far off, his horse was hanging its head, close to exhaustion.

"Damn you, anyhow," Willy growled.

"What are you upset about now?" Jenna wearily asked.

"The same thing as before," Willy said.

"How many times do I have to tell you? I didn't do it on purpose. I was trying to get away from you."

"I'm beginnin' to regret takin' you," Willy growled. He'd noticed that, although he'd forced her to ride double, she'd made it a point not to let her body touch his, except for her hand on his shoulder. Now and again he'd leaned back against her, wanting to feel her bosom on his back, but she always pulled away. Her message was plain, and he resented it.

"Then let me go," Jenna said. "Just leave me and ride on. When my father finds me, I'll convince him not to go after you. You can get clean away."

Willy snorted. "Your pa won't agree to that. I know him. He'll want me dead, and he won't give up this side of the grave." More likely, Willy thought, Cal would send a couple of the others to do the actual deed. Burt Alacord and Weasel, maybe. Alacord was the shootist of the bunch, although the others were deadly in their own way.

"I can persuade him, I tell you."

"Just shut up," Willy said in disgust. "I'm not lettin' you go. Not after all the trouble I've gone to." He looked over his shoulder at her, and smirked. "In fact, later on, you and me are goin' to become better acquainted than ever."

"Touch me in that manner and I'll kill you," Jenna said coldly.

"You gave your word," Willy said. "To do as I please for puttin' your mare out of its misery." All afternoon he'd been daydreaming of him and her under the blankets. It stirred him, down low. He was hungry to consummate his desire. "I expect you to abide by your promise."

"I didn't think you meant *that*," Jenna said.

"Yes, you did," Willy called her lie. "You knew exactly what I meant."

She said nothing.

They were winding among low, grassy hills, and Willy was on the lookout for a spot to camp. Somewhere not in the open. Somewhere he could have his way with her and not worry about being interrupted.

They went around yet another hill and Willy grinned in pleased surprise.

Long ago, part of the hill had collapsed and a large

swath of earth had cascaded to the bottom. A dirt avalanche, as it were, leaving a gap about fifteen feet wide and twenty feet deep that ran from near the top to the bottom, with a flat space in the middle. The grass had since regrown, creating a pocket perfect for his purpose.

"There," Willy said, and gigged his horse. "Our own little love nest."

"I'm warning you," Jenna said.

Willy laughed. He took delight in putting her in her place. She needed to learn that she must do as he said.

They climbed to the flat space and Willy alighted. Grabbing hold of Jenna's arm, he went to pull her off but she resisted. To teach her a lesson, he wrenched, hard, and had the satisfaction of seeing her tumble to earth and lie gritting her teeth in pain.

"Quit fightin' me, and you won't be hurt."

"I'll tear out your throat with my teeth if you lay a finger on me," Jenna said. "So help me."

Willy had to hand it to her; she was a scrapper. He believed she'd do exactly as she threatened, so he'd make it a point to gag her when the time came. "Keep makin' things difficult and you won't like what happens. There's only so much bother I'll let you put me to."

"True love, is it?" Jenna mocked him.

"I wouldn't know true love if it bit me on the ass," Willy admitted. "All I know is that I want you like I've never wanted a female before in my whole life, and I'll have you, one way or the other."

"They call that lust," Jenna said in contempt.

"Lust. Love." Willy shrugged. "It's all the same to me."

"It would be."

Willy almost kicked her ribs in. He was tired of her insults. "Sit up and rest while I strip my saddle. We're not making a fire. It would give us away."

"What about food?" Jenna said. "I'm starved."

"Jerky, and water from my canteen."

"Wonderful."

There she went again, Willy thought. She pricked and she pricked. He'd have to knock that sass out of her once they were in the clear.

Tucking her knees to her chest, Jenna draped her bound arms over her legs and rested her chin on her knees. "I never imagined I'd say such a thing, but I hope my father kills you nice and slow."

"Keep makin' me mad. That's real smart."

"I don't care how you feel."

"You will," Willy said.

Spreading his bedroll and hobbling his horse didn't take long. The jerky had been in his saddlebags for months, and the pieces had become more brittle than he liked. After only a few bites, he stopped. It wouldn't hurt him to go hungry.

Jenna didn't have much interest in hers, either. She ate part of it, and went back to sulking.

As much as Willy would like to throw her down and have his way, keeping his hide intact came first. "If you're not goin' to eat, you can crawl under those blankets and turn in."

"And have you crawl in with me once I'm asleep? No, thanks."

Rising, Willy stood over her, his hand on his Colt. "I wasn't askin'. You do it, and you do it now, or so help me, I'll knock you out and throw you under them."

"I hate you," Jenna said, but she did as he'd demanded, lying on her back with the blanket up to her chin. "Happy now?"

"Not a peep from here on out, you hear me?"

"What are you up to?"

Willy didn't answer. The sky had darkened to where

stars were blossoming. Retreating into a patch of black shadow, he hunkered.

The trap was set.

Jenna Grissom was tired and hungry and miserable. She needed rest but she refused to go to sleep. Not with the threat of Willy forcing himself on her. She would stay awake, and when he tried, fight him tooth and nail.

She half-expected him to come swaggering over the moment she lay down. When he didn't, when he moved off into the shadows where she couldn't see him, she assumed he was heeding Nature's call. That he was being polite about it and not doing it in front of her was a welcome surprise.

Minutes went by, and Willy didn't reappear. Jenna wondered what he was up to. After all his talk about ravishing her, this made no sense.

Jenna wished her father would hurry up and overtake them so she could be free of the nightmare.

The moon rose, casting the prairie in a pale glow.

Jenna's eyelids grew heavy. She had gone without sleep for so long, she dearly needed rest. Her eyes closed, and she started to slip under. With a start, she snapped them open and gave her head a vigorous shake. Should she fall asleep, she might wake up with Willy on top of her.

Jenna craned her neck but couldn't spot him. Here she was, out in the open for anyone to see, and he was hiding somewhere. Then it hit her. Willy wasn't hiding. He was lying in wait, and using her as a lure to draw her father and the others in.

No sooner did the truth dawn than Jenna heard a rustling that suggested furtive movement, from below. Raising her head to peer over the blanket, she nearly gasped at the sight of something or someone slinking toward her on its belly. She took it for an animal, a cougar, maybe. She went to yell for Willy to come to her aid when the "cougar" rose on its elbows.

It was several seconds before Jenna recognized Tom Kent, without his hat. He looked all around, and resumed crawling. The glint of metal told her he had a knife in each hand.

Jenna knew how skilled he was with those knives. She'd seen him practice throwing them into trees and stumps. He never missed.

Her hopes soared. If Kent was there, her father and the others must be, too. She imagined they were covering Kent while he snuck in to cut her free and get her out. Kent was taking an awful chance.

Jenna needed to warn him about Willy. Sliding her arms out from under the blanket, she motioned to get Kent's attention. He didn't seem to notice. She dare not speak; Willy would hear. Rolling onto her side, she wriggled around so she faced Kent and moved her arms back and forth. Once again, no reaction.

Jenna took a gamble. "Don't come any closer!" she whispered. "Willy is nearby."

To her consternation, Tom Kent kept coming.

"Didn't you hear me?" Jenna anxiously whispered. "Willy could be anywhere."

At last Kent stopped. He nodded to show he understood, then put a knife to his lips to enjoin her to silence. And on he came.

Jenna glanced at where she had last seen Willy. Was it her imagination, or was there a hint of movement? Frantic that Kent would come to harm on her account, she slid out from under the blanket and crawled toward him. She would meet him halfway.

Tom Kent stopped, apparently in surprise.

Expecting at any instant to hear the boom of a six-shooter, Jenna crawled faster. She scraped a knee, and didn't care.

Kent was waiting for her, an arm cocked to throw a knife should he have to.

Jenna looked over her shoulder. No Willy anywhere. She wondered if he had fallen asleep. But that would be too easy.

Kent was scanning the darkness.

Pumping her arms and legs, Jenna scrambled the last several feet. "Mr. Kent," she whispered. "Where's my father?"

"Hush, girl," Kent whispered, and began to slide backward. "We have to get you out of here. Follow me."

Jenna eagerly complied. Soon she would be reunited with her father, and her ordeal would be over. She stayed close to Kent, her face inches from his. "Thank you for coming for me."

"Quiet, I say," Kent whispered.

Jenna nodded, and swallowed. A feeling of dread had come over her. She wanted to rise and flee. But Kent stayed down, so she did, too. They were on the bottom part of the slope, moving faster now.

Tom Kent pushed up into a crouch, slid his left-hand knife into a sheath, and held out his hand for hers.

They ran.

Jenna looked for her father and Burt Alacord and the others, and the awful truth dawned. "Are you alone?"

"You don't listen worth a damn, girl," was Kent's response.

Jenna could go faster if her hands were free. It was awkward with them tied. "Cut me loose," she urged. "Please."

Without breaking stride, Tom Kent flicked his right-hand blade and the loops around her wrist parted.

Jenna flinched, thinking he would cut her, as well. But the knife never broke her skin. Marveling at his prowess, she moved her arms in rhythm with her legs. They flew on down the hill to a waiting horse—her father's bay—its reins wrapped around the saddle horn.

"Get on," Kent said, turning to watch the slope behind them.

"It *is* just you," Jenna said.

"Your father sent me on ahead. I'm taking you to him."

"More of you should have come."

To Jenna's annoyance, Kent shoved her. "Climb on the damn horse."

Grabbing the saddle horn, Jenna swung up and slid back to make room. "Now you." She was anxious to get out of there.

Tom Kent gripped the saddle horn with his free hand, and mounted. He was careful not to hit her with his leg. Once in the saddle, he unwrapped the reins and wheeled the bay. "Soon you'll be safe and sound with your father," he said, and smiled.

"I can't thank you enough," Jenna said. He sounded proud at having rescued her. "But I won't breathe easy until we're there."

"Quit your worrying, girl."

Those were Tom Kent's last words. A revolver cracked, a single shot, and the side of his face sprayed every which way, showering her with gore. Jenna recoiled in horror. "No!" she cried.

Kent was falling, his body gone limp. Jenna felt sorry for him but she had to think of herself. She pushed and sent him tumbling, and grabbed the reins. All she had to do was jab her heels and she would be gone.

That was when a grim apparition materialized beside the bay, a revolver pointed at her head.

"I'd think twice, were I you," Willy Boy Jenkins said.

Her legs half-bent, Jenna froze. She didn't doubt for a second that he would shoot if she made him.

"Good girl." Willy took a step back. "Now climb down."

"Are you fixing to kill me?"

"Why are you still on that horse?" Willy thumbed back the hammer. "You don't want to make me madder than I already am."

Fearing the worst, Jenna alighted. She had been so close. So very close. Her eyes moistened, and she blinked tears away.

Willy stepped to Tom Kent and kicked the body. "Silly man with his silly blades. Only a jackass brings a knife to a gunfight."

"What now?" Jenna said. "You have your way with me?"

"I should, but no." Willy gazed to the south. "Your pa and the others must be close. They'll have heard the shot and come on quick."

"I pray they do," Jenna said.

Willy Boy Jenkins did a strange thing. He grinned and said, "You and me both."

30

"We should stop," Weasel Ginty said. "Our horses need rest."

"No," Cal Grissom curtly replied. "Not until I have her back safe."

Weasel glanced at Burt Alacord, thinking Burt would side with him, but as usual, whatever Cal wanted, Burt did. Weasel refused to let it drop. "Somethin' must have gone wrong. Kent should have been back with her by now."

"I have a hunch we'll catch up to them soon," Cal said.

Weasel could have pointed out how foolish it was to rely on a feeling, but he held his tongue. It wouldn't do any good. When it came to saving his girl, Cal was like a wolf after a bone.

They were winding through low hills, a canopy of stars sparkling in the firmament. From time to time coyotes keened, and once a wolf gave voice to a long, wavering howl.

Cal pulled ahead, which suited Weasel just fine. He brought his horse alongside Burt's and said so only Burt would hear, "This is a mistake and you know it."

"Could be," Burt said.

"Why aren't you speakin' up? He'll listen to you if he'll listen to anyone."

"Cal does trust me more than anyone else," Burt agreed.

"Then tell him," Weasel said, inadvertently raising his voice.

Cal glanced over his shoulder. "Something the matter back there?"

"We're fine," Weasel said. To Burt, much lower, he remarked, "If you don't count ridin' into the gun sights of a natural-born killer."

"Are you sayin' I can't take him?"

"Don't put words in my mouth. Willy Boy doesn't stand a snowball's chance in hell against the four of us. . . ."

"Five," Burt corrected him.

"Four," Weasel insisted. "If Tom Kent was still kickin', he'd have brought Jenna to Cal by now."

"I'm afraid you might be right."

"That's not all. Our horses are beat. They could give out on us anytime. You need to talk to Cal. Tell him our animals need rest."

"So it's the horses you're worried about," Burt said, "and not your own skin?"

"That was harsh," Weasel said. Even if it was true. "Just remember I was against this when it turns sour."

"You and your sunny disposition."

Weasel was about to say that he knew a lost cause when he saw one when Cal Grissom drew rein.

"Look yonder!"

The hills were coming to an end. Beyond spread

more prairie. And not a quarter-mile off, a fire flickered.

"Willy the Boy made camp, *ja?*" the Prussian said in that thick accent of his.

"Out in the open like that?" Weasel scoffed. "Willy is a lot of things, but stupid ain't one of them."

"That's where we'll find Jenna," Cal said. He stopped and waited for them to come up on either side. "I've changed my mind about whittling on Willy slow. We'll gun him down like the cur he is."

"It could be a trick," Weasel said. "It could be he's waitin' for us."

"You fret and you fret," Cal said.

"Doesn't he, though?" Burt agreed, chuckling.

Weasel resented their smugness. Whether from worry or lack of sleep, Cal Grissom was making a rare mistake. "Will you listen to me? Can we do this slow and careful?"

"We should charge," Spike Davis suggested, "like Prussian cavalry."

"You hardly ever say two words to anybody," Weasel said, "and *now* you decide to throw in your two bits?"

"I like his idea," Cal said, drawing his revolver. "We charge in and it's over, and I have Jenna back safe."

"Burt?" Weasel made one last try.

"Whatever Cal wants."

"Of course." Weasel slumped in his saddle. He was wasting his breath. But he'd be damned if he'd get himself killed on the girl's account. When the others fanned out, he did, too. When they started forward, so did he. But not at a trot, as they were doing. He went slower.

Cal and Burt and the Prussian bore down on the campfire in a thunder of hooves.

The idiots, Weasel fumed. Willy Boy would hear them

and be ready. In all his years of riding with Cal, Weasel had never seen Grissom do anything so foolhardy.

Weasel made out someone on their knees by the fire. As he drew closer he realized it was Jenna Grissom, bound hands and feet, with a bandanna over her mouth. A rope had been thrown around her neck and tied to a stake that had been pounded into the ground.

"Jenna!" Cal Grissom roared, and galloped to her rescue.

Burt and the Prussian followed his example.

"Hell in a basket." Weasel still hung back. He refused to commit himself until he was sure it was safe.

Jenna Grissom was shaking her head and trying to scream through the gag. Tears glistened on her cheeks, and she struggled fiercely to stand.

Cal only had eyes for his daughter. Looking neither right nor left, he hauled on his reins and was out of the saddle while his mount was still in motion. He stumbled, caught himself, and reached Jenna.

Burt and the Prussian came to a stop on either side of them. Burt's hands flashed and both his pistols gleamed in the firelight. The Prussian already had his Mauser out and was swinging it right and left, seeking a target.

Weasel had been so sure disaster was about to befall them, he wasn't the least bit surprised when a muzzle flashed and a rifle boomed.

Jenna tried to warn them that Willy Boy was waiting for them, that he'd used her as bait, *again*.

A slug struck the Prussian's helmet with a loud *spang* and knocked it askew. Somehow Davis managed to stay on his horse, stunned but otherwise unhurt.

In a blur of living lightning, Burt Alacord twisted in his

saddle and cut loose with his twin Colts. He fired four shots in such swift cadence, they almost sounded like one. Jenna had never seen anyone shoot so fast. Weasel came riding up—reluctantly, she thought—and he fired, too.

Then her father was on his knees in front of her and ripping the bandanna from her mouth.

"Jenna! Jenna!"

"Willy Boy . . ." Jenna tried to get out.

"Don't worry about him," her father said, and turned to the stake that held her fast. Gripping it in both hands, he strained to pull it out.

Jenna *was* worried. They were in the firelight. Willy Boy wasn't. "He can pick us off."

Continuing to strain, her father shouted at Burt Alacord. "Go after him! I'll take care of her."

Swinging down, Burt hollered at Weasel Ginty and the Prussian. "You heard the man! Davis, come with me. Weasel, protect Cal and Jenna." Burt melted into the night, the Prussian hurrying after him.

Jenna expected Willy Boy to keep firing but for some reason he didn't. Weasel Ginty dismounted and came over and stood with his back to her father.

"Hurry it up, Cal. We're sittin' ducks."

Her father stopped straining against the stake, and scowled. "I can't get this damn thing out. Help me."

"One of us needs to keep watch," Weasel said. He had crouched and was turning from side to side.

"I need your help, damn it."

"Burt told me to protect you two and that's what I'm doin'."

"Who runs this outfit? Burt or me?" her father demanded.

"You do," Weasel acknowledged. "But I won't let that get us killed."

Every moment they bickered was an eternity of worry for Jenna. "Kick it," she said.

"Eh?" her father said. He didn't seem his usual self.

"Kick the stake," Jenna said. "That should loosen it."

Her father sat, cocked his legs, and slammed his boots against the stake. It moved, but only slightly.

"Keep at it," Jenna urged.

Cal kicked again and again and again. He swore, and kicked some more. "How on earth did he pound this in?"

"He used a rock," Jenna recalled. And it had taken a long time, as hard as the ground was. Willy had taunted her while doing it, saying that thanks to her, her father would soon be dead.

Cal resumed kicking, throwing all his weight into it. The stake shook. It moved a little. Grabbing hold, Cal pulled, but once again, he couldn't get it out. Furious, he sat and attacked it with a frenzy of kicks.

"Hurry," Weasel said.

"I'm doing the best I can," Cal snapped.

"Do better."

Jenna was surprised that Weasel was giving her father sass. It was obvious the little man was scared, and fear had made him bolder.

Her father swore a mean streak, then kicked with both boots at once. There was a loud *crack*.

"Careful," Weasel said. "You break that stake off with the rope still in the ground, and we'll have to dig it out."

"You're commencing to annoy me," Cal said.

"He's right," Jenna said. Willy had tied the rope to the bottom of the stake, not the top. She'd wondered why, and now she knew. To make it harder for them to free her.

All three of them stiffened at the sudden sound of a

horse. But it was moving away from them, not toward them.

"What the hell?" Weasel blurted. "Is Willy runnin' away?"

Boots pounded, and into the firelight hastened Burt Alacord and Spike Davis. "He lit a shuck," Burt informed them.

"That doesn't sound like Jenkins," Cal said. "He's not yellow."

Burt had holstered his left Colt, and he held his left hand out to show that several of his fingertips were smeared red. "I must have hit him. We heard some sounds and were movin' toward them when I put my hand down and touched somethin' wet."

"His blood!" Cal exclaimed.

"From what we could tell, he's bleedin' pretty bad."

"Good," Cal said.

Burt looked at Jenna. "Why is she still trussed up?"

Cal kicked the stake. "I can't get this out."

"Are you thinkin' straight tonight?" Burt said. Turning to the Prussian, he motioned. "Davis. Use that pig-sticker of yours."

The Prussian nodded and drew a bayonet he wore attached to his belt, behind his left hip. A single slash, and the rope parted.

"All you had to do was cut it," Burt said.

"Well, hell," Cal said.

Jenna would have laughed except that something had occurred to her. "What happened to those lawmen? To that young one, Robert Grant?"

"Why bring them up at a time like this?" her father said, bending to undo the rope around her ankles.

"They had escaped, remember?" Jenna said.

"And good riddance." He pried at a knot.

"I'd like to know," Jenna persisted. She'd grown

fond of Grant those last couple of days. It had been fun riding together and talking about everything under the sun. With all that had happened since she was abducted, she hadn't thought about him much. Now she was worried. Terribly worried.

"We lit out after you in such a hurry, we left their horses behind," Cal related. "I sent Fletcher back for them but he never caught up to us. Which makes me suspect they made worm food of him."

"They're still alive, then," Jenna said more happily than she intended.

Her father glanced up. "You can do better than a tin star. That young one isn't for you."

"I'll say who is and who isn't."

"No daughter of mine is going to marry a lawman."

"Who said anything about marriage?" Jenna said, her temper flaring. "I like him, is all."

Burt Alacord stepped up. "What's gotten into you two? Save the love talk for later. If Willy's not as badly hit as we think, he might circle around and use that rifle of his." He turned to Ginty. "Wease, lend Cal a hand."

In no time Jenna was on her feet, rubbing her chafed wrists. Her horse was brought and her father gave her a boost up. They headed south but only went a mile or so. In the lee of a bluff her father drew rein and announced they'd spend the rest of the night there.

"We'll go without fire. Willy Boy or those lawdogs might see it."

"Do you reckon the tin stars are after us?" Weasel asked.

"That old one struck me as having a lot of bark on him. So yes, I do."

Jenna smiled to herself. The likelihood of seeing Robert Grant again pleased her greatly. Deputy Stone was another matter. The old lawman had said he was going to arrest her for her part in the Unionville Bank robbery and that stage holdup.

Had she been saved from Willy Boy Jenkins, only to face the prospect of years behind bars?

Lord, she hoped not.

31

Alonzo Pratt had never done so much hard riding in his life. Usually he took his sweet time getting somewhere. With Jenna in danger, Stone and him pushed their animals to the point of exhaustion.

Stone complained about Alonzo's packhorse. It slowed them. Stone wanted Alonzo to leave it behind, but Alonzo refused. Everything he owned was in those packs. The more he thought about it, though, the more he came to realize that the old lawman was right. It boiled down to which was more important, Jenna or his impersonations?

When, shortly thereafter, they stopped to give their lathered mounts a breather, Alonzo came to a decision. Without a word to Stone, he began undoing the packs and setting them on the ground.

"You've come to your senses, I take it?"

"This isn't easy for me," Alonzo said, lowering a pack.

"Don't you reckon that pretty gal is more important?"

"Why do you think I'm doin' this?" Alonzo said. Once he had everything in a pile, he stepped back and sadly reflected that he might never set eyes on them again.

"You're doin' the right thing, son."

In his heart Alonzo knew that. It was his head that balked at leaving everything behind. It was as if he was leaving a part of himself.

"I wouldn't hobble the horse, if I were you," Stone advised.

Alonzo didn't need to ask why. Not with all the things that might do the animal harm. He didn't look back when they rode on. He had a sense he'd never see his belongings, or the horse, ever again.

Not long after, a distant shot brought them to a stop. They listened for more but there was just the one.

Deputy Stone rose in his stirrups. "I believe I see hills yonder," he announced. "I can just make them out."

They pressed on. Once amid the hills, they rode warily, their hands on their six-shooters. When Stone's horse nickered and shied, they investigated a cut in the side of one of the hills. If not for the moonlight, they would have missed the body lying in the grass.

"Well, now," Stone said, leaning on his saddle horn, "Tom Kent, dead as can be. One less for us to have to deal with."

"Willy Boy's handiwork?"

"That would be my guess. Wouldn't surprise me if we hear more gunfire before too long. Cal Grissom and the rest are still after him."

The old lawman's prediction came true when a flurry of shots cracked not that far away.

"What did I tell you?" Stone said. "Let's go." With a lash of his reins and a jab of his spurs, he was off to a gallop.

Alonzo spurred Archibald, who was showing signs of faltering. Beyond the next hill spread a plain. He spied a campfire a ways off and figures moving about.

Deputy Stone had seen them, too, and hauled on his reins. "Climb down! Hurry!"

"Make up your mind," Alonzo grumbled as he wearily slid off.

"I don't think they've seen us," Stone said. Crouching, he motioned for Alonzo to do likewise.

"You're not fixin' to rush them?" Alonzo wouldn't put it past him.

"There are four left, and one is Burt Alacord," Stone said. "Rushin' into his guns is suicide."

Alonzo squinted, trying to make out details. "I can't tell much. What are they doin'?"

"I don't rightly know. But they're movin' around a lot. We'll wait for things to quiet down and then sneak in close."

Presently, though, a new development presented itself.

"They're leavin'!" Stone exclaimed. "Headin' south, from the looks of things. And the girl's with them."

Alonzo was suddenly all interest. "Are you sure?" The old man's eyes put his to shame.

"Unless one of the men has sprouted long hair, I'm sure, yes. They've rescued her from Willy Boy." Stone rubbed his stubble. "But if he's dead, why aren't they campin' there?"

"We shouldn't let them get too far ahead," Alonzo said.

"Don't worry. We won't lose them. But we have to do this smart. Pick the time and place to make our move."

Alonzo didn't argue. Stone had a lifetime of experience at this sort of thing. And Jenna would be all right, now that she was reunited with her father.

"We'll wait for the sun to come up."

That suited Alonzo. He was so tired, he could curl up right there and sleep the day away. As it was, his eyes kept closing and he'd struggle to snap them open again. Slumped in fatigue, he let his chin dip to his chest. The next he knew, a hand was on his arm, shaking him.

"Time to go," Stone said.

Alonzo was stunned to see the sun half-up. "Sorry," he said, struggling to shake off his lethargy.

"You young'uns today," Stone said, chuckling. "You've got the stamina of kittens."

The lawman had them advance riding ten yards apart, their revolvers at the ready. Wisps of smoke rose from the charred embers of the fire. Nearby, a stake jutted from the ground, and a few pieces of rope were scattered about.

Other than the high grass swaying slightly in the cool morning breeze, all was still.

"How about we rekindle that fire and treat ourselves to some coffee?" Stone proposed.

"We can't take the time," Alonzo said. "We have to get after Jenna."

"As tired as we are, we wouldn't be much good," Stone said, shaking his head. "The coffee will wake us up. Besides, I doubt Cal Grissom will go far before he makes camp, not with them having ridden all night."

Alonzo considered that, and changed his mind. "I have a better idea. Why not sleep until noon or so?"

"That's what they'll be doin'," Stone said. "It's our chance to take them by surprise and rescue your girlfriend."

"Quit callin' her that."

Stone climbed down. "I'll get the coffee goin'."

Dismounting, Alonzo stretched. He was almost out on his feet. "I hope I can hold up."

Jacob Stone had vigor to spare. He used water from both their canteens to fill the coffeepot, and rekindled the fire. Hunkered there, he smiled and rubbed his hands in anticipation.

"You must want that coffee awful bad," Alonzo said.

"It's not that," Stone said. "It's the Grissom gang. Two dead for sure, and a third likely. With your help, I can put an end to them, once and for all."

"You're forgettin' I'm not a lawman. Why should I lend a hand when you're only goin' to throw me behind bars when we get to North Platte?"

Stone stared at him for so long that Alonzo began to feel uneasy.

"What?"

"I have an idea," Jacob Stone said.

"So do I," another voice declared, and out of the grass rose an apparition with a bloodstained shirt and a pearl-handled Colt in its hand. "So much as twitch, either of you, and I'll blow you both to hell."

Deputy Marshal Jacob Stone would have tried for his revolver except that Willy Boy Jenkins was pointing that Colt at him, and not at Alonzo Pratt. Evidently Willy Boy considered him more dangerous, which was shrewd on Willy's part.

Stone saw that the blood staining Willy's shirt came from two wounds, not one. Willy had taken a slug high on his chest and another lower down, about where the ribs began. Willy came toward them slightly hunched over, his face slick with sweat, his elbow pressed against the lower wound.

"You!" Alonzo Pratt exclaimed.

Worried that Alonzo would try for his six-gun, Stone said, "Stay calm, son. Don't do anything rash."

Willy Boy grunted in pain as he came to a stop. "Listen to the old geezer and you'll live longer."

"You abducted her!" Alonzo said, his fists balled.

Willy Boy cocked his head in perplexity. "What does that matter to you? Sounds like you're takin' it personal."

To draw Jenkins's attention to himself, Stone remarked, "I figured you were dead by now."

"I almost was, thanks to that damn Burt Alacord," Willy Boy growled. "The bastard must have eyes like a cat to hit me in the dark."

"Did you fire first?" Stone imagined. "He probably shot at your muzzle flash." He'd done the same thing on a number of occasions.

"I was crouched down," Willy Boy said. "I thought they'd shoot over my head." He looked at his blood-drenched shirt. "I was out for a while. My horse ran off, too."

"And here you are, aimin' to take ours," Stone said. He was surprised that Jenkins hadn't simply shot them dead.

"I want some of that coffee you're makin'," Willy Boy said. "To keep my strength up."

A suspicion came over Stone that there was more to it, that Willy hadn't gunned them down because Grissom and the others hadn't been gone all that long, and might hear the shots and come back to investigate.

"First, you'll shed your hardware," Willy Boy said. "Startin' with you, old man. Use two fingers and toss your six-shooter as far as you can."

Stone did as he was told. It was either that or be shot. He threw his revolver a good ten feet, then placed his hand on the handle to the coffeepot.

"Now you, boy," Willy said to Pratt.

"Don't call me that," Alonzo bristled. "You're not much older than I am, if you're older at all."

Willy Boy's jaw muscles twitched. "I'll call you any damn thing I want. Throw that smoke wagon, now."

Alonzo's own jaw worked as he plucked his six-shooter and cast it barely four feet. "There? Happy?"

"You call that far?" Willy Boy said.

"You want it farther, throw it yourself," Alonzo said.

Stone wished the boy would behave. He was ready to make his move but couldn't with Willy's Colt now trained on Alonzo. "Quit givin' Willy Boy a hard time."

"Whose side are you on?" Alonzo angrily replied.

Stone was watching Jenkins. Willy Boy's Colt was cocked, Willy's finger curled around the trigger. All it would take was the slightest of squeezes to send young Mr. Pratt into eternity. "When an enemy has the better of you, you do as he says."

"The hell I will."

Willy Boy said, "You ought to listen to him, boy. The old buzzard knows what he's doin'."

"Not if it means kowtowin' to the likes of you," Alonzo spat. "Who knows what you did to Jenna, all that time you had her."

"Why do you keep bringin' her up?" Willy Boy said. "What's Jenna Grissom to you?"

"My friend."

"I wonder," Willy Boy said, his brow puckering. "Sounds to me as if you're smitten."

"She's a decent gal," Alonzo said. "Much too good for the likes of you."

"Insult me one more time. I dare you."

Alonzo opened his mouth to say something.

Stone's every instinct warned him that Pratt was about to provoke Jenkins into shooting. In order to save him, Stone did the only thing he could; he hurled the coffee into Willy Boy's face. The coffee wasn't as hot as Stone would have liked but it splashed full into Willy's eyes and Willy stumbled back, cursing, and swiped at them with his sleeve. Stone sprang as Willy Boy's Colt went off. He felt a searing pain, and then he had hold of Willy's wrist. Hooking his foot behind Willy's leg, Stone tripped him. They both went down, Willy Boy growling like a wild beast and struggling to break free.

Stone tried to pin him, but something was wrong. He suddenly felt weak, and his legs wouldn't move as he wanted them to. A fist caught Stone on the cheek. Willy Boy drew back his arm to strike him again, but Alonzo Pratt pounced on Willy's free arm and slammed it to the ground.

Despite his wounds, Willy fought fiercely: he bucked; he rammed a knee into Stone's back.

Stone grew weaker. He lost his grip on Willy Boy's wrist and Willy thrust the Colt at him. It was Alonzo who swatted it aside as it went off, the blast nearly deafening Stone in his left ear. Alonzo grabbed Willy's wrist with both hands, and they grappled for control of the Colt. Stone tried to help but his arms were as useless as his legs. He fell onto his side.

The world blurred. Stone was aware of the struggle taking place beside him but he was powerless to help. Gritting his teeth, he tried to rise onto his elbows. He got partway and saw that Alonzo had bent Willy Boy's arm and the Colt was pointed at the bottom of Willy's chin.

In a desperate bid to fling Alonzo off, Willy Boy thrashed fiercely. When his Colt went off, the shock on his face matched Alonzo's own. The slug tore through the soft flesh between the jawbone, up through Willy's face, causing scarlet to spurt from each nostril, and burst out the top of Willy's head, taking his hat and some of his brain matter with it.

Stone collapsed.

Alonzo bent over him, concern in the younger man's eyes. "You were hit? How bad is it? What can I do?"

"Save her," Stone gasped. "Get the girl away from them."

"But you . . ." Alonzo said, clasping Stone's hand.

"I'm dead, son," Stone said.

"No! You can't! I need you!"

"Sorry." Jacob Stone smiled, and was engulfed in blackness.

32

———◆———

Shock numbed Alonzo Pratt. "Deputy Stone?" He felt for a pulse in the lawman's wrist and couldn't find one. "No!" he cried, and pressed his fingers to Stone's neck. Still nothing. The terrible realization that Stone was gone washed over him and he sat back, shaking his head in denial. "No, no, no, no, no."

Alonzo gazed blankly about. This was the worst thing that could happen. Jenna needed to be rescued, and the one man most able to do that was gone.

"What do I do?" Alonzo addressed the empty air. His thoughts were in such a jumble, he sank onto his back, closed his eyes, and sought to compose himself.

First off, Alonzo told himself, Jenna wasn't in any danger. She was back with her father. But she'd told him that she didn't want anything more to do with the outlaws, and, in fact, wanted to return to California.

The problem with that, Alonzo reflected, was that the outlaws might not let her go. Spiriting her away wouldn't be easy, not when the four still alive would kill anyone who tried.

Opening his eyes, Alonzo turned his head toward Jacob Stone's body. "You picked the worst time to die on me, consarn you."

Alonzo had a choice to make. He could go after Jenna. He could risk his life for her. Or he could take Stone's horse and collect his packs, and continue on with his life of living hand to mouth, impersonating folks.

Alonzo had a sense that he was at a crossroads. He adored Jenna Grissom. And he had a strong feeling that she liked him, too. Could he turn his back on her? On the only woman to ever show an interest?

If he did go after her, Alonzo decided, and by some miracle succeeded in getting her away from the outlaws, and by some bigger miracle she and he stuck together, things would have to change. He'd have to find real work. He'd have to live an ordinary life, as other people did. Was Jenna worth that? Alonzo surprised himself at the answer that popped unbidden into his head. *Of course she was.*

"Well, then," Alonzo said, and stood. He didn't need the coffee. Fighting Willy had set his blood to racing and cleared his head better than the coffee ever could.

He must head out after the outlaws while their trail was still fresh.

Alonzo collected the lawman's and Willy Boy's revolvers and placed them in his saddlebags, then went through their pockets and helped himself to their pokes. In Willy's he found two pokes and guessed that one might have belonged to Tom Kent. Together, the total came to six thousand dollars, a staggering sum. Their pokes went in his saddlebags, too. Finally, Alonzo took hold of the reins to the lawman's horse, and climbed on Archibald.

Alonzo stared down at Stone's body. "Sorry I can't bury you." The ground was so hard, it would take hours to dig a grave deep enough. "So long, Jacob," Alonzo said, and gigged Archibald.

Alonzo reckoned the outlaws must be miles off by now. But he hadn't gone all that far, and was nearing a bluff with a flat crown and sheer sides, when Archibald raised his head, pricked his ears, and nickered.

Alonzo drew rein. Archibald usually only ever did that when he caught the scent of other horses. "Surely not," Alonzo said out loud, and then smelled smoke. A tingle of excitement ran through him. The outlaws must have stopped sooner than he reckoned. Climbing down, he led both horses on foot, moving slowly, and as quietly as possible. The bluff swelled until it towered above him.

The outlaws' tracks bore to the left. Alonzo went to the right, his mouth suddenly dry, the enormity of what he was about to do sinking in. He was pitting himself against the Grissom gang. Notorious man-slayers who thought he was a lawman and would shoot him on sight.

Alonzo imagined Jenna in his mind's-eye, and it firmed his resolve. For her he would do this. For her, and the prospect of something he'd never had before: a future.

He took another step, bumped a rock with his boot, and his spur jingled. Stopping, Alonzo broke out in a sweat. Mistakes like that could get him shot. Sitting, he removed both spurs and added them to his saddlebag collection. As an afterthought, he took out Stone's revolver, checked that it was loaded, and stuck it under

his belt, close to the buckle. Two revolvers were better
than one.

His chest hammering, Alonzo worked his cautious
way around the bluff. With boulders and broken
chunks of earth littering the bottom, it stood alone and
aloof in the middle of the prairie, its own little world.

A drop of sweat trickled into Alonzo's left eye, and
stung. He thought of the canteens on the saddles, and
dearly thirsted for a swallow of water.

The outlaws were on the south side of the bluff.
Alonzo came to a boulder as high as an outhouse and
as long as Archibald, and peeked around it.

Gray tendrils rose from a campfire. Alonzo couldn't
see the fire because of the intervening boulders. He
didn't see the outlaws or Jenna, either, but he did spy
four hobbled horses.

Alonzo left his own horses behind the boulder and
cat-footed forward. Drawing both revolvers, he cocked
them. He supposed the smart thing to do was wait until dark when he could sneak in unseen. But nightfall
wasn't for nine or ten hours yet. And with any luck,
he'd catch the outlaws sleeping.

Alonzo skirted a pile of loose rock. The smoke smell
was so strong, he smothered an impulse to cough.

Sometime in the past a rift of dirt, shoulder high,
had broken from the bluff and spilled a dozen feet onto
the plain. Alonzo started around it and was almost to
the end when a figure in a metal helmet suddenly rose,
hitching at his pants, and moved toward the fire. They
both set eyes on each other at the same instant.

Alonzo stopped and pointed both six-shooters.

Spike Davis turned to stone, his hands on his britches.

"Not a sound," Alonzo whispered. He didn't want
to shoot; the others would hear. And the Prussian's revolver was in its holster.

Davis arched an eyebrow as if to say, "Well?"

"Hands in the air," Alonzo whispered.

The Prussian let go of his pants and they fell down around his knees. As they dropped, he grabbed at his revolver and brought it to bear with his arm extended, military-fashion.

Alonzo squeezed both triggers. He did it without thinking. The twin blasts, magnified by the bluff, resembled the crash of a cannon.

Spike Davis, or Ladislaus Dowid, or whatever his real name happened to be, was slammed back as if kicked by an invisible mule. His legs buckled and he oozed down, his revolver drooping to his side. He stared at Alonzo as if he couldn't believe what had happened, and went limp.

Alonzo could scarcely believe it, either. The Prussian was supposed to be formidable, yet he'd died as easy as anything. He kept thinking Davis would raise his arm and try to shoot, but no, the man was truly and really dead.

A shout brought Alonzo out of himself. Crouching, he ran to a boulder and sank to his knees.

Someone began yelling, "Davis! Davis! Where are you?"

Alonzo recognized Weasel Ginty's voice. Boots thudded, coming closer. Alonzo bent so low, his hat brushed the ground. He saw the boots, scuffed and caked with dust, come around the boulder and stop, and he looked up.

Weasel Ginty was gaping at the Prussian, his revolver in his hand, his back to Alonzo.

"Drop your six-shooter," Alonzo said.

Weasel half-turned, and caught himself at the sight of the twin muzzles of Alonzo's revolvers. "You!" he exclaimed. "Where's the other one? The old one?"

"Covering you," Alonzo lied, and when Weasel looked all around, he said, "I told you to drop that six-gun."

"Damn you," Weasel hissed. But he let the pistol drop and raised his hands, fingers spread.

Alonzo's elation at disarming him lasted all of ten seconds. That was when he realized Burt Alacord and Cal Grissom were somewhere close, and hadn't made Weasel's mistake. "Where are your friends?"

"Wouldn't you like to know?" Weasel looked around again. "I don't see that old lawdog anywhere."

"Take a few steps back," Alonzo commanded to keep Weasel from jumping him.

His features a mask of resentment, Weasel obeyed.

Alonzo rose high enough to peer over the boulder. The smoke still rose and the horses were still there. But no one else. Alacord and Grissom could be anywhere, concealed behind any of a score of boulders, or in rents in the bluff.

"You and that old man have bit off more than you can chew," Weasel said. "Burt will snuff your wicks."

Alonzo was trying to think what to do. Should he march Weasel in at gunpoint and demand the others throw down their guns? "How fond are they of you?"

"Burt and Cal? What kind of question is that?"

"Holler to them," Alonzo said. "Tell them to come out with their hands empty or I'll put lead into you."

Weasel laughed.

"You think that's funny?"

"I think *you're* funny, boy," Weasel said. "How long have you been wearin' that badge? Any tin star worth his salt knows they'd never do that. They're my friends, sure. But they're not dumb."

Alonzo was stymied. His rescue attempt was falling apart. "Listen. All I want is Jenna. Yell for them to send her to me and I'll let you go. The three of you can head wherever you want."

"What's Grissom's gal to you?"

"Damn it." Alonzo was losing his temper. "Quit stallin'. They send her over and you go on breathin'. That's fair."

"Except that her pa ain't about to turn her over to you or anyone else. He's powerful fond of that girl of his."

"I don't want more blood to be shed," Alonzo said.

Weasel tilted his head quizzically. "What kind of lawman are you? Sheddin' blood is what you do for a livin'."

"No, lawmen enforce laws," Alonzo said, and the ridiculousness of it struck him like a slap in the face. Here he was, a pretend lawman, arguing with a notorious lawbreaker about what real lawmen did.

"Boy, you beat all," Weasel Ginty said.

"Tell them anyway," Alonzo grasped at a straw. "Yell to her father."

"You're plumb loco," Weasel said, but he cupped a hand to his mouth and bawled, "Cal? You hear me? The young deputy shot Spike Davis and has me dead to rights. He wants me to make you an offer."

Every nerve aflame, Alonzo waited for the reply. He thought that maybe Cal Grissom wouldn't want to give his position away by answering, but then a shout rose from boulders thirty feet away.

"What the hell do you mean by an offer?"

"The deputy says the three of us are free to go if you'll give him your daughter."

"What the hell?" Cal Grissom said, sounding as if he thought he hadn't heard right.

"If you give him Jenna, the rest of us can go free."

"What does he want with her?"

"Beats me. But that's the deal. You hand her over and no more blood has to be shed. His very words."

There was a long pause; then Cal Grissom responded with a question Alonzo never would have expected.

"Is he drunk?"

"Doesn't appear to be," Weasel hollered. "Just stupid."

"Where's the old one? Deputy Stone?"

"The young one says he's around somewhere."

"Deputy Stone?" Cal Grissom shouted. "Deputy Jacob Stone, wasn't it? Answer me, old man."

Alonzo had to do something. They'd figure out right quick that he was alone, and close in. "Enough stallin'," he said, holding both revolvers steady on Weasel Ginty. "Have them send Jenna Grissom over or I'll send you straight to hell."

"You're bluffin'," Weasel said.

To show that he wasn't, Alonzo reared up and rammed the barrel of his Colt into Ginty's gut. Weasel cried out and doubled over, clutching himself. Dropping down again, Alonzo jammed the Colt against Weasel's temple. "Still think I am?"

"Damn your miserable hide," Weasel snarled.

Taking a desperate gamble Alonzo slipped behind Ginty, jerked him upright, wrapped his left forearm around Ginty's throat, and gouged his Colt into Ginty's ear.

"You see this?" he hollered.

"I see it," came Cal Grissom's shout. "Let him go, boy. I'm not handing my daughter over to you no matter what you do."

So much for Alonzo's bluff. He stood there not knowing what to do next, and distinctly heard the clicks of twin gun hammers behind him. He didn't need to look to know who was there.

"You'll oblige me by takin' your six-shooter out of my pard's ear," Burt Alacord said.

Weasel Ginty chuckled. "About time you showed."

"I was nosin' around for the old one," Burt Alacord said. Then, "I'm waitin', boy. But I won't wait long."

Alonzo racked his mind for a way of turning the tables. The only thing he could think of was, "You shoot me, the lead might go clean through and hit your friend."

It happened frequently to bystanders during shooting affrays, which was why when bullets commenced to fly, savvy onlookers were quick to hunt for cover.

"Not if I shoot you in the foot," Burt Alacord said. "And when you fall, I'll finish you with a shot to the head. Get shed of those six-guns while you still can."

With no other recourse, Alonzo threw his Colt to one side, then tossed Stone's to the other. Hiking his arms, he turned. "Do your worst," he said, hoping he sounded braver than he felt.

Weasel stepped around him, rubbing his ear. "I should bust you in the mouth."

Instead, he went to reclaim his revolver.

"Where's Deputy Stone?" Burt Alacord demanded. "I haven't seen hide nor hair of him."

It was pointless for Alonzo to continue to deceive them. "Dead," he said, "thanks to Willy Boy Jenkins. Willy Boy is dead, too."

"I'd celebrate if I had some whiskey," Burt said. He glanced past Alonzo. "Did you hear, Cal? That backstabber got what was comin' for takin' Jenna."

"I heard," Cal Grissom said. Striding past Alonzo, he stood next to Alacord. "You have a part in Willy's dyin', boy?"

"We were fightin' over his six-gun," Alonzo confessed, "and it went off."

"Then I owe you," Cal Grissom said.

"That you do, father."

Alonzo hadn't heard Jenna come up, yet suddenly she was at his side, a Winchester in the crook of her arm. She gave him a warm smile that he swore made his ears tingle.

"Did I hear right?" Jenna said. "You shot Spike Davis, too?"

"He was tryin' to shoot me," Alonzo explained.

Weasel returned, brushing dirt from his revolver. Satisfied it was clean, he shoved it into his holster and moved to the other side of Burt Alacord. "What are we to do with this tin star, gents?"

"Nothing," Jenna Grissom said.

"That's not for you to decide, daughter," Cal Grissom said.

"I'm afraid it is," Jenna said. "I happen to like him, father. He's always been nice to me, always treated me with respect. Fact is, I'd like him to escort me to North Platte. I'd feel safer with him along. He fought the Sioux, he shot Willy, and now he came to save me from you."

"I'd never harm a hair on your head, or let any of my men harm you, either," Cal angrily declared.

"That didn't stop Willy Boy, did it?"

Cal Grissom flushed with indignation. "Is that why you're so all-fired set on parting company?"

"I want my old life back," Jenna said. "I'm tired of always being on the move. I don't like robbing people. I don't like seeing people hurt. I talked myself hoarse pleading with you to give this life up, but you refused."

"Daughter," Cal Grissom said, and took a step.

Jenna leveled the Winchester. Not at any of the three in particular, but in their general direction. "Stay where you are."

"What's this?"

"You're going to hear me out. Then I'm leaving, and Deputy Grant is going with me." Jenna shook her head when her father went to move. "Don't. I mean it. I want you to listen, and that's all."

"You're being unreasonable," Cal Grissom said.

"*Me?*" Jenna said. "Who came all the way from California to see you? Who had high hopes that at long last we could be together? Not just for a few months but for the rest of our lives? Who would have done anything to make that come true?"

"Things aren't always as simple as—"

"Don't," Jenna said, cutting him off. "You say you care but you're not willing to change. Your outlaw ways means more to you than I do."

"There's more to it than that."

"Oh, really?" Jenna said. "Suppose you explain it to me. Explain why a father would rather rob and kill than be with his own flesh and blood?"

"It's the only thing I know."

"*That's* your excuse?" Jenna said, incredulous. "You can change. People start new lives all the time. All it takes is the will to try something new. Is that too much to ask?"

Alonzo had seldom seen anyone look as miserable as Cal Grissom. The outlaw gazed sadly skyward, then bowed his head and let out a sigh.

"I've been at this too long to give it up. It's not that I love it more than I care for you. I don't. But I've done it for so long, it's more than a way of life. It's me, if that makes any sense."

"It doesn't."

"I'm not a virtuous man, Jenna. I'm not like that young lawman, there. Or Jacob Stone, for that matter. I don't see anything wrong in helping myself to things that don't belong to me. I don't see anything wrong in having to shoot someone now and then. I live as a I please, beholden to no one. And I do it because it's who I am. Just as wearing that badge and upholding the law is who your friend is." Cal looked at Alonzo. "Tell her, boy. Tell her I'm right. That we're born into this world with our natures already set, and nothing we do can change that."

Alonzo thought of all his impersonations. Of being a parson, a gambler, a Civil War veteran. A lawman. He thought of how easy it was to go from one role to the next. All it took was a change of clothes, and a change in how he presented himself. Jenna was right. Anyone could do it. All it took was the will. Cal Grissom was wrong, dead wrong.

But if he said that, Cal might rethink things, might decide to give up the outlaw life and go with her to start anew. And where would that leave him? Nodding, he said, "You're absolutely right, Mr. Grissom."

"There," Cal said, vindicated. "You heard him."

"I still don't agree," Jenna said. "But it's your life. Live it as you will. As for me, I'm leaving, and my friend is going with me, and no one, not Burt nor Weasel or you, is to try and stop us."

"Uppity, ain't she?" Weasel said.

"No," Cal said. "Let her go. Him, too. It's the least I can do after all she's been through."

"Glad that's settled," Burt Alacord said, and twirled his pistols into their holsters. "But it doesn't seem right, him shootin' the Prussian and we don't do anything."

"I've made up my mind," Cal Grissom said. "He gets to live."

"Then that's what we'll do," Burt said.

Jenna held her Winchester out to Alonzo, went to her father, and embraced him. "Thank you," she said softly, and kissed him on the cheek.

Cal Grissom coughed, then said, "I'm sorry things didn't work out."

Jenna turned, squared her shoulders, and walked past Alonzo, saying, "Are you coming, handsome?"

"You bet," Alonzo said. He figured he'd wait a few days to tell her he wasn't really a deputy, and if she was still interested, follow her to the ends of the earth. He quickly caught up, his arm brushing hers.

Jenna gave him a sheepish grin. "This didn't end as you thought it would, did it?"

"It ended just right," Alonzo Pratt said.

Also available from
David Robbins

Badlanders

When Alexander Jessup moves with his two
daughters to the Badlands to run a ranch, he's
unprepared for the West's deathly perils. But
despite the dangers, his daughter Edana is
determined to manage the Diamond B. And it
may be possible, thanks to ranch's foreman,
Neal Bonner, and his partner, Jericho, an
expert gunman.

But Edana's headstrong sister, Isolda, has other
plans. She has no interest in herding cows—or in
polite society, for that matter. So she latches onto
cutthroat conman Beaumont Adams, and the two
scheme to take over the Diamond B with the
help of the worst criminals in the Badlands. Now
Edana, Neal, and Jericho must face down a pack
of stone-cold thieves and murderers to save their
ranch—or die trying.

National bestselling author
RALPH COMPTON

"A writer in the tradition of Louis L'Amour and Zane Grey!" —*Huntsville Times*

Available wherever books are sold or at
penguin.com

No other series packs this much heat!

THE TRAILSMAN

Available wherever books are sold or at
penguin.com